03/13

Fay Weldon

was born in England and raised in New Zealand. Her work is translated into most world languages: she lives in London.

D1375733

Fiction

The Fat Woman's Joke
Down Among the Women
Female Friends
Remember Me
Little Sisters
Praxis
Puffball
The President's Child
The Life and Loves of a She-Devil
The Shrapnel Academy
The Heart of the Country
The Hearts and Lives of Men
The Rules of Life
Leader of the Band
The Cloning of Joanna May
Darcy's Utopia
Growing Rich
Life Force
Affliction

Children's books

Wolf the Mechanical Dog
Party Puddle

Short story collections

Watching Me, Watching You
Polaris
Moon Over Minneapolis
Wicked Women

Non-fiction

Letters to Alice
Rebecca West
Sacred Cows

FAY WELDON

Splitting

For Karen,

with best wishes,

Fay Weldon

Flamingo
An Imprint of HarperCollinsPublishers

Wigton

04.10.08

Flamingo
An Imprint of HarperCollins*Publishers*
77–85 Fulham Palace Road,
Hammersmith, London w6 8jb

Special overseas edition 1995
9 8 7 6 5 4 3 2 1

First published in Great Britain by
Flamingo 1995

Photograph of Fay Weldon by Isolde Ohlbaum

ISBN 978-0-00-729187-8

Set in Linotron Baskerville

Printed in Great Britain by
HarperCollinsManufacturing Glasgow

To
JANE WYNBORNE
for whose skill and dedication over the years
I am profoundly grateful

Grateful acknowledgement is made to
the following to quote from copyrighted
material:

The Literary Trustees of Walter de la Mare, and
The Society of Authors as their representative.

PART ONE

A Perforated House

Edwin's Divorce Petition

There was trauma in the air.

Sir Edwin Rice has decided to divorce Lady Angelica Rice. Sir Edwin alleges in his affidavit to the Court – a document which the lawyer Brian Moss was now dictating to his secretary Jelly White – that Lady Angelica has behaved intolerably. And would the Court therefore put the couple asunder.

Jelly White's hand trembled.

Angelica, claimed Sir Edwin, committed adultery with one Lambert Plaidy; being discovered in flagrante delicto by Sir Edwin, and in the Rice family four-poster bed. This behaviour, typical of much similar behaviour on the part of Angelica Rice, was unreasonable and intolerable to Sir Edwin.

Yes, it was intolerable for Edwin Rice to live with Angelica Rice: his health, his happiness was at risk.

The Petitioner claimed that his spouse had acted in various other ways unacceptable to him: that she had been abusive and violent, pinching him while he brushed his teeth and otherwise molesting him; he alleged that her kissing of the family dogs amounted to bestiality, and her embracing of female guests to lesbianism. He petitioned the Court to let him go free of her.

Brian Moss heard Jelly White take in a breath of outrage between her teeth, and looked at his secretary sharply, but her face remained unmoved and her hand was steady again as it continued to race across the sheet. He went on dictating.

The Petitioner claimed that Lady Angelica made excessive sexual demands on him; that she refused to have children; that she had dirty habits; that she was drunken, and took drugs; that she failed to provide proper food for his guests, thus humiliating him. And that, all in all, her behaviour has been intolerable and unreasonable, and he wanted a divorce. Now.

'Goodness me!' said Jelly White, looking up from her shorthand pad. 'Did you write this for Sir Edwin? Doesn't it smack of overkill?'
'How well you put it,' said Brian Moss. 'But overkill is our stock-in-trade. It's our trademark here at Catterwall & Moss. We like to offer the Court offences in all available categories of unreasonable matrimonial behaviour. Offer the minimum, as too many firms do to avoid unnecessary trauma, and you risk the Court's rejection of the petition. What pretty white fingers you have!' And his strong brown fingers slid over her pale, slim ones, and Jelly White let them stay. Brian Moss did not, in any case, interfere with her right hand, only with the left, which was not observably making him money.

'Lady Rice sounds a dreadful wife for any man to have,' remarked Jelly.

'The Court will certainly believe so,' said Brian Moss. 'As it happened, I did have some trouble finding an example of physical assault. We had to make do with the bottom pinching.'

'But Sir Edwin was happy enough to allege it?' enquired Jelly, as if idly.

'Certainly,' said Brian Moss. 'With a little help from the new lady in his life.'

And he told his secretary how once, in the days before her employment, Sir Edwin had brought Lady Anthea Box along to an appointment: not the kind of thing Brian Moss usually approved of but, as it turned out, her presence had been useful. Anthea had spoken for Sir Edwin, who was not as coherent or determined as she. Bestiality, still one of the major and useful categories of matrimonial offence, had been quite a problem until Anthea reminded Sir Edwin how he had never liked the way his wife kissed the dogs.

'Perhaps he was just nervous of his wife catching something,' suggested Jelly White. 'Perhaps the fear was to do with hygiene, not sexual rivalry?'

'Country men seldom worry about things like that,' said Brian Moss, brushing the suggestion away. 'I hope you can get this document in the post today.'

'Of course,' said Jelly White, but it was two days before she did, and even then she put the wrong postal code on the envelope, so it was four days before the document reached Barney Evans, solicitor to Lady Rice. In the meantime Lady Rice had presented her own petition. She 'got in first', thus giving herself some minor advantage in the game that is divorce. The Rice couple, as Brian Moss observed, were not the kind to wait peaceably for a 'no fault, no blame' arrangement. Fault there was, blame there was, and fault and blame they'd have.

Jelly White was, as it happened, Lady Angelica Rice in disguise – or, to be more precise, in her alter ego. It was only lately that Lady Rice had begun to fear that the voices in her head had separate and distinct personalities. Dress up as Jelly White, and Jelly White, to some degree or another, owned her. All Lady Rice could do was whisper in Jelly's ear. They shared the ear, but Jelly it was who turned the head. It was unnerving.

Lady Rice concluded that she was suffering from a perforated personality: worse, that if any further trauma occurred, she would develop a full-blown split personality: she would become a clinical case. Lady Rice tried to maintain a calm attitude, and not to blow up more storms than were unnecessary, which was why she allowed Jelly to allow Brian Moss to fondle her and made no protest. She preserved herself for worse emergencies, and in any case, she might not be heard. Jelly was a strong and wilful personality.

In her petition for divorce, Lady Angelica Rice alleged adultery between Anthea Box and her husband over a six-month period previous to the date on which she, Lady Rice, had left the matrimonial home.

Lady Rice claimed physical assault, over-frequent and perverted sexual activity; drunkenness, drug-taking and financial irresponsibility; she asserted that her husband's relationship with his dogs was of a sexual nature. That she had been eased out of her home, Rice Court, to make way for Sir Edwin's paramour, Lady Anthea Box. Lady

6

Rice, on the other hand, had throughout the marriage been a good and faithful wife.

Sir Edwin had behaved intolerably and she wanted this reflected in any property settlement.

'An out-of-London court!' exclaimed Brian Moss, this seeming to be the part of Barney Evans' letter-plus-enclosures which most affected him. 'What a nightmare! I have no influence whatsoever in the provinces. A nod in London is simply not as good as a wink anywhere else. How ever are we to get this case settled? And how strange: the wife has claimed almost the same unreasonable behaviour as has the husband.'

'I expect it's because they were married so long,' said Jelly. 'They can read each other's minds.'

'Eleven years isn't a long marriage,' said Brian Moss. 'There was a couple in here the other day in their nineties wanting a divorce by consent. I asked them why they'd left it so long and they said they'd been waiting for the children to die.'

He laughed; a deep, hoarse, unexpected laugh at a pitch which made the many racing prints on the wall rattle, and Jelly laughed too, at his joke. Her tinkly little laugh made nothing rattle, but he pinched the swell of her bosom where it disappeared under her blouse. Just a little pinch: friendly. She had taken off her white woollen sweater. It was a hot day.

Outside the elegant Regency windows, London's traffic flowed, or tried to flow. Only emergency vehicles seemed able to make progress – police, fire, ambulance. Their sirens approached, passed, faded, with enviable speed.

'I make a good living,' observed Brian Moss, 'out of other people's need to be in the right; they like to claim the privilege of being the victim. Who's at fault in the Rice debacle is of no importance. The property is all that matters, and we'll make sure she doesn't get her greedy little fingers on too much of that. Clients assume that conduct during marriage will have an effect on a property settlement and veer it in the direction of natural justice, but it's rash to make any such assumption. Or only in the most extreme cases.'

'You don't see the Rice divorce as extreme, then? Merely run-of-the-mill?' enquired Jelly.
'Very much run-of-the-mill,' said Brian Moss, 'other than that both parties do have to go to considerable lengths to hide their income.'
And he explained that Lady Rice was once a pop star and no doubt had large undisclosed sums put away. And as for Sir Edwin, his accountants had naturally been working overtime, losing their client's assets in the books – fortunately for Sir Edwin the Rice Estate had books of enormous and wonderful complexity.
'I imagine they are,' said Jelly.
'Otherwise,' said Brian Moss, 'it's just a normal divorce. Both parties vie for the moral high ground, never noticing that a major landslip has already carried the whole mountain away. And both parties enrich me, thank God, by arguing.'

'You are a very poetic kind of man,' said Jelly White. Some of her hair had fallen free of her headband. Brian Moss caught up a strand or so between his fingers and tugged, and Jelly White smiled obligingly. Lady Rice sighed.

Thus Lady Angelica Rice had once smiled at Sir Edwin, her husband. Only now she smiled with measured guile, not an overflow of innocence. Trust and amiability had done Angelica Rice no good at all. She understood now that the transparency of innocence protected no one. She learned fast.

Lady Rice had a problem with lies and cunning. Jelly White had no such problem: they were intrinsic to her persona. Angelica had a story to tell.

2

The Velcro That Is Marriage

I was married to Edwin for eleven years, and the Velcro that's marriage got well and truly stuck. The stuff is the devil to wrest apart: it can rip and tear if your efforts are too strenuous. The cheap little sticky fibres do their work well. 'Overuse', they say, weakens Velcro. If 'overused' – a strange concept: should you fasten only so often? – is there some moral implication here? – you can hardly get Velcro to stick at all. But I was not overused in the beginning. On the contrary. When Edwin and I married, when I stopped being Angelica White and became Lady Rice, I was seventeen and a virgin, though no one would have known it. Chastity is not usually associated with leathers, studs, boots, crops, whips and the more extreme edges of the pop scene which I then frequented. But my velcroing capacity to be at one with the man I loved, in spite of appearances, was pristine, firm, ready for service. Velcro hot off the loom. I 'waited' for marriage. Extraordinary!

Edwin and I have now been apart for some months: he stayed in the matrimonial home; I left in disgrace and disarray. When it became apparent that I was in danger of having nothing whatsoever to show for my eleven years of marriage – not love, nor property, nor children, not even friends I could endure – I reckoned I had better get as near the legal horse's mouth as possible, to retrieve what I could of property and reputation; that horse being Brian Moss, and a fine upstanding ungelded beast he is, at that. Barney Evans, my own solicitor, is rather like a pit pony; forever squidging up his poor dim eyes in the sudden glare of his opponent's intellect. See me, Angelica Rice, as a bareback rider: high-heeled, fishnet-stockinged, wasp-waisted, leaping from saddle to saddle as the two blinkered legal steeds run round and round their circus ring. Jelly White running after with a bucket and spade, shovelling up the shit.

On a good night, tucked up in my high, soft bed at The Claremont, a stone's throw from Claridges, with its pure white, real linen sheets, I see myself as an avenging angel. Then I laugh aloud at my own audacity and admire myself. Fancy getting a job with your husband's lawyer's firm! On a bad night, when the fine fabric of the pillows is so wet with my tears that the down within gets dark, matted and uncomfortable, when I feel tossed about in a sea of dejection, bafflement, loss – a sea that keeps me buoyant, mind you, made extra salty by my own grief – why, then I know I am just any other abandoned and rejected woman, half-mad, worthy of nothing. Then I see that taking a job at Catterwall & Moss, in the heart of the enemy camp, is mere folly, presumption and insanity, and not in the least dashing, or clever or funny. And I worry dreadfully in case I'm found out. My moods are so extreme I feel I am two people. How is it possible to contain both in the same body?

Yet apparently it is. At least three of me look out of my two eyes. Lady Rice, Angelica and Jelly: Lady Rice and Angelica fight it out for ascendency: Jelly is Angelica's creature.

Lady Rice is a poor, passive creature in my, Angelica's, opinion. That's what marriage made of her, once it began to go wrong. She'd lie about in The Claremont suffering all day if I let her. She wouldn't even bother to answer Barney Evans' letters. I, Angelica, am the one who has to get her to work each day, dress her up as Jelly White, take her to the gym, keep her on a diet, stop her smoking. I am, I like to think, the original, pre-married persona. Why she maintains she's the dominant personality round here I can't imagine. Perhaps it's because she has a title: perhaps it's because she can't face the small-town girl that's me, which is part of her and always will be.

3

Lady Rice's Sea Of Sorrow

Each night Lady Rice rocks in a sea of sorrow, half-sleeping, half-dreaming. The sea is so salt with tears she can never sink: see how she is buoyed up by her own grief. Sometimes the sea grows wild and stormy, whipped by winds of anger, hate, violent resentments: how she turns and tosses then. She's afraid: she will be sucked down into whirlpools; she will drown, in a tempest of her own making. All she can do then is pray; much good it does her. Dear Father, dear God, save me from my enemies. Help me. I will be good, I will be. Let the storm cease. She takes a sleeping pill.

Ghostly barques glide by, in fog; pirates' swords, the swords of wrath, glinting, slashing, disembowelling, castrating. Steady the mind, steady the hand, in case the sword turns against the one who wields it. Lady Rice is pirate and victim both. She knows it. Lady Rice rocks in her nightly sea of sorrow. In her head it is called the Sea of Alimony. It might be on the moon, for all she knows, like the Sea of Tranquillity; she might be in her mother's womb. She might be in some drowned church, knocking up against stone walls, as the current pulls her here and there; her father's church. Certainly she is bruised, body and soul. Dear Father, dear God, forgive me my sins. Let the weight of Thy wrath depart from me.

Sometimes the Sea of Alimony is calm; the rocking sensuous, almost sweet. She is sorry then to surface. She is a mermaid, stunned, beached up upon the white sands of The Claremont's linen sheets, rolled back by waves into the sea, tossed up again, to surface with the dawn, to wake to the World of Alimony, Brian Moss, work, and the parts of the self still quarrelling: but also to alimony, healing, sustenance. Grief nourishes; it is a drug; she is dependent upon it now, all three of her or is it four? She sleeps as one, she wakes as many. The sea of sorrow sucks her in as one, whirls her down, washes her up fragmented; or is it the telephone which thus shatters her? A man's voice.

'Good morning, Lady Rice. It's seven thirty. This is your wake-up call.'

Lady Rice looks in her morning mirror at a face puffy with restless sleep: last night she did not take off her make-up. She collects cold water in cupped hands: it gushes plentifully from large-mouthed taps, antique or mock antique, who cares? The antique leak lead into the water, the new do not. Lead is good for the complexion, bad for the brain. She splashes her face: she does not use the white face flannels provided in some number. She despises them. They are too small. This morning she will despise anything.

She goes back to bed. But the voices in her head are loud; clear enough for once to distinguish one from another; not pleasing in what they say. She would rather just be in bed and weep: they won't let her. They are full of reproaches, complaints, eggings on to action, all unwelcome. She is beached, beached. She has tried to incorporate these bickering women, these alter egos, back into herself, but she can't. She must listen to them, and answer them.

> 'It's too bad,' moans Jelly. 'Can't you even clean our face off at night? This is the quickest way to a bad complexion, and you don't even care.'

> 'I was tired,' explains Lady Rice feebly. 'I've been so distressed by the divorce, surely I'm allowed to be tired.'

> 'You can't afford to be tired,' says Angelica. 'We've got to get out of this mess somehow. How are we going to live? We can't stay in this hotel for ever. Sooner or later they'll throw us out.'

> 'They'd never do that,' says Lady Rice. 'I'm a member of the Rice family. Edwin would never let it happen.'

> 'Of course he would,' says Angelica. 'You have a replacement. You're old news. What does he care about you? Nothing as ex as an almost ex-wife! The most hated object.'

Lady Rice dissolves in further tears: the grief is harsh, not languorous.

> 'Get her up, for God's sake,' says Jelly. 'You have more influence than me. I hate being late for work. You just deliver me and go away. You don't have to stand around to receive the flack.'

> 'I think if I had a fuck,' says Lady Rice, surprisingly and suddenly, 'I'd feel better. Brian Moss will do very well. The only cure for one man is another man.'

'Don't use that language,' says Jelly, shocked. 'And surely you can do without a man for a month or so? Men are the source of the problem, not the cure.'

'I don't know what came over me,' says Lady Rice, remorseful. 'But now it's said, it might be true.'

'Perhaps Brian Moss is our karma,' says Angelica cunningly. 'Shall we just get up and go and meet our destiny?'

And Lady Rice finally drags herself from her bed, just to shut them up, since they won't leave her alone. She can see they might make good company. She need never be lonely: and loneliness, for all that others speak of aloneness, is what she most fears.

4

Initial Transformations

Angelica rose and dressed. She left for work in black leather jacket, black wig and dark glasses, looking she hoped not at all like Lady Rice – that wronged, tearful, virtuous, needy creature – but like some important guest's rather ferocious and determined mistress. She carried a holdall in which, neatly folded (by Jelly: Jelly was good at folding: Angelica was not), were Jelly's working clothes.

Angelica it was who would step into her chauffeur-driven, hired Volvo at exactly seven forty-eight. Nearly every morning the car was there, parked in Davies Street. She would step into the Volvo as Angelica, step out as Jelly. Once in the car, she would take off Angelica's wig to reveal Jelly's short, shiny, straight blonde hair: she would take off her leather jacket and put on a pale blue blazer with brass buttons, made in a cheap, uncrushable fabric. She would drag her hair back behind a pale pink satin headband, and hang a long string of artificial pearls round her neck, to fall over her tight, white woollen jumper. She wore a bra which under-played her breasts: the tightness of the sweater was more to do with fashion than sexuality. She would wipe off her more extravagant make-up and put on owl glasses. She would become Jelly White, with Angelica's knowledge and consent.

But occasionally the Volvo was not there, not waiting in Davies Street when she left the hotel. The car service was stretched that time of the morning, they would explain. Or they were short of drivers; there was a flu epidemic. Could she wait? Half an hour, perhaps? And she could not, and would have to travel to work by public transport. Then she would make the ego change in a Ladies' room at the Inns of Court, so boldly entering the passages marked 'Private', passing without shame through doors marked 'Staff Only', to find this safe, high, private, empty, well-disinfected, slightly odorous place, leaving with so prim and self-righteous a mien that in neither personality was she ever challenged.

But she preferred the back of the Volvo: the darkened windows, the stiff back of the driver the other side of the glass, leather upholstery made sticky by the contact of flesh, albeit her own.

And there she would be as Jelly White, she of the highly developed super-ego, the eye for detail, the capacity to distinguish between right and wrong, and the self-righteousness, the priggishness that goes with it; a clean, tidy, cologne-scented, unambitious young woman with a self-image not high, not low, but realistic, well aware of her own virtues, her own faults; Daddy's girl, the one who stays safe for his sake, who never ventures far, who marries someone reliable and nice on the right day at the right time, the one in whom incestuous desires are decently repressed, the one in whom deceit runs rampant, the one to whom lies come naturally, and are always justified, the one to whom rank and order of authority matter; Jelly, for this reason, fit to be under-paid and overworked, the one who stays late to get the mail done, the one just occasionally to pursue the flir-tation with the boss, and sue for sexual harassment later. Office bait: a sweet smile, a gentle look, but an eye for the main chance. Daddy never frowned on that. 'You get what you can out of it, my girl! Never *be* the boss; no, *use* the boss.'

While you're at the office, incognito, Jelly is the girl to be. No use being Angelica, anyway: life would be one long error, Tippex spill and misfiling: one long chafing under instruction: a yearning for freedom, a throwing open of windows to let the air in, and letting wind and rain in instead, to everyone's dismay.

Angelica would threaten Brian Moss's marriage to the sweet and domestic Oriole as Jelly never would. The Jellys of the world, sealed off from real emotion, seldom create it in others. Lust, yes: yearning, no. They sit at the office desk and one might be another. Angelicas come singly, and because they suffer, also inflict suffering.

Angelica tried out Jelly's role for size, and found that not only did it fit, but could be discarded easily. Jelly put up no resistance: she was wonderfully practical: good at emergencies; never dithered: nor threw her hands in the air nor acted like a startled child.

Sir Edwin arranged a meeting with Lady Rice and her solicitor Barney Evans at Brian Moss's office. It was easy enough for Jelly to allege a sudden migraine, pretend to take a taxi home, then slip into the powder room and turn into Lady Rice: take off the owl glasses, pull a little black velvet hat down over her hair, change the city high heels for a steadier, more country kind, put on blue eyeshadow and bright red lipstick, adjust the expression on her face and there she was, an unhappy version of a once happy Lady Rice, and all Sir Edwin's fault.

The powder room where Jelly achieved this transformation was one of the original back bedrooms of the pleasant Georgian house where Catterwall & Moss made their home, haphazardly converted. The room was high and large; plaster flaked from the ceiling. Thick cream paint covered the walls and ancient plumbing alike. Draughts whistled under the doors. Go into the loo as typist, adopt the body language of those who command, rather than those commanded, and come out the client.

As it happened, Sir Edwin had not turned up.
> 'Just as well,' said Jelly. 'There'd only have been a scene.'
> 'Chickened out,' said Angelica, and retired for a time, defeated, disappointed in spite of herself.
> 'I love him,' moaned Lady Rice. 'If only I could just see him, meet him, talk things over, he'd realise that he really loves me; he couldn't possibly prefer Anthea to me.'

And so on. Lady Rice went back to the powder room and changed into Jelly again, by-passing Angelica. Jelly realised she need not defer to Angelica. She had her own existence.

5

Office Business

Both solicitors had been trying to persuade Lady Rice to accept an out-of-court, once-and-for-all, clean-break settlement, which Lady Rice was not prepared to do. Prompted and nudged by Angelica, she was prepared to fight.

'Such settlements may suit the Courts and the lawyers,' said Lady Rice boldly to Barney Evans. 'They save the Court time and trouble, but they don't suit me. Why should I let Edwin get away with his crimes against my life, my spirit? Let my husband be answerable to me for the rest of his life: let him support me for ever. He can disguise his assets temporarily, but in the end truth emerges. Doesn't it?'

Barney Evans, now acting like a fine dray horse, sniffed and trumpeted and avoided saying, 'No. In my opinion and experience truth rarely emerges.' Clients had to be protected from the world, allowed to keep their illusions. Yes, justice exists: yes, heaven exists. This was the task of the lawyer, as it was that of the priest. 'Lo, there shall be no corruption, no mortality!' was their constant cry.

'I demand justice,' Lady Rice persisted in crying, as did

so many. 'I will never rest till I have it, and nor should you!'

Oh, Lady Rice was a nuisance, Barney Evans and Brian Moss agreed, by a look exchanged, a soft sigh of common understanding.

'I'm sure I've seen Lady Rice somewhere before,' said Brian Moss to Jelly White after Barney Evans had shared a sherry with him and departed, and the Rice v. Rice files were put away.

'She was almost a celebrity once upon a time,' said Jelly White, head turned towards the computer, stretching and bending her fingers so as to save herself from Repetitive Strain Injury (Wisdom v. Argus Telephones) which can so wretchedly affect the computer worker. 'That was before she married Sir Edwin, back when she was a pop star. She was number one for eight whole weeks with "Kinky Virgin", and on TV a lot. After that she was lead singer in a group of the same name; they toured quite successfully. But that was all. Marriage put paid to her showbiz ambitions.'

'I don't look at TV,' said Brian Moss. 'I don't have the time. When I get home I have to bath the babies. I'm a New Man. Why did Edwin Rice marry a pop star in the first place? Didn't he need someone he could take to point-to-points? It's so much easier to marry a woman other men ignore. That's what I did when I married Oriole. I knew I would be safe; Oriole would always be faithful: I make a real effort to be the same. Well, Anthea Box will suit Sir Edwin much better than his first wife ever did, so long as she can stay off the drink. Those are hard-drinking circles, I believe. She's out of the same stable as he is, that's the main thing when it comes to marriage. Isn't she some kind of cousin? I hope there's nothing unfortunate in the genes. I find Barney Evans a very pleasant and helpful guy. I was at school with his brother. Heart of gold.'

'Aren't you meant to be antagonistic,' asked Jelly, 'on behalf of your client? I was surprised you were so friendly.'

'We go through the motions,' said Brian Moss, 'but, like anyone else, all we really want is as much profit and as little fuss as possible. We professionals are all on one side, the punters on the other.'

The pace of the divorce and the property settlement was laboured and slow. Lady Rice withdrew her petition and let Sir Edwin's stand, since a nod and a wink from Brian Moss suggested to Barney Evans that Sir Edwin would be generous if she did. Sir Edwin's refusal to communicate directly with his wife continued. Lady Rice complained of undue influence from Anthea Box. And indeed, a letter from Brian Moss's office suggesting that Sir Edwin make another attempt to meet Lady Rice and sort things out in a friendly fashion was fielded by a phone call from Anthea, saying it was out of the question. Jelly, who took the call, said she'd let Brian Moss know. She did nothing of the kind, of course, since Brian Moss was unaware of the initial letter: she had written it herself and signed it per pro Brian Moss.

Lady Rice received a letter from Barney Evans saying it was in her interests to move the hearings from the provincial Courts to London, since they would get a better hearing there with a more sympathetic judge. Lady Rice wrote back to say no, the provinces would do her very well. She would rather trust an impartial judge than a sympathetic one. Sympathy could sway like a tree in a high wind; first here, then there. Lady Rice did not know whence this wisdom sprang: sometimes she felt she was older than her years.

Lady Rice remained vague as to her whereabouts. She gave Barney Evans her mother's address for correspondence. Let Edwin have a sense of her as Lilith, whom Adam discarded; the original, wronged wife, who wanders the outskirts of the universe, bringing trouble to mankind, never resting, for ever spiteful, for ever grieving, making others feel bad.

The best place to hide, she knew, is beneath the nose of the searcher. It was obvious to Jelly White that such staff at Catterwall & Moss whose job it was to look after Sir Edwin's private finances would have neither time nor inclination to look through the files when The Claremont Hotel's bill came. Who would be bothered to check that Rice, Sir E, didn't have 'and Lady A' tucked in next to it? No one. Nor would The Claremont think it prudent to point out to anyone that Lady A, according to the newspapers recovering from bulimia and anorexia in a nursing home somewhere in the Midlands, was to their knowledge living in their Bridal Suite. It suited The Claremont well enough to have a titled lady in residence, although that lady went incognito.

6

Angel Is Born

One Tuesday morning Lady Rice woke from her sea of sorrow and went to work as usual, getting into the Volvo as Angelica, preparing to leave it as Jelly, when she found herself howling aloud. She howled as in films the man who turns into a werewolf howls, body and mind stretching and deforming: they had gone into overload. She was giving birth to yet another self. Its name was Angel, and no angel, it.

Ram the chauffeur, seated behind the glass partition which cut off employer from servant, stopped the car, turned his head and fixed Angelica/Jelly with startled eyes. His eyes were dark, well-fringed, kind, albeit male. Angelica's dress was up to her knees. She was changing her slimming black stockings to Jelly's ankle-thickening beige. But her leg from ankle to knee, whatever she wore, remained long, slim and fetching.

'Is that my exhaust holed?' the driver asked. 'Or is it you?'

Lady Rice, Angelica, Jelly, Angel howled again. They howled because it was a Tuesday morning, and on Monday nights Anthea often stayed over at Rice Court, so Lizzie, Lady Rice's detective, had told her. (These days Lady Rice had detectives as other people might have hairdressers, astrologers, chiropodists, aerobicists. It is the most urgent desire of the divorcing person to know what goes on behind closed doors.) It had been the habit of the female combo that was her to drug herself to sleep on Monday nights, so heavily that it would be nearly Tuesday lunchtime before the three awoke. But the exigencies of employment had made that impossible, and here they were, caught halfway between Angelica and Jelly, at eight thirty on a Tuesday, knowing that this was when her husband's enjoyment and capacity for sex was at its highest – many's the time she had slipped out of bed early so as not to encounter it, as she remembered to her pain – and, worse, the chance thereby increased of his saying something intimate, loving, and kind to her rival. And at that very moment, if she thought about it, that rival, like as not, would be in the marital bed. Of course the entity howled.

They made no further effort to move their legs together. They were in any case wearing French knickers which hardly hid a thing. In fact they found themselves moving their legs further apart.

'For God's sake, what are you doing?' pleaded Angelica, suddenly alarmed. 'This is no answer to anything.'

'You don't know this man from Adam,' warned Jelly. 'Remember AIDS.'

'I do as I like,' said Angel, for it was she, moving her legs further apart. 'And I have what I want, and what I want, as ever, is sex.'

'What is going on in here?' demanded Lady Rice, who had been dozing, but was startled sufficiently to be back at least notionally in charge. 'I know

I said I wanted a fuck, but I was speaking theoretically.'

'Oh no you weren't,' said Angel.

'We don't want you interfering,' said the other two. They were already ganging up on her. 'You had your chance and a fine mess you made of it.'

And Lady Rice retired, part hurt, part glad to have been given permission, to some brooding part of her being, to rock in her sea of sorrow and absorb its nutrients. She was glad now she'd been an only child, had never had sisters.

'Please don't make that noise,' Ram pleaded. 'It makes it difficult to drive.' He was, Angel supposed, for she was looking at him closely, as Jelly never did and Angelica never would, in his late twenties. He was fair-complexioned and had well-manicured nails which rested with confidence on the well-padded wheel; he was blessed with the strong jaw and sharp eyes of a business executive. Only the chauffeur's cap suggested that the car was the tool of his trade, not the badge of his status. But the emergent halfway woman didn't really care who he was or what he said, or indeed what he saw – one stocking half rolled off, the other un-suspended, and the suspender straps with their plastic button device falling loose – tights are tricky to change in confined surroundings: stockings less of a problem, but still provide some difficulty. That person halfway between a couple of I's and a you uttered another howl, and tears ran down her face.

Ram turned the Volvo without so much as a comment, let alone asking for permission from his multi-faceted employer, into an underground car park. 'Spaces' flashed out in red lights in the narrow street outside. As the car turned in, the barrier to the entrance rose, apparently of its own accord. The electronic world is so much in tune, these days, with the living one, it is not surprising we get confused, see ourselves programmed, incapable of political or social protest, as we go about the routine of our lives. The car approached, access was willed, the barrier rose: the horror of the scene thus revealed – the dark mouths of concrete stalls, the puddled floor, the scrawled tormented walls, the stench of urine – seem an inevitable consequence of that very willing. Forget it, don't argue, don't fight, don't attempt to reform; technology doesn't, why should you? You are less than the machinery which serves you, and by serving you controls you; more prone to error, the ramshackle entropy, than when you were poorer but more in control. The human spirit splits and fractures, it has to, to make an amoeboid movement round technology, to engulf it, as flesh forms round a splinter, the better to protect itself. The four-fold entity of Lady Rice is not yet commonplace, but may well yet be.

Ram took his vehicle deeper and deeper underground. Angel swayed, first this way, then that, as the car traversed the descending levels, the bare stretch of thigh above her stocking tops sticking, first this side, then that, on hot leather, until there was nowhere else for the car to go but the furthest, deepest, blackest stall, after which the entrance signs turned to exit signs. Ram McDonald reversed the Volvo into this small space, with considerable skill. The vehicle's windows were of darkened glass. The occupants could see out: no one could see in. The rich like to travel thus, and the journeys, after all, were on Sir Edwin's charge account. Ram left the front seat and joined Angel in the back. She did not protest. Anthea clasped Edwin, Edwin clasped Anthea: the sun did not go out, let alone society disapprove. What matter then who clasped whom, in lust or love, since decency and justice had foundered anyway?

The core of the amoeba is fluid; its outer parts jelly-like. When the amoeba wishes to move, fluid is converted to jelly at the leading end of the body, and jelly is converted to fluid at the other end, and so the whole animal moves along. The concept of 'wish' is vague, and there seems no point within this single cell creature which could generate an emotion, or drive, yet 'wish' it does. It wishes to move, or chooses to move, or fails to remain still. However you put it, the amoeba demonstrates intent: just so Lady Rice's body, flowing, incorporating, changing from fluid to jelly, jelly to fluid, announced to her and demonstrated to her parts its joint intent to experience a unified and unifying orgasm, as Ram strove and stroked.

'That's better,' said Angel to the others, shuddering and juddering. Ram pulled her close to him. 'That's what you lot needed. A good fuck.'

'Speak for yourself,' said Angelica. 'It was the last thing I ever wanted,' and she turned her mouth away from Ram's. 'Edwin and I always got on well enough without. I liked being wooed and I liked being kissed, but I hate being out of control.'

Angel made Angelica turn her mouth back to Ram's. His lips were heavy on hers and Jelly could feel the bristles of his chin roughening the delicate skin of her cheek, but had to let the matter rest.

'He's not even wearing a condom,' agitated Jelly

into Lady Rice's ear: surely that would make an impact. 'For God's sake, put a stop to all this –' 'It's beyond me,' murmured Lady Rice. 'My mother used to tell me there was no stopping a man once he's begun, or you get yourself raped. Just get it over. Aren't you going to be late for the office?'

Jelly and Angelica wept, Lady Rice sulked, Angel responded to Ram in kindly fashion, though her own gratification had been long since gained.

'We must do this again,' said Ram.
They wondered what to reply.
'Get involved with a chauffeur?' demanded Angelica. 'You must be joking.'
'Impossible. I must keep my mind on my work,' said Jelly. 'I can't afford diversion.'
'Never, never, never,' cried Lady Rice. 'Edwin might find out.'
But they discounted her. She was the one who loved Edwin. The others had long given up. Love, they could see, was a luxury they could ill afford. The humiliation of love spurned was what made women on the edge of a divorce give up their rights so easily.
'Take it all,' they cry. 'I don't want a thing.'
Later, when love's over, they can see their mistake. He has no such qualms. Winner takes all.

'We'll do it again tomorrow,' said Angel, and, as she had use of the mouth and the whole body felt good and at ease, it was Angel Ram heard.
'Unless you're free this evening. But shall we concentrate on now?'

'Slut, whore, bitch! Anybody's! Stone her to death,' came Angelica's response.

She *was* in a temper. Angel bit her own lip and let out a yelp. Ram licked the sore place better.

'And what time of the month is it?' Jelly asked.

'Forget AIDS, what about pregnancy? Christ, you're irresponsible.'

Lady Rice just gave up and thought about other things. Let Angelica, Jelly and Angel emote; it left her free to reflect in tranquillity. She had wanted a fuck and got one but, when it came to it, this was no kind of answer. She supposed she was in the power of the statistic, yet again. She was one of the thirty-four per cent of women who engage in untoward sexual activity when first apart from their husbands and suffering, as a consequence, from low self-esteem. Her own behaviour, she could see, was nothing to do with her, not her responsibility at all.

Interesting, she noted, that Angel's stretched arms fell apart from around Ram's neck at the moment of orgasm. Jelly would have clasped hers the tighter, in surprise. Angel, on orgasm, felt gratification, not surprise. Angel's body fell automatically loose and languid at such a moment. Angelica would have tautly stretched and side-stepped: first the stretch to better experience, but then the last minute sidestep to avoid the fluid to jelly, jelly to fluid of orgasmic takeover. Fidgeting, defensive Angelica; self-interested, manipulative Jelly; serve them both right to be overwhelmed by the desires of lustful, conscience-less Angel!

What pleasure then, and what rejoicing should there not be, as out of the sepulchral gloom which surrounds the death of marriage, this brilliance dawned, this angel, sweeping away humiliation, self-interest, discrimination, with such powerful wings. This new source of lustful energy now streamed out waves of stormy, light-dappled dark; and in the flickering blackness that still was light, Ram McDonald gained his power; hairy male arms and legs entwined with her own smooth white limbs. Or, look at it this way, a king crab crawled out from under a rock, perfectly at home in his watery parking lot; monstrous yet everyday; the handsome, healthiest crab you ever saw; king of the rock pool, all-important till you got a glimpse of the ocean. A chauffeur today, but whom tomorrow?

If Angel fluttered through clouds of sexual glory, it was to rejoice in their turbulence. Good Bad Angel, thought Lady Rice; her little sister Angel, who loved to feel the stickiness of hot leather on naked thighs, who rejoiced in the rush of non-identity to the head, the feel of long skinny legs opened, the satisfaction of the thrust of strange hard flesh felt between; and the familiar flurry and panting begin, the search for the soul of the other, buried so obtusely in flesh. Leave it all to Angel.

Then Angel cried out in the sheer delight of her coming to birth.

> 'Be quiet,' begged Jelly. 'Don't make that dreadful noise.'
> 'Don't overdo it,' said Angelica. 'He'll think you're faking.'

Good Bad Angel, little sister! Lady Rice denied maternal status. She would be Angel's sister; that much she could allow, but she could never see herself as mother in charge. She had had enough of all that, in marriage. In charge of Rice Court, in charge of her husband's happiness, in charge of everyone's morals, as good wives are: inexorably, little by little, simply by virtue of knowing best, being turned into mother. What even halfway decent man could allow himself to stay married to his mother, once that status had become unequivocal?

'By the way,' said Angel into the quiet of spirit which follows orgasm. 'My name's Angel Lamb.' (Lamb was Angelica's mother's maiden name.) 'I am the Angel and the Id together,' she introduced herself. 'I am the internalised sibling of Lady Rice, Angelica Barley (a passing stage name) and Jelly White, our father's daughter. Now just shut up and let me get on with this. There's no stopping me now I'm here. The time you've wasted; the journeys you've taken with this gorgeous hunk of manhood and done nothing about it! Too bad!'

Angelica winced at the phraseology, and Jelly lamented the folly of what had been done, and Lady Rice drowsed and sniffed her unhappiness, and they all adjusted their dress and Ram took his place in the front seat and took them to the very door of the office.

7

History

Back in the Sixties, Prue Lamb, aged seventeen, married Stephen White, aged fifty-two, and gave birth soon thereafter to a little girl they named Angelica, who was both dutiful and ambitious, cute and swift. Sometimes they called her Jelly, for short – in affection and dismissal, 'Oh, Jelly, you are being a pain; what husband will put up with you?' – and occasionally they called her Angel, as in 'Angel, dearest, fetch me this; Angel, dearest, fetch me that. Angel, dearest, put pennies on your poor dead father's eyes. He, too, is an angel now. If only you hadn't chosen to sing that rock and roll stuff, if only you'd stuck to Handel's Messiah, you could have risen to soprano lead and your father might not have got so upset and died. Not that I'm blaming you, my Angel, both our Angel, indeed you were your father's Angel, with a voice that carolled like a lark, in whatever mode you chose, and at least he didn't live to have to listen to "Kinky Virgin". At least you preserved your virginity, for his sake, until he'd croaked, pegged it, passed over, fell off the perch. It was only to be expected, he being thirty-five years older than me, but I can tell you expecting makes no difference. It's still an outrage to be left without a husband.'

Larks and lambs, and pure white rice: add a soupçon of barley; all good things. Why do they go wrong? Nothing's ever over, that's the answer, not even the giving of names. They should have called her Jane: it is a name scarcely open to division, perforating, or outright splitting. Angelica was just asking for trouble.

8

Anthea In The Linen Room

As Ram leaned over Angel, shuffling off his blue serge trousers in the back of the Volvo, and she inclined further backwards on the real leather seats – with their added spray of real leather scent – pulling her narrow skirt further up around her hips to demonstrate her assent, to quieten her howling, Edwin did indeed enter Anthea, not in the marital bed but in the second floor linen room of Rice Court. Here the shelves were neatly stacked with bedding of the old and tasteful kind, linens and cottons well-washed to a delicate flimsiness, folded neatly and flatly: woollen blankets likewise: not an acrylic duvet or a man-made fibre in sight.

Edwin, massively built, broad-shouldered, a softness of flesh covering muscle and nerve, smooth-chested, warm-skinned in spite of his blue blood, a chin naturally commanding but with a nature perpetually retreating, appearing to the outside world as a man extremely fortunate in his heredity, both physical and financial, supremely rational, calmly confident, pleasant, co-operative and intelligent, with untold shares invested in mysterious companies abroad, leaned back against the slatted laundry shelves, parted Anthea's knees with his, pushed up between her thighs and with no ceremony entered her. Anthea barely blenched. She wore her head-scarf of heavy cream silk, with a splatter of anchor chains and horses upon it. Edwin liked Anthea to wear the headscarf in the house and out of it, and Anthea, conscious always that her hair probably needed washing, usually made no objection. She wore only the headscarf. She was narrow-hipped to the point of skinniness. An observer would have found the woman wholly eclipsed by the man, by so many inches did his width surpass hers. Mrs MacArthur too often surprised them: bringing their breakfast on a tray. Here they were safe, for at least an hour or so.

Anthea was the natural Lady Rice, everyone agreed, well-suited to be mistress of this splendid house: she was plain, horsey, straightforward, blunt, boring, practical, with the wealth of generations behind her: she would tell him what to do while appearing to be told.

It was understood, but seldom said, that Edwin had succumbed to a passing infatuation when he married Angelica, married someone hopelessly unsuitable; a young woman with no background, who not only wouldn't ride to hounds but spoke up for the hunt saboteurs; who, or so it was said, would refuse her husband his marital rights on one pretext or another, while still claiming his title. But Anthea understood that the way to keep a man happy was to give him as much sex as possible and give him no intellectual challenges. Men liked to rest, once adolescence was over. See Anthea now, leaning back into pieces of soap-scented linen, arms outstretched as if crucified against the shelves, hands clenching and un-clenching; eyes rolling, gasping: more, more!

Oh darling! They seldom kiss – it seems too personal. That's how Edwin likes sex; so does Anthea. Lots of sex, and all of it impersonal. The original Lady Rice, Angelica, ex-Kinky Virgin, turned out to be over-fussy. She required wooing; she had a notion of romance: she liked kissing, endearment, sweet words, tired easily, and in the end would rather plainly not fuck at all if she could help it. A man can grow weary of that kind of thing. Seduction and persuasion, foreplaying and tantalising, are all very well for a year or two, but ten years into a childless marriage can begin to seem to be onerous.

Trauma had rendered Lady Rice uncomfortably telepathic. And even as in the second floor linen cupboard of the ancestral home her rightful husband shuddered within her rival, Angel let out the bellow which was her birth-cry. The umbilical cord that tied Angel to Lady Rice was cut. Angel understood, as Angelica had not, or Jelly either, that life could be good. You just had to accept what it offered, and if the offering was male, you'd take it.

Jelly At Work

'I'm sorry to be so late,' said Jelly to Brian Moss of the velvety smooth voice, cunning eye and beautifully cut suit. 'I had to go to the doctor. I hope you haven't opened the post,' she added. 'You always get everything in such a muddle.'

'I leave detail to you, my dear,' he said. 'I look after the major issues, the wider sweep, as befits the male. Shall we have coffee now?'

'You mean will I make it?' she asked, and did.

These days a good legal secretary is hard to find and, if they are found, are usually elderly women – the young ones decline to take work both so responsible yet so poorly paid. Legal secretaries often start out with crabby natures – those with an eye to detail often have these – and impatience with human folly gets the better of them, and feeds into the original disposition. It is not easy or pleasant to get correct, day after day, the detail by which human beings try to wrest justice from a world determined not to deliver it. People, it soon becomes clear to the legal secretary, veer either to the delinquent or to the boring. At the delinquent end of the scale – criminal or family law – there is too much distress; at the boring end – contractual or constitutional law – there is just yawning boredom. And even that boredom exists as a fragile, if opaque, lid on a bubbling cauldron of iniquity and roguery; scams so great, from the stealing of pension funds to the selling of junk bonds to the hijacking of nations, it is hard to believe it is happening. The detail of fraud is not so much interesting as incomprehensible to the non-criminal mind. Spelling mistakes creep in. Negatives where negatives should not be. The computer operator, the legal secretary, to whom the shameless effrontery of others so often is initially apparent, tends to stay silent. A bad dream induced by boredom, they tell themselves. It can't be happening. Shut up, stay quiet, don't rock the boat, look after yourself, keep the job. The world can't be as bad as this, nor the people in it so villainous, so confident in their grey-suited villainy: the stories unfolding before my eyes upon the screen must surely be fiction.

And, after all, then the legal secretary, the computer operator, has, by virtue of training and inclination, no need for desperate action, seldom any personal craving for wealth or power, and finding so little villainy in themselves, even on close self-inspection, is not looking out for it in others. This may be a pleasant characteristic, but it is also dangerous. 'I didn't believe it; I didn't want to rock the boat,' are the initial pleas. 'I thought they must know what they were doing; I was only obeying orders,' the final ones. Good legal secretaries come too expensive to have their time wasted on coffee-making, but Brian Moss, a New Man in the home, was a Former Man in the office and liked Jelly to do it. Nor, when it came to it, did Jelly much mind. Brian Moss was too impatient to let the water boil and the coffee he made was lacklustre.

'Excuse me,' said Jelly later in the morning, when she was taking dictation.
'Well, what is it? Grammar? Correct it as you go along. We have a lot of post to get through.' Brian Moss was impatient. She liked the way his fingers tapped upon the table: imperative and irritable. It seemed to her the proper way for a man to be. He had just concluded a letter to a would-be father suing a Health Authority for causing his wife's infertility. 'My best regards to your wife. I hope the poodles are keeping bright and bushy-tailed.'
'Poodles get their tails docked at birth,' said Jelly. 'Perhaps "bushy-tailed" is inappropriate.'
'Replace it with some similar jocularity,' said Brian Moss. 'I leave it all to you.'
He stood behind Jelly's chair and his hands slid round beneath her breasts, feeling the weight of each one. She felt her identity scatter as her pearls had scattered earlier in the day in the back of the Volvo. Sexual desire was inimical, it seemed, to single-mindedness.
'You're not wearing your pearls today,' he said. 'I like your pearls.'
'They broke on the way to work this morning,' said Angel, speaking through Jelly's lips.
'Please,' begged Angelica, 'not this too! Don't mess this job up, as you did my marriage.'
'Who, me?' enquired Angel, all innocence. 'I wasn't even born when you were married.'

41

Angelica managed to manoeuvre the wavering Jelly out of the room and back to her desk. Brian Moss followed them both, believing them to be one.

The secretarial quarters at Catterwall & Moss were small, high-ceilinged squares of rooms looking out onto a soot-blackened wall, requiring always artificial light. Jelly's was the partitioned end of the former Georgian library which served as Brian Moss's office, which was grand, formal, old-fashioned, panelled in oak, but disproportioned as a result of that very partitioning. Brian Moss seldom entered the small room. He found it gloomy, not surprisingly. He spoke through the intercom and summoned whoever it was sat there: they changed with the years. Now he followed Jelly.

'We've nowhere near finished the post,' Brian Moss complained. 'Some of these letters really have to go off today. You will just have to excuse the inexcusable, Miss White, if so it was, come back into my office and get on.'

Brian Moss looked at his secretary pleadingly, little-boy like. He had blue eyes and a face reckoned handsome, in the English manner: clean cut and under apparent control; his expression imbued with a gentle melancholy. At first Jelly did not reply: she was busy collecting personal belongings from her desk drawer; saving what was on the computer; evidently preparing the place for her successor.

'Please,' said Brian Moss. 'I really am sorry. I shan't lay hands on you again. Promise.'

It was in Brian Moss's favour, Jelly told Angelica, that he was prepared to talk about his infringement of her body space. Many a man would maul you and then say nothing; would prefer to pretend, if the advances were rejected, that the advance had never occurred. Many a man, come to that, put in Angel, would spend a night with you and never refer to that event again either, and the woman, feeling rejected and diminished, would all too often collude and fall silent too. As if the very past were male, defined by the man's memory of it, forget the female's.

'Do stop looking at me like that,' he said. 'Say something. Or, if you won't, couldn't we just get back to work?'

'I doubt it,' said Jelly. 'According to the small print of my agency contract with you, I am free, in the event of sexual harassment, to terminate my employment without penalty.'

'You'd have to prove sexual harassment,' said Brian Moss, 'and that would be difficult, even impossible. Your word against mine. Why do you think we agreed to that clause being there in the first place? Because it is meaningless, and because women like to see it there. It makes them believe they're being taken seriously. But all that is by the by. I am actually a perfectly decent guy and don't want to take advantage of you. You had your blouse unbuttoned so far down that I could see your nipples. And you're not wearing a bra. So I didn't think you'd mind. I'm sorry. It won't happen again.'

Jelly quickly buttoned her blouse, which was indeed undone, but not to the extent Brian Moss suggested. Angel had no doubt managed to slip a button or so through a hole or so when she, Jelly, was thinking of something else. And how did she come to be bra-less? What Angel did was only vaguely recalled by Jelly, Angelica or Lady Rice, but the marks left upon the body – their nipples were sore and there were bite marks on their neck – stood between them and total forgetfulness.

43

Jelly conceded that she might, albeit unknowingly, have provoked him, and consented to go back to work.

Brian Moss told Jelly a little about his wife, Oriole, whom he loved but who was so forgetful she would never even remember to comb her hair in the mornings, and would collect his children from school in a car into which she'd forgotten to put petrol. She was a danger to them. Once she'd left the iron on so it burned right through a ceiling; it was a regular occurrence for Oriole to let the bath overflow.

'Would that count as unreasonable behaviour in a divorce court?' Jelly asked, and Brian Moss looked quite disconcerted at the thought, and said he and Oriole were Catholics so there was no question of that anyway. But she now understood why he watched her own smooth, quick, certain movements with a kind of longing, a subdued passion for what was effective, efficient and reliable. She was pleased to see it. It was part of herself which had never in the past been properly appreciated.

Jelly worked late; so did Brian Moss: both of them in their separate rooms. The building was darkened. Computer screens gave off a luminous sheen; pot plants seemed to breathe, and to swell and diminish minutely with each breath.

Jelly could feel Angel whispering and nudging her: saying,

> 'Look, here's your chance. Do something! Take off your clothes; but leave on your suspender belt and stockings. Very nice too. And then just walk into Brian Moss's office.'

44

'But why?' Jelly asked. 'What would be the point of that?'

'You'd get a rise,' said Angel. 'And you could make him do what you want.'

'For someone as brazen as Angel,' said Angelica, 'she's extremely naive. You'd just as likely find yourself fired by morning.'

'You're not here to earn a salary,' murmured Lady Rice. 'You're here to make sure I get proper alimony from Edwin.'

'What about revenge?' asked Angel. 'Edwin's having a good time with Anthea. Anthea's living in our house, sleeping in our bed –'

'Don't make me think about it,' said Jelly, bile rising in her throat.

'Brian Moss could stop you thinking about it,' said Angel. 'He could stop you thinking about it for at least two hours. Think how well Ram did only this morning. If one man fancies you, another man will. Make the most of it.'

'Brian Moss has a wife at home,' said Jelly. 'I don't do things like that. I don't go with married men. Because Lady Rice is unhappy, why should Oriole Moss be unhappy, too?'

'For that very reason,' gritted Angel, bad Angel, avenging Angel, in Jelly's ear. 'If you spread the misery wide, you make it thinner for yourself,' and Angel bit into the base of Jelly's thumb so hard there was a mark for days, almost as sore as her breasts where Ram had pecked and nibbled at them.

'I won't do any such thing,' said Jelly. 'Angelica is right. I'd only get fired. That's what happens in office romances.'

45

'This is not an office romance,' gritted Angel. 'It is you fucking your boss in your own best interests.'

'No,' said Jelly.

'But I want to. I mean to,' yelled Angel in her head, drowning out reason. 'I want Brian Moss *now*, you mean old bitch, and I'll have him.'

'Shut up,' said Jelly, biting the other thumb. Lady Rice was humming to herself somewhere else; some sad, melancholy tune. 'Don't put this pressure on me. I'm tied to the mast, understand? And I'm not listening to you. I can cope with Lady Rice, I can cope with Angelica, but you – you're a menace! Get out of my life!'

'The ingratitude!' shrieked Angel. 'After all I did for you! You'd never have had the nerve and you know you loved it!'

'I'm going home now,' called out Brian Moss to Jelly White. 'Must be home to bath the babies.'

'That's fine,' called his secretary in reply. 'I'll turn the lights off and set the alarm.'

Brian went home by train. Jelly took the Underground, squashed with a thousand others into a space fit for a hundred, the smell of despair adding humidity to the air she breathed. How do I escape, how do I not do this? How not to be herded, squashed, insulted, abused? See, there's the hem of my coat caught in the door: it will brush through the soot of ancient tunnels: that woman's high heel driving between my toes, removing skin: that man's crotch, that woman's arse, rubbing against mine. We share the same torment, rebreathe each other's air, use the strategies of the traumatised to escape all remembrance of the journey: as the slaves were whipped to the pyramids, simply for the fun of it, the pain of it, for a whipped slave works half as well, but a man must know when he's beaten. So have his masters from the beginning of time insisted on the humiliation of their workforce. These days, through their Lodges and Confederations, they have got together over champagne and devised the public transport they never travel in to whip the workers to work: and are not jobs short and is not the living hard and precarious, and who can argue any more?

Do we not suffer? – the multi-voiced air of the metro rose to heaven, spoke to heaven – 'Who will save us?' But there came no reply. Suffering does not necessarily suggest its own relief: because things start does not mean they must end: oppression does not necessitate the rise of the hero, nor sin its saviour. And besides, everyone disliked each other too much to do anything about any of it. White hated black, black hated white, and all stations in between: parent hated child, child hated parent; police hated citizen, citizen hated police, man hated woman, woman hated man, the old hated the young, the young hated the old, and everyone hated the men who cried aloud, 'Mind the doors, please,' and sometimes with a strong hand in the middle of some wretch's back – serve them right! – shoved yet another human unit to judder up against the sighing, sodden, juddering mass inside. In London, in Tokyo, in Moscow, or New York, in Sydney, Johannesburg or Toronto, in Seoul and Samarkand it is the same.

Thus Jelly travelled to Bond Street Station where she alighted. By the time she arrived at The Claremont she imagined she would, as usual, be Lady Angelica Rice again, albeit incognito, albeit with bruised and painful breasts and a sore chin. It had been a long day, starting with Ram, ending with jam. Angel laughed at the thought. She skittered into The Claremont and the door-man looked after her, not recognising her as Lady Rice, and wondering what agency she was from and why he had no commission.

'You can't live at The Claremont for ever, paying your bill by false pretences,' said Jelly to Lady Rice. 'A girl needs her own house and home, if only to put a red light above the door; write "model" on the wall. You don't take enough notice of your own predicament.'

But Lady Rice wasn't listening. She was weeping again.

10

Post Coital

Lady Rice broods on alimony. Lady Rice will not really be deflected by Angel as a source of entertainment, though she appreciates the usages of sex. Lady Rice still wants her pound of flesh, but is grateful to Angel for trying.

To do without unhappiness, Lady Rice explains to her sub-sisters, would be to do without the nourishment she has come to expect. These days she relies on the bread of outrage, well spiced by bitter gall rising to the throat. It is bread buttered and slavered with hatred of Anthea. Unholy, unhealthy emotions all, but satisfactory: knife between the teeth of the embattled warrior; an unchancy weapon, metal against ivory, sharp edge turned outward, but, of course, if you fall, that's what disembowels you: your own enmity, forget the enemy. Hate, like sex, is an addiction, explains Lady Rice: you feel you can live on it for ever; that you're born one fix of hatred under par; but of course all the time it's enticing you, luring you, killing you. And it can kill you quick, if you overdose, as heroin does: you can choke pretty fast on your own bile. It's the opposite of a quiet death – it's death by intemperance, spite, righteous anger, the nausea of revulsion. Or else it can kill you slowly; you can retreat howling, as Jelly did in the Volvo, parking in a concrete stall, leaving the field to others, licking obviously fatal wounds, a savage beast holed up in a rancid cave, pitiful but dangerous. If anyone demonstrates kindness, Lady Rice sneers, she who once gave such nice dinner parties; if anyone goes near, the creature will repay that kindness, that approach, by tearing the innocent to bits in its death throes. Beware the howling of the injured. Angel, don't feel too safe in the body you think you control. You may be out of your depth. Jelly does nothing to annoy; Angelica is almost a friend; but Angel has left Lady Rice with her knicker elastic snapped and Lady Rice may not like it; let Angel not rely on the gratitude of Lady Rice, divorcee-in-waiting.

11

Alimony As Justice

Barney Evans, represent us as well! Try and understand what we are saying, this complex creature who is your client.

We need alimony! We want nourishment: we are cracking and splitting. We are thin and brittle for lack of love: we have lost two stone in six months. If our husband won't help us, then society must come to our aid: law courts and lawyers must stand in for a corrupted individual conscience.

We are not motivated by vengeance or greed. On the contrary. No. Our plea is that if the scales of justice are to remain in balance there has to be brought into perpetual existence, recreating itself moment by moment, the proper, decent, material reflection of 'spiritual good' (or 'Goods to the value of' – as we say, aptly). The lost goods – love, illusion, hope (worse than lost, this latter: stolen!) have an equivalent in money; this equivalent needs to be paid monthly to the end of time. That is to say, 'in her lifetime', which for the individual, of course, is the same thing as 'the end of time'.

The great wonderful construct which is marriage – a construct made up of a hundred little kindnesses, a thousand little bitings back of spite, tens of thousands of minor actions of good intent – be they the saving of a face, the rescuing of an ant, the plucking of a hair, the laughing at a bad joke, the forgiveness of sins, the overlooking of errors – this cannot, must not, as an institution, be brought down in ruins. Let the props be financial; if this is all that remains, it has to be so.

If we don't get alimony from Edwin, the whole caboodle will crumble: I can feel it. A lot rests on this. The stars themselves will implode. The scales which balance real against unreal will be shoved so far out of kilter they will tip and topple and the point of our existence, and therefore existence itself, will be gone. We will all vanish like a puff of smoke. Or implode like a collapsing marshmallow man. In the end it is money which keeps us in being, inasmuch as money is the only recognised good which we have.

And of course I may fail. A Court might decide, as Edwin hopes it will and as Barney Evans tells me may happen, that I'm perfectly well equipped to look after myself, and since the doctrine of No Fault prevails in our divorce courts, and the great injustices one human being can render to another are now apparently neither here nor there, the Court may say what the hell, who is this hopeless wife, this ex-pop star who never rode to hounds at her husband's side, who was found in bed with her best friend's husband? – who can possibly believe her account of how she got to be there, or how little happened in it? – give her nothing! Yes, they are capable, I hear, of awarding me nothing at all, since even the Matrimonial

Home was in the gift of the husband's family, and the husband is unemployed and, according to his accountants, has no assets whatsoever. Should all my hopes for justice fail, how will any of us live? Why, as the birds do, picking at nothing. We could always take to blackmail. We may yet have to.

'Blackmail's out of fashion,' said my employer Brian Moss to me one day, 'because no one's ashamed of anything any more,' and I nodded and smiled politely, but other people's imaginations clearly don't run the way mine do, and these days I have a pocket full of tapes, stolen from the office, the way others have pockets full of rainbows, or claim to. And in my shopping bag I bring home files containing letters and transcripts of bugged conversations, depositions and affidavits from many sources, not just those relating to Rice v. Rice, matrimonial. People do chatter on to their solicitors.

Lady Rice doesn't react, can't react: she is too stunned by events to marvel at anything, even her alter ego Jelly's delinquency, or Angelica's pickiness, let alone Angel's whorishness. What she can see is that, when it comes to it, she's no lady.

The Perforated Personality

Don't get this wrong. Angelica, Jelly and Angel are not three split-off parts of Lady Rice. Each can and should be held responsible legally, fiscally and spiritually for the other. There is no question here of the one hand not knowing what the other is doing; one personality dominant, controlling lesser ones, capable of taking the others by surprise. In classic cases of split personality, respectable A will wake in the morning and discover herself, say, bruised and smeared with honey, be puzzled and distressed, and have no notion at all of what her other persona B was up to during the night, or where B went, or what she did – indeed that B even exists. But B does exist and, what is more, exists alongside, quite probably, C, D and occasionally emerging others, E, F and G; who will either know all about the others, or know nothing about the others, or have some degree of knowledge, depending on whether they are, as it were, on A's or B's team, and to what degree trusted by their controllers. The main split, the A/B split, lies between the steady, the good, the nice and the cautious, and the licentious, delinquent, spiteful and spontaneous.

In the case of Lady Rice, the split is better described as a perforation: not yet complete: a rather extreme case of voices in the head. Only if torn will the actual split occur, as when you tear your round Road Tax disc from its embracing square. As it is, if Angelica murders someone, Jelly and Angel cannot be excused: they ought to have controlled her, and had the capacity so to do. If Jelly develops repetitive strain injury at Catterwall & Moss, Angelica and Angel can hardly complain: it was their own fingers they overworked, in excessive zeal. If Angel gets herpes, or AIDS, Angelica and Jelly can hardly be surprised: they should not have colluded: the truth is that they, too, were sexually tempted. The three must, and should, take their place together, as one, in the eyes of the world, if not themselves: perforated, not split, merely holding endless speculative conversations amongst themselves. A phenomenon not yet clinical, and with any luck never to be clinical. Each knows everything about the other and individual parts continue to make up a recognisable whole. The square still contains the circle. So far.

Now the conglomerate persona that consists of Angelica, Jelly and Angel, which on marriage formed itself into Lady Rice, received nothing but affection and kindness – so far as any parent is capable of wholly admirable and pure behaviour – from her parents Prue and Stephen White. Evil, psychosis, trauma, do not necessarily fit the equation; they are not necessary to the creation of a perforated personality. Split is clinical and distressing, morbid: perforation is a far more common occurrence. Many of us suffer from mild perforation, a vague feeling of disassociation, the gentle murmuring of voices in the head. Poor me, poor me, with variations: for example, I don't know what came over me! It happens to the most sensitive, not those most oppressed by worldly misfortune.

To be thus divided into three is what many women report. When they stare at themselves in mirrors, twirl on delicate toes, they are Angelica: when they go to work, industriously, impersonally, they are Jelly: when they go to the bad, take another drink, smoke an illicit joint, leave the child un-babysat, leap at the genitals of another sex, why then they are Angel. They sign their letters Lady Rice with a kind of conjoined formality.

When a woman says 'if only I could find myself', all three personae speak at once: they feel over-Jellyfied, Angelicised, or Angelated, and don't like it: they search for a balance.

When she says 'I must fulfil myself', it is the Jelly in her speaking, (looking up from her work, wondering what the matter is, deciding it's lack of babies), trying to leave Angelica behind and get Angel out of her system somehow.

When women keep husbands as pets to fetch their handbags, won't have sex with them and affect a general air of moral superiority, then Angelica predominates. It is Angelica who says all men are rapists at heart and are nasty, messy, aggressive creatures in general. Animals!

When a woman runs off with her best friend's husband and says this thing is bigger than me, or all I have to do is snap my fingers and I'll have your boyfriend, why that's Angel, and she probably will have him. Beware.

Her heart is kind, but her passions are great and her morals few.

Lady Rice has 'trouble coming to terms with her situation', as the newspaper therapists calmly put it; that is to say giant stars in her psyche implode and black holes yawn: reeling, she takes refuge in Angelica, Jelly, Angel.

But times are worsening. Trauma approaches. Where and how will rescue come? The union soul is under attack; the confederation falters; the flag is torn – poor Lady Rice can't tell good from bad, nothing seems real, nothing can be trusted, her past has become meaningless, her future is obscured; even friends are no longer friends. The very plates from which she is accustomed to eat are apparently not hers at all, but Rice family heirlooms, or so Sir Edwin writes to Brian Moss. Lady Rice has no access to her satin sheets, neatly folded in the master bedroom press; worse, her rival Anthea leans up against piles of healthy, folded, natural fabric in the second floor linen room to be pleasured by her husband. She has a vision of it happening. She is telepathic in her anguish.

Poor Lady Rice. See how now she goes through her life stunned, flickering out of one persona, into another, as men and women do when they discover that concepts of love, of home, of permanence, are not placed on rock, but on shifting sand. When the Velcro splits and tears and the trousers and the knickers fall down and everyone laughs, even those who live in hotels can be pitied.

No wonder people put their trust in Jesus. Jesus never fails. Upon this rock this Church is built, if only you can overlook a little historical evidence, a South Sea Scroll

57

or two. South Sea Scroll, that phrase being the melding of South Sea Bubble, that great financial scandal, and the Dead Sea – that arid waste, that bitter pond. South Sea Scroll, article of lost faith.

Alimony is the rock, in Lady Rice's eyes, on which such future as she can have will be founded; Angelica planning, Jelly working and Angel fucking.

13

Breaking Out

Lady Rice, that perforated personality, that collection of identities loosely bound in the one body, sat in The Claremont in her silk wrap, bought from the hotel boutique, paid for on Sir Edwin's charge account, looked in her mirror, felt lonely, wept and could no longer contain herself. 'I can't stand it!' she cried, and indeed she could not. Most people say they can't stand it, and lie: they do stand it, having no choice. But the spasms of emotional pain that overwhelmed Lady Rice were so intense that she was driven not out of herself but into more of her selves.

Perforations deepened.

> 'Pull yourself together, for God's sake,' Jelly said to Lady Rice, out of the mirror. But she added, more kindly, 'It's been a long, hard day.'
> 'In future,' said Angelica, 'we'll go home by bus, not Underground. It's easier on the nerves. And do stop crying, before our eyes get red and puffy. Jesus! What a sight!'
> 'Let's go downstairs to the bar,' said Angel, 'and make out with some rich businessman. Have a fun night out, some sex – good or bad; I grant

you that's a risk. We'll score if we can and make ourselves some money.'

'Score?' asked Lady Rice.

'Drugs,' said Angel.

Lady Rice uttered a little scream.

Lady Rice found herself looking out her best lingerie and trying it on, while Jelly agitated.

'You'll do no such thing,' said Jelly. 'You need a good night's sleep. You have to go to work in the morning,' at which Angel pinched Jelly's arm and left a nasty little bruise, so Jelly shut up, while Angelica just looked on in horror, and Lady Rice screamed again and collapsed altogether into her separate parts and there seemed nothing left of her at all.

She lay down on the bed and left it to the others to get on with the night.

14

Angel's Outing

The bartender smiled at Angel. He was young and Greek; he had soft brown eyes, a snowy white shirt and tight trousers; he leapt about from one end of the bar to another at the behest of his slow-moving customers. Angel, considering his small, muscular buttocks, actually licked her lips. She allowed the edge of her small pink tongue to show, running around her carmined mouth.

Angelica seldom wore make-up: Jelly went in for soft shadings and a discreetly artificial look: Angel just liked lots and lots of everything. Her skirt was up at her thighs, her silver shoes high-heeled; her midriff showed: black leather jacket fastened with an enamelled rose, the kind of thing a sheik might buy at Aspreys for a very lucky girl.

The barman nodded to an empty table in the panelled corner, softly lit. The bar was done out in tasteful pinks and greys. Angelica loathed it, Jelly loved it, Angel didn't notice: excited even by the feel of her own tongue on her own lips. Who cared now about Edwin, marriage, injustice, alimony, law: all that was another world.

'I'm supposed to discourage single ladies,' said the barman, 'but you might do business some good.'

Jelly began to say that this was outrageous – an affront to her principles, if not single women then why single men? – but Angelica and Angel made her hold her tongue. Angel sat down with her drink, and casually slid her skirt even further up her legs, stretching them to show them to advantage. The elderly, well-coupled rich who this evening, more's the pity, frequented the bar, looked, and looked away, and the wives looked at the barman for help, but he had his back to them, and a couple of the husbands sneaked a speculative after-glance or so.

> 'Oh God,' said Jelly, 'this is so crude and shameful.'
>
> 'What do you expect?' asked Angelica, bitterly. 'Angel's a very crude person.'
>
> 'She'll be sorry in the morning,' said Jelly. 'That's all I can say. We all will.'
>
> 'Just shut up, the pair of you,' said Angel, hitching open her leather jacket so that more swelling bosom was revealed. 'I certainly won't be sorry.'
>
> 'I don't believe this,' said Jelly. 'Angelica, this is intolerable. Shall we go?,' and Angelica made an effort and stood up, but the stiff drink had weakened her legs – Lady Rice rarely drank anything stronger than tonic water – so she had to sit down again quickly.

At last two men without women came into the bar: in their late forties, solid, red-faced, probably American; not the suave, moneyed, boardroom types on better days to be found in the bar, nor the eloquent, quick-moving, dangerous Arabs who moved in groups, liked a big-breasted girl and had her in order of precedence; these two were more like, say, engineers who'd started out as practical men, good with their hands, and ended up on the executive floor, and perhaps had a share in their company's fortunes; steak-and-chips men, not the caviare kind; more prone to simple human affections, to weeping not beating, who had solid, plain wives whom they loved: more at home in the bar than the nightclub. Angel sighed.

'Two little lambs who've gone astray,' murmured Angelica, reviving, 'in unknown pastures, and God knows when they last changed their underpants. Angel, how can you?'

'Shut up,' said Angel, so fiercely that Angelica did. 'If I want to be the reward, their good night out on the town, that's my privilege.'

A murmur in the barman's ear: he nodded towards Angel. The two turned to stare at her, speculatively.

'Hang on a moment, Angel,' reasoned Jelly. 'Jesus! I know that kind of barman. He just wants you out of here. You're bringing down the tone of his bar. He could have fixed you up with anyone. It's an insult, an outrage. At least settle for a millionaire. For God's sake, Angel, don't just throw us away!'

'Fucking shut up,' said Angel, and pinched Jelly's arm again, and had to smile through her own grimace as the two approached, carrying two whiskies for themselves and a double gin for her. 'At least I give good value for money.'

The punters would, after all, get three of her for the price of one, though no doubt Angelica would be reluctant, and Jelly a wet-blanket; but sex is sex: the moment the body was engaged in its instinctive business the other two shouldn't prove too much of a problem; might even add a frisson or so to Angel's own entertainment.

Lady Rice slept. Where did she get her worldly wisdom? She had led an emotionally trying but narrow and sheltered life – enough to make you believe in the group unconscious: delve too deep into it and you find the accumulated wisdom and experience of not just three but all the women in the world; and all the false assumptions and conditioned responses too, and no sense yet made of any of it. She's no angel: that much you can be sure of. No jelling yet, but that comes later.

Michael, with thick silver hair and the single gold tooth, sat at Angel's left. David, with thinning red hair and crinkly blue eyes, sat on her right. Glad to make her acquaintance, they said. They were strangers in town. She smiled and said nothing in particular. They were staying, they said, in an hotel down the road. That figured: their suits did not have quite the flat smoothness of the ones usually seen at The Claremont. They had been packed, unpacked, and not made good by a first class valet.

Michael and David pressed more gin upon Angel, intently watching her drink. She told them her name was Angel; that she was a private nurse. That she was employed to look after a stroke victim, an elderly lady currently a guest at The Claremont. It did not do to present herself as either too up-market, or too obvious in her profession. Amateurs did better in this game than professionals.

'Angel by name,' they said, 'Angel by nature.' They expected she needed something to cheer her up, and she agreed that she did.

Michael laid a well-manicured hand on one arm, David on the other.

> 'Ask them if they're married,' said Jelly in Angel's ear.
>
> 'For God's sake, leave me alone,' said Angel, aloud.

'Did you say that to me?' asked Michael, surprised.

> 'I'm sorry,' said Angel. 'Sometimes I talk to myself.'

David leant over and squeezed her lips gently together with thumb and forefinger.

'That's to stop you,' he said. 'Women shouldn't talk too much. It gets them into trouble.'

She could see the gold wedding band on his third finger: there was no avoiding it. He had a wife.

> Angelica said, 'Don't you have any respect for anything?'
>
> Jelly said, 'Oh, give up, Angelica. There's no stopping her. Let's just go with the flow,' and for a time they did.

Michael said to David, concerned, 'If you hold her lips together, she won't be able to drink,' and David took his hand away and Angel beamed happily from one to the other. The barman held the door open for them, and they helped her across the room.

'I'm so drunk I can hardly stand,' she confessed to the barman, giving him a little kiss for good measure.

'Wrong man!' said David, pulling her away.

'Isn't that Lady Angelica Rice?' asked the doorman of the barman, in the marble foyer, as the three went off down the road, in search of their lesser hotel.

'Of course that's not Lady Rice,' said the barman. 'That's some pick-up, using and abusing my bar. I just get them drunk and out as fast as possible.'

'Lady Rice is here incognito,' said the doorman, 'so in theory it's not our concern. She'll just have to look after herself.'

On the way down Davies Street, towards Oxford Street, Jelly kept looking over her shoulder.

'Why are you doing that?' asked Angelica, annoyed. 'I need to concentrate. I'm trying to keep her steady on her feet.'

'It's all too easy,' said Jelly. 'I'm nervous. We've been set up. Supposing we've been recognised? Supposing Edwin gets to know? Supposing we're being spied on? Supposing it affects our alimony?'

'You're being paranoid,' said Angelica. 'Personally, I'm glad of the opportunity to widen the field of my experience.'

'You're a hopeless little slut at heart,' said Jelly, bitterly. 'No better than Angel.'

Angel tripped and nearly fell, and was buoyed up on either side by Michael and David. Michael had his hand inside her jacket, she noticed, fingering her bosom. She liked that.

'This goes too far,' said Angelica, and shut her eyes. 'I've changed my mind. I'm going to join Lady Rice.'

'So am I,' said Jelly. 'Angel, you're on your own.'

Before she retired, Jelly managed to extract one of her high heels from a grating, instead of merely leaving the whole shoe behind as Angel was happy enough to do. Angel was neither prudent nor scrupulous. She enjoyed waste. The shoes were silvery net – an expensive pair Lady Rice had seldom had opportunity to wear: in Rice circles shoes were usually plain and serviceable. Presently Jelly became aware that Lady Rice was lying semi-clothed on a bed, not in The Claremont but in some strange hotel: the less she knew about any of it the better. She just hoped to live. Casual sex was insane. Serial killers, HIV rapists were at the outer edges of the sex-with-strangers experience: further in, nearer home, sadists, bullies, men on power trips, men anxious to humiliate. If Jelly knew this, how come Angel so readily took Lady Rice into danger? Or perhaps Angel thought horror a small price to pay for sex. What did two men want with one woman? Or did one woman merely save the cost of two?

When it came to it, David and Michael seemed more interested in one another's orifices than in Angel's. Angel served, as Angelica acidly observed in the morning, safely back in The Claremont, as witness to passion, even love, and as a kind of soft, sweet, fleshly jam spread on harder, crusty, rather stale bread, in the hope that the latter would be made appealing. To which Jelly replied, 'You are such a mass of euphemisms, Angelica. It was disgusting. Men are beasts. They just wanted somewhere extra for a ramrod to ram, should it run out of places. There was no love in it, none.' To which Angel murmured but they seemed to love each other: who cared

67

about love, anyway? She, Angel, had a good time and earned herself a hundred pounds cash; and then, as Angelica filled and scented the bath and Jelly folded the clothes and tut-tutted over the scuffed heel, Angel lapsed into exhausted silence and went into hiding.

When she was gone, Jelly said to Angelica, 'What are we going to *do* about her? She'll get us into terrible trouble,' and Angelica, anointing her sore parts with healing jellies, said, 'I don't know. I don't know.'

Over breakfast, Angelica said, 'I thought I saw that nice barman when Angel came in. I had the feeling he'd been waiting up. It was obvious what we'd been up to. Drunk, unescorted, skirt torn, four in the morning. Supposing he took a photograph?'

Jelly said brusquely, 'Nonsense. We'd have seen the flash.'

Angelica said, 'We were in no condition to notice anything.'

Jelly said, brightly, 'At least we're "we" again. A good night out can work wonders.'

Angelica said, 'Speak for yourself. I'm ashamed and humiliated. But I expect it's no more than I deserve.'

They enjoyed their coffee. It was black and strong. The croissants were fresh, and there was a Danish pastry, well-filled with apple and quite delectable. Sun shone in. 'Only four hours' sleep,' said Lady Rice, herself again, 'and a full day's work ahead! God knows what comes over me, sometimes.'

As a day, of course, it was a dead loss. Lady Rice stumbled through it as Jelly, hungover and sleepless, but the speculative pain was muted, the outrage and blind fury that Edwin preferred another woman to her, that that other woman had so easily taken her husband, her property, her home, her very life from under her nose, had somewhat abated. Lady Rice used her alter egos as strategies for survival. What else was she to do?

Jelly forgot to save a file on her computer and lost a whole day's work, including a letter to Barney Evans which she omitted to mention to Brian Moss. If a letter came in complaining of undue delay, she could lose that one too, when it arrived. She had stopped being in a hurry: there seemed all the time in the world. While she had her freedom, she should enjoy it. Nothing to it. She had to put off Ram by telling him she had a period pain: Angel was exhausted after her night out and had to sleep

PART TWO

An Attempt At Diversion

1

Family Attack

I, Lady Rice, offer the scene to you because it's a relief to me. These days any flights of my imagination tend to end up with visions of Edwin in bed with Anthea, and are intolerable. This one, triggered by Tully Toffener, Member of Parliament, another of Brian Moss's clients, ended safely enough, with mere doubts about the nature of reality. Perhaps I am beginning to heal.

Tully called my employer Brian at the office and I listened in, with (for once) Brian's permission. Mostly Jelly eavesdrops, records and take the tapes home secretly. She used to pilfer when she was a child: look through keyholes, listen in on extensions, collect little piles of stolen goodies: with trauma the habit has returned.

'That poor old man,' said Tully of Congo, his step-grandfather-in-law. Sara's grandmother Wendy had re-married at an unseemly age, and hopes of Sara's inheritance were dashed. Wendy and Congo seemed bent on getting rid of as much wealth and property as possible before they snuffed it. Tully's voice was unctuous with hypocrisy. That is to say it sounded pretty much as usual. 'That poor old man!' said Tully Toffener. 'He's begun to see things. He needs to be shut away for his own good. He's senile. Alzheimer's, I expect.'

Last weekend, instead of weeping and watching Sky TV, I wrote up the scene as I imagined it. I used the word processing skills Jelly had recently developed in my fingers. It's not a skill I ever wanted to acquire, but needs must when alimony drives. And The Claremont will produce a personal computer for a small extra charge.

Bedouins swung from trees to attack the poor old man. Communards, their sashes red, their rags grey, wormed up over the bare boards towards him to set fuses for their gelignite. A pirate, his jacket tattered velvet, his cap skull-and-crossboned, spurred cowboy boots on his feet, slept propped up against the tallboy.

Every now and then Peter Pan's Tinkerbell would flit by in her froufrou, screaming abuse, striking out with what looked like an extended sparkler. A skinny man in skin-tight black leather paced like a kind of moving cut-out in the window alcove, silhouetted against the thin sheets which served as curtains. He carried a rope garotte in his strong hands, and occasionally would jerk it tight, looking at Congo with horrid meaning.

The visitors came at dusk: with the dawn they went away. Congo would leap and flail with his broom all night and be exhausted by morning, but at least Wendy could sleep. He kept her safe. When she woke, she would look at him with adoring eyes and say something simple and to the point, like 'my hero', and murmur that her glass needed filling, and he would make the dangerous journey to the bathroom and fridge to bring back vodka. The freezer compartment grew its muzzy ice blobs and sparkling tentacles further and further out into the world: the hatch door of the ice compartment no longer closed: soon the door of the fridge would no longer close – then what?

There was no point in worrying about the future. The hazards of the present were enough to be getting on with. Most things in the apartment were by now sold – once all were gone, that would be that. Every week or so Congo would show Wendy the empty housekeeping purse and she would point to something in the room – she seldom spoke: at ninety-two, words had finally begun to fail her – Persian rug, original Regency curtains, Tiffany lamp, escritoire – and Congo would call Arthur, or Bob, or Alice – they kept adding their names and numbers to the list on the pad – and someone would come round with cash and take whatever it was away. Sometimes other things would go as well – the six silver spoons in their soft dark blue wrap had gone from their drawer, and eight miniatures from the wall, and what else? But the dealers seemed cheerful; they'd smile and chat and were not disapproving or surprised by the smell and the mess.

And was not property theft? Had not Marx so described it? Neither of them, Wendy or Congo, had worked for its acquisition. Wealth had come to them: they had not earned it. You could not take objects beyond the grave, however valuable or beautiful: why should the dealers not have them, to make an honest or dishonest living as they chose? If the dealers didn't get them, Sara and Tully Toffener would. Relatives were more dangerous and distressing by far than dealers ever were. Relatives traded love and hate, using possessions as both weapons and symbols: dealers merely traded.

What could the motive of the nightly visitors be, in so attacking him, so abusing him? That was the real problem. Did he deserve it? Was hell sending out its messengers? The visitors used language in a way Congo never had in all his life, thus persuading him the more of their reality.

'Get that fridge thawed out, you fuck-head,' the executioner would snarl, while Congo kicked and poked him away with the broom.

'I got your false teeth in my pocket,' jeered a Communard one day. 'We're stewing them up for food because we ain't got nothing else. You fat bastards are starving us out.' And he wormed, halfway between adder and human in his grey rags and red silk sash, over the oak floorboards, and caught and ripped the sash on a nail which had often bothered Congo, catching as it would on the dry skin of his old toes. It was the detail that so impressed. And Congo could swear he once heard Tinkerbell snipe, as she swung by, 'I used a dildo on Wendy when you were asleep', and as she swung back, 'She loved it, darling, absolutely loved it. Filthy old thing!'

He tried to maintain a dignified silence, but sometimes it got to be too much.
'Get out of here!' he'd yell at them. 'Who are you? What

do you want? This is my home –' but they didn't seem
to hear, as if he were the apparition, not they.

One night the executioner put the noose aside to sharpen
a guillotine blade. Screech, screech. Congo's ears hurt.
An edge of the blade caught in the thin fabric and ripped
it. The tear revealed a perfectly ordinary Chelsea street
scene outside: the good Georgian houses of Lodestar
Avenue, the decorated street lamps which the tourists
loved; the headlights of occasional passing traffic. And
Congo could hear the sheet ripping. There was no discern-
ible difference between that reality and this. What was he
to make of it? And when he looked out of the window he
saw a row of Arabs squatting by the garden wall, staring
up at him reproachfully. They seemed hungry. What was
Congo meant to do about it? There was no food in the
house, only ice and vodka. The whole world was needy: in
old age especially, the rich as well as the poor.

Anyway, this was the scene I envisaged, on the strength
of one phone call from Tully Toffener. I had no understanding at the time of how later it would relate to my
own affairs. It is strange how these things happen. The
scenes that stay in your mind for years, for no apparent
reason, can later turn out to have great relevance to your
life. A passing meeting with a stranger by the lake: lake
and stranger engraved into your memory, though you
can't imagine why: the stranger turns out to be your
future husband's brother; the lake where your best friend
inherits a house, so you come to know both well. The
examples of portent are so often trivial and gossipy; it's
as if, in the Platonic sense, they were mere shadows of
Portent itself. But I digress.

Congo had to sleep, that was the trouble. God alone knows what goes on while you sleep and in the end everyone has to sleep.

If I understand the culture of the aboriginals correctly, human beings are the mere result of dingoes dreaming in the dreamtime, before the power of those dreams made the world take actual form. Well, that figures. Dreamt up by a dingo. I can deal with that. And at least for a time I was out of my own predicament, and into Congo's, and learning to despise and dislike Tully, as well as Anthea. Spread outrage more thinly, and it's easier to swallow.

2

The Wicked And The Good

'Congo sees things,' Tully Toffener repeated disin-
genuously to Brian. 'He needs to be shut away for his
own good. So does the old woman, before he manages
to kill her off. Because that's what he's up to. And it gets
up my nose. Not that I have a vested interest in keeping
the old girl alive, on the contrary, but why should Congo
Warby get away with it?'

'Get away with what?' asked Brian Moss, cautiously, in
his soft, lawyer's voice. He always spoke slowly, the
better to wrong-foot both client and opposition should
need arise. His mind moved quickly enough. Three
thoughts for every one word.

'Robbing my wife Sara,' said Tully Toffener, 'of her
rightful inheritance.'

'How is Mr Warby doing that?' asked Brian Moss, as if
he really wanted to know. Oh, he was good!

'If the old bitch hadn't remarried,' said Tully, 'Sara
would have stood to inherit the tenancy of Lodestar
House. Wendy's her grandmother, her mother's mother.
Sara's the only living relative. I mean to fight it, you
know.'

Brian Moss allowed himself to sound puzzled.

'But Congo Warby is the husband,' he said, 'and in residence, and your wife and yourself are adequately housed. More than adequately, if I may say so. I am not sure that you have much of a claim.'

'Warby only married Wendy to get his hands on the Lodestar Avenue property,' said Tully. 'Everyone knows Wendy was in her dotage even then and that was twenty-eight years ago. I don't see why Sara and I should be doomed to live in second class accommodation when Lodestar's ours by right. Look, I'm calling from the House. I've got to get back to a Division in a mo: it's a three-line-whip.'

Tully Toffener lived at a perfectly good address in Livermore Gate, W8. His round figure and bald pate appealed to the cartoonists; his whiny voice made him sound both earnest and honest; his clamping jaw intimidated: he had a full soft lower lip, very bright and pink.

'What I was trying to say, Brian,' said Tully, more reasonably, 'is that when Sara goes round to see Wendy, Congo won't let her in. He's barricaded the place. He won't even open the door to the social workers. They're only trying to earn their living, poor bitches. Sara's worried stiff about her Gran. The only people Congo lets in are the vermin, by whom I mean the dealers. They're allowed to run in and out like mice, you bet they are, dragging the goodies away. You've got to do something.'

'No one is by law required to answer the door to anyone,' said Brian Moss temperately. 'And we have no evidence that either of the parties is mad, bad or a danger to themselves or others.'

'They're a fucking danger to me,' shouted Tully Toffener. 'They're disposing of my wife's inheritance. Don't
give me that shit about old people not being paper parcels, having a will and rights of their own. If I had my
way, everyone in this country over eighty would be tied
up with string like the parcels they are, and put out of
their misery. Get this pathetic old couple certified. Lock
them up where they can be properly looked after. Get
me power of attorney, Brian. There's the division bell.'
And the phone clicked down.

Brian Moss turned to Jelly and said, 'Human nature is
a remarkable thing.' As if Jelly didn't know.

And Brian told Jelly what she knew already, for anyone
can read the legal column in *The Times*, but Brian loved
imparting information, about the shocking new legislation under which long-term tenants could buy the property in which they lived, at the price the property would
have fetched at the time the tenancy began. 'The old
woman's a socialist; she doesn't believe in owning property. Drives Tully mad.'
'What happens if she just does nothing?' asked Jelly.
'The property reverts to whoever owns it,' said Brian.
'And the opportunity of making a million or so simply
vanishes. These days the law punishes non-activity when
it comes to the possibility of making money for nothing.'
'So, what will you do?' I asked.
'Tully's the client,' said Brian Moss cheerfully. 'Ethi-
cally, my duty is to look after his interests. So I'll do
what I can to get the old folk out of their home. I'll try
and get Sara power of attorney so she can take over the
tenancy, sell the property at a vast profit and inherit the
money. The place is falling down, anyway. Gloomy old

house. It needs to be developed. The future has to sweep away the past, sooner or later.'

It was becoming clear to Jelly that Brian Moss had the ethics of a buck rabbit. He was all too likely to screw her, in both senses of the word, with a clear conscience, as man and employer. Nor would he see either way as mutually exclusive. She was prepared to put up with it. She had an interesting and comparatively well-paid job, and had to earn a living somehow, though she had been advised by Barney Evans not to let it be known just how capable of doing such a thing Lady Rice was. Women claiming alimony must present themselves in two different ways at the same time, said Barney Evans, as hopelessly incompetent yet with expensive tastes. If a woman shows herself to be strong, independent and practical, she will be penalised. The less she can manage on, the less she will be given. The law, while preaching gender equality, favours the old tradition: that women are mythical creatures who can't live without a new hat and who scream at the sight of a mouse. The more a woman conforms to this archetype, the better a judge will look after her.

Property disputes are almost a relief after the tangled distresses of matrimonial cases. The 'different perspective' of the different and differing parties in all kinds of litigation is to me, as it is to Brian Moss, a source of perpetual wonderment. If Toffener and Warby fight over property, it is because there is no space in our society left for fisticuffs, for physical confrontation, and so the law has to do it for us, metaphorically. But Rice v. Rice, matrimonial, is war against the self, and there can be no real victory in it on either side.

'Except I suppose for Anthea,' said Lady Rice to Jelly one evening, 'horse-faced bitch; running her fingers up and down my husband's spine, taking away what's mine by right. What is this preoccupation of yours with Tully Toffener?'

'I don't like him,' said Jelly, childlike, as if disliking justified everything. As happens with so many not very likeable to themselves, she spent a good deal of time disliking others. Lady Rice liked most people but, as she kept saying, to bored looks from such friends as she still had, 'Much good has it ever done me.'

'Let her get on with it,' advised Angelica. 'Jelly's obsession with Tully seems to keep Angel away. We don't really want any more of this Ram business or nights out on the tiles with strangers. Angel could get us all into real trouble. I'd encourage Jelly if I were you. Let her get on with Toffener v. Warby and Lodestar House.'

'I'm a very insecure kind of person,' lamented Lady Rice, with a rare flash of self-knowledge. 'Really I have very little or no influence on anyone, not even myself. But I don't like the way Jelly seems to be taking over. She's competent but without imagination. Couldn't you have a go, Angelica? I don't suppose you like Tully Toffener either. Who does?'

3

Tully Toffener And
His Powers

Tully Toffener sits on the Government Front Bench of the House of Commons, but only when his superiors don't think it prudent to sit there themselves, when they don't want to have to answer difficult questions. Then he acts as the Department's spokesman. He is the one who takes the blame, carries the can. He is the one who gets hated. Tully it is who recommends, if only by proxy, that little old ladies should pay more for their heating, that the lame should be obliged to limp to the dole office, that the poor should drink the rain from heaven, not water from the taps. Yet at the same time Tully must profess to love the old, the lame, the poor. Tully is politically ambitious: he would not want his hypocrisies made public: he would not want his desire to euthanase all unfortunates made known. I might blackmail him.

Tully is quite attractive. His fleshy face has a well-fed glow; his eyes are bright and intelligent; he knows he is powerful, and so do the girls he meets at parties, on tap for his benefit and entertainment. I think he mostly goes home to his wife Sara, whom he loves, though perhaps not always. They have no children.

Once I took the nastiness of people like Tully for granted. Part of me still does. Part of me might even have agreed, just a little, with his views; that the rich deserve to be rich and happy, and that the poor deserve to be miserable. But I am changing. I am more censorious of the Tullys of this world than I used to be. I have joined the ranks of the persecuted. I have grown kinder in one way, crueller in another. It's not so much, as Lady Rice says, that hell hath no fury like a woman scorned: it is that a woman scorned is thrust into hell and must work her way up out of it, and her antennae as to what is good and what is bad, and where hypocrisy lies, and who most deserves her sympathy, become sensitive and acute. And she might as well turn that to her advantage, says Lady Rice.

The guardians of our society have lost their way, says Angelica. The law refuses to condemn, our politicians need to be liked.

> 'Leaders of the people by their counsel
> Wise and eloquent in their instruction –'

Oh yes, oh yes. Tully Toffener, leader of the people. Brian Moss, eloquent in his instruction. Villains! Bastards! cries Angelica.

I am led, I am instructed, and it does me no good at all, says Lady Rice. Edwin loves Anthea; he no longer loves his wife. And when she remembers it she is all to pieces and different personae again. Anthea has stolen my husband from me, and she is so much lesser a person than I am. How can he possibly prefer her to me? My head hurts as the alter egos kick and writhe within it.

4

Welcome To Our Wonderful World

'Wise and eloquent in thei-ei-eir in-struct-shun.'

My father made me sing soprano solo in Handel's Messiah before the days of my defection to rock'n'roll. How easy admiration and adoration once seemed, before we realised men were merely men, not heroes; before we got to see our leaders on TV.

'Welcome to the club,' as the experienced divorcees say to the new arrival. 'Welcome to our wonderful world!'

What a wonderful world, as Disney says, Mickey Mouse gliding on liquid waters between faery parapets opening out on chubby kings and cute princesses, yellow curls and pink cheeks, and perhaps Prince Othello to keep us in officially correct countenance, with a gnarled tree or so and a witch for an enemy: between English hedges and Swiss mountains and Rhine castles and Mowgli jungles. Eskimos tend to get left out.

People in cold climates need their energies for survival: they need other humans if only for warmth: why argue, kill and render cold when the fun of doing that is as nothing compared to the enjoyment of just being warm: of touching another person and knowing they're part of the living world, not the dead? The difficulty is that the chilly folk don't have the energy of the warmer folk, let alone the time left over, after the demands of survival have been met, to weave cute costumes and develop intricate dances. In the realer world – I don't say 'real', notice, these things are all comparative – in the realer world out there, in the arctic wastes, a stamp or two on the ground to bring a seal to its airhole will do for a dance, and the greatest kindness is to offer your wife to a passing stranger.

Does the wife say to the husband over the seal-stew meal, 'Nudge, nudge, he'll do'? An unwilling wife wouldn't be much fun for the stranger. What are the divorce laws like in the far tribal Arctic? Does adultery count? What does alimony consist of there? Do they have their own equivalent of Catterwall & Moss? Does a calm, handsome Brian lookalike offer his tissues to the chilly, lonely, weeping, un-velcroing men and women of the Arctic wastes? Men weep, too.

'Welcome to the club!' as the velcro rips and tears. 'Welcome to our wonderful world. Divorcees unite; you have nothing to do now but compare notes.'

Unlike many a member of the club, I am not living in humiliating circumstances, but that is due to my cunning, not Edwin's will.

'Not a penny will she have from me,' I heard him tell Brian Moss on the phone. He'd got fed up waiting for letters which never came. 'Not a penny, the slut. She'll have to take me to Court before she gets a penny!'

This is the voice that once spoke lovingly, protectively.

It is sad for me to have to call The Claremont home, but I grant you it's better by far than to live in a cardboard box. One must do without the world's sympathy, it seems, damned by the standard of my accommodation, whilst attempting to save that world from self-destruct. The whole universe, willy nilly, has focused down on Catterwall & Moss, and its humble, legal assistant, Jelly White. Everything, everything, is at stake. Justice must be exacted, wrung out of the world like water out of a stone. It can be done.

5

No Grand-Daughter Of Mine

'Is there anyone there?' asked Sara Toffener to the closed and wormy door which faced her, and then murmured aloud, as memory dictated, the words of the Walter de la Mare poem:

> ' "Is there anybody there?" said the Traveller,
> Knocking on the moonlit door;
> And his horse in the silence champed the grasses
> Of the forest's ferny floor.'

She spoke the words as she would a charm. When Sara was little, her grandmother would give her two shillings for every poem she learned by heart. Sara had always favoured Walter de la Mare because his lines were so short. Still the door did not open. She took up the yard broom which stood, witch-like, by and beat upon the disintegrating wood: paint and dust flew everywhere. There were movements in the air behind her; a stirring of her hair. It was probably a bat; she would not be surprised at all if it were a vampire bat.

'Bats in the belfry!' she chanted, opening the letterbox, putting her lips to the rusty, metal-lined slit. 'Bats in the belfry!' Why not? Inside, they were all deaf as posts.

They must be, or they would surely have opened to her knocking. In the end, people did.

Wildlife conservationists, as well as social workers, had long tried to gain access to Lodestar House. Bats – protected by an Act of Parliament and a rarity in London – nested in the folly at the end of Lodestar's garden. A barn owl had been sighted in the line of ragged trees – once a neat hedge that had divided the orchard from the paddock, but now grown into rampant and crude disorder. It was absurd, Sara said, and Tully agreed, and not only absurd but unnatural and disagreeable; firstly that nature should have this hidey-hole in an urban area, secondly that no one was allowed in to supervise, let alone make a profit from it.

The Physic Garden down the road from Lodestar at least put its few acres to good purpose, cultivating natural medicinal herbs according to scientific principles, showing visitors round for a fee, attracting tourists. But Lodestar's garden had simply been let go, and cities could not put up with neglect for long. Every year that passed, the environmental lobby became more powerful, inquisitive and interfering, and if old Lady Wendy wasn't careful, didn't act soon or, better still, die soon so Sara and Tully could take over, some law would be passed making it illegal to turn urban green into concrete, or giving bats precedence over human beings, and Tully's plan to build studio apartments facing the river would come to nothing.

'And a bird flew up out of the turret,
Above the Traveller's head,' said Sara Toffener.
'And he knocked again upon the door a second time.

"Is there anybody there?" he said.'

Now Sara took off her high-heeled shoe and banged it upon the door of Lodestar House, this place of crumbling turrets and dried-up moats within the head.

'And no something something something,' Sara went on, at the top of her voice. Who would hear? A woman could be raped in this hooded brick doorway and no one be any the wiser. Or she could be swept away by sudden floods. If Sara had anything to do with it, this entrance would be boarded up, the old front door restored. Down here was just a Black Hole of Calcutta, whatever that might be.

'No voice from the something stairs –'

Why hadn't her grandmother, the vampire bat, just given her daughter a couple of shillings and not made her dance for her money, learning lines. It had been humiliating. Her whole childhood had been humiliating; a training in bohemian family traditions she wanted no part in.

'Open the door, you stupid old bats,' yelled Sara Toffener through the little grated window in the door. The spring in the letterbox was heavy: it might have snapped back and trapped her lips. This was safer. 'I'm family. I wish you no harm.'

Sara knocked again upon the castle door. What goes to make an obsession? She had been born in this house and cast out of this house before she was three: her mother Una prevented from returning, for reasons as clear as a pikestaff, whatever a pikestaff may be, which Sara refused to see, and why should she, for it was no fault of hers that she was the daughter of her grandmother's husband Mogens, and at her mother Una's clear instigation, not her father's. Una did the seducing, not Mogens. Sara saw herself cast out for no good reason, out of spite and whim; this door hers to open when she chose, and as she chose; this house to burn if she so decided.

You couldn't see in. The windows were too clouded with dirt.

What I'd like to do this very moment, thought Sara, is to bring a bulldozer to bear on this problem. How pleasant to charge the door with heavy iron, driven by clanking gears: to just burst in, carrying lintel and frame along with the giant shovel; to open up; to beckon in teams of policemen, social workers, psychiatrists, dustbin men, rat exterminators, cleaners; to set to work, to clear the house of its present occupants, its past, ghosts; to rid it of trauma, dirt, pests, vermin; to throw out everything broken, chipped and dusty, human and inhuman; to clean the place out, hose it out if necessary – as one of Wendy's cousins had allegedly been hosed out of a rear gunner's cockpit in the Second World War. Only the antiques would be spared from the cleansing onslaught, and a team of restorers and valuers would come close behind – Tully would insist. He couldn't bear waste, let alone scandal. If Wendy and Congo survived, they'd be well looked after in a nursing home, given the psychiatric care they needed. That would take money.

Tully was in the House of Commons. It was a late-night sitting. Whenever was it not? It was Sara's custom, when Tully was away, to drink a bottle of wine or, if there was nothing else to do, to go round and visit her grandmother. Or so she described it to friends. She was a very family kind of person. She said so, often. What she normally did was what she planned to do tonight: to bang upon the door and make her presence felt, and go. But the moon was full, the tide was high, so tonight she quoted poetry.

The hate, the resentment, the discordance of body and mind that Wendy's behaviour gave rise to, Sara revealed to no one except Tully, who, amazingly, understood. Only Tully, pink in the face, tight in his body to the point of bursting, seemed to understand the power and purpose of indignation, outrage, when it related to principle. It was not right, simply not right, that Wendy Warby, although in her nineties, should refuse to make a fortune when all that was needed was for her to sign a simple piece of paper. A fortune which Tully and Sara would then inherit. Something is due from family: if not love, why then possessions.

A window on the first floor opened and Congo stuck his head out and shouted in his hoarse old voice:
'Go away, or I'll call the police. This is private property.'
'But whose property?' called up Sara. 'Shall I just come up and we'll discuss it?' She spoke as sweetly as she could manage, remembering Tully's advice. If you act as loving family should, you're not likely to end up disinherited, no matter that the deceased had willed the wealth away. Courts can, and often do, override the wishes of the departed in the interests of the living. As in matters of alimony, so in inheritance law; those who have most get most. Let's all speak well of the dead: their shekels are more likely to be ours.

The old man was gibbering and pointing down at the wall behind her. Sara looked. Only bricks, pavement and weeds which shouldn't be there: no flood water. He beckoned her closer. She gazed up at him. She feared spittle might fall from his barely-toothed mouth.

'You brought them in with you,' he hissed.

'Brought who?'

'Arabs,' he said, more calmly. 'Twenty of them behind you. Don't look now but they're sitting just behind you. Men, women, children too. The women are wearing black, the men are in white. What do they mean? What do they want?'

'I don't know,' said Sara. 'They didn't tell me.' Encourage him in his delusions: the sooner he'd be certified insane.

'They're waiting for me to die,' said Congo. 'But why Arabs? Why the robes? What will happen to Wendy when I'm gone?'

He scraped open the door for her. Sara pushed past him and went up the wide staircase to see her grandmother. Cobwebs brushed her face. It was like being in the Ghost Train. Una had once taken her to a funfair; that was the day before she left for ever. The smell in the vaulted room was oppressive – vomit, urine, stale food, alcohol, acetate upon ancient breath. But Wendy sat upright in bed against yellowed Victorian cushions; she seemed a long way from death. She waved her glass about, cheerfully.

'Who are you?' asked Wendy.

'I'm your grand-daughter Sara,' Sara said.

'What big teeth you have,' said Wendy – and indeed Sara had protuberant teeth and a bad bite. Una had given up on Sara's looks early on: there was hardly enough to work on, as she'd told Mogens, in Sara's hearing.

'I have no grand-daughter. I had one once called Sara, but I didn't like her, and anyway she died.'

Sara tried not to be hurt, tried to stay angry; noted that the refrigerator in the bathroom had grown so much ice the door no longer closed and counted the empty vodka bottles on the floor, the better to build up her dossier for the Social Services, for when the time came to send for the men in white suits and a compulsory order for their admittance.

Do not suppose that just because a young woman with the sweet name of Sara knocks upon a door and has difficulty gaining entrance, and quotes poetry, and visits her grandmother, that the young woman has a sweet nature. If I were Congo, I just would not have opened the door. My husband's defection has taught me to trust no one: Brian Moss's files confirm the lesson.

6

Trouble Brewing

'I don't like Sara Toffener much either,' said Jelly into the tape recorder, 'but I'll try. She's a woman and I must do my best for sisterhood. I daresay she, too, is what marriage has made her.

'The File Room at Catterwall & Moss is in a mess. I like to sit there and consider my situation. Sometimes, just for the hell of it, I mix up the files still further. Will anyone care?

'Stapled to Toffener v. Toffener (Tully and Sara) divorce documents – Tully started and withdrew divorce proceedings five years back, on the grounds of Sara's adultery – vigorously denied – were further depositions and statements relating to the Musgrave family, all of them illuminating, none of them particularly happy, but suggesting why there might be grounds for forgiving Sara who, before she became Toffener, was a Musgrave.

'The dusty filing cabinets of solicitors' offices bear witness to the energetic and tumultuous nature of human relationships, which no amount of legal language – as it sucks out the sweat of passion, best and worst endeavour, sexual indiscreetness, misadventure, good will and malice – can render dry of import. Attempt to fit us all nicely in under one law, render ruly the unruly, and you must in the end fail: diversity triumphs for ever over the law's desire to universalise the ordinary, contain the exceptional.

'1899. Violet Musgrave begat Wendy at the turn of the century, who begat Una at the beginning of the Great Depression, and Una was clearly a trouble to everyone, and begat Sara, whose father was described as "unknown" – being married to her grandmother and therefore unclaimable – on her birth certificate. When Sara was five, Una sued her residential nursery for damages: they had given Sara meat to eat and the child was a vegan. The nursery's defence was that Sara was returned to them so pale and thin after the Christmas holidays they felt it necessary to feed her up with whatever came to hand. Sara had been at the nursery for two years, returning home only for three weeks every Christmas. Una lost her case.

'There in the file was the Deed of Gift by which the property at Lodestar Avenue was given to Violet Musgrave in 1904, in token of Sir Oscar Rice Musgrave's natural love and affection. Oscar Rice Musgrave was Violet's cousin: Wendy no doubt Violet and Oscar's child, in spite of his being married to one Alice.

'Wendy grew up to believe that property was theft. She had lived through the age of Marx: she thought that sacrifice on her part would somehow make others happy. Perhaps Wendy's ardent socialism was what made Violet disinherit her: perhaps these views of hers were held to spite her mother, to diminish any sense of maternal achievement, rather than existing as a cool and disinterested conclusion as to what to do about society. Men do it often enough – the stockbroker's son throws a million dollar bills from the top of the Empire State building, to prove the inconsequence of money: the old hippie's son goes into the SAS – why not women?

'There in the file was Violet's Deed Poll changing her name from Bonham to Musgrave in May 1903. There was Alice Musgrave's action contesting the Deed of Gift after her husband's death in 1915. That failed, too.
'Finger through the yellowing sheets and find Oscar's death certificate. Killed in Action in 1915. Alice didn't manage to get hold of that, either. Una's birth certificate – Mother, Wendy Musgrave: Father, Philip Grace, medical practitioner. The one and only mention, but at least he must have turned up in person to declare himself the father, thus lessening the force of the illegitimacy. In 1935 Wendy married one Mogens Larsen, a Danish engineer. In 1949 she divorced him, changed her name back to Musgrave and left Lodestar House. Mogens continued to live there with Una, his erstwhile stepdaughter. Sara was born. Three years later Una left Lodestar; two months later Wendy returned. Tied in ribbon, a bundle of love letters written by Gerald Catterwall to Una in the late nineteen fifties. Una was clearly a goer.

'Gerald Catterwall's portrait hangs in the waiting room. The painter's art has done little to disguise his piggy eyes and flabby chin. Perhaps the artist was underpaid? It was perfectly likely. Catterwall & Moss – Gerald Catterwall was one of the founders of the firm – are not known for their handsome payment of staff; on the contrary, and I wonder if this was one of the causes of the firm's general incompetence. If you underpay the filing clerk you must expect files in such a state as these. Jelly, of course, now deliberately adds to the confusion.

'Holly, the accountant in charge of paying tradesmen's bills for various scions of the Rice family and now inadvertently meeting my hotel bill, once told Jelly that Gerald had taken his own life some twelve years earlier, being in financial difficulties to do with the clients' money. The circumstances of his death had been understandably hushed up. He was seventy-eight at the time, and still practising. He saw retirement as defeat.

'Then I came across, and unfolded with difficulty, a document so seriously faded I doubted that anyone other than myself had referred to it since the turn of the century. It related to the issuing in 1899, to Oscar Rice Musgrave by the Rice Estate, a hundred-year leasehold on the Lodestar property. The Deed of Gift, by which Oscar so generously passed the freehold property on to Violet, presumably after Wendy's birth, do not allude to the forms of tenure, it being a mere leasehold. "Have it, my dear. Take it, for you and your child," no doubt sounded a better phrase than "Have it for ninety-five years, my dear; hang on a minute while I consider the legal implications."

'In 1954 Violet had innocently bequeathed the house to Una, bypassing her daughter Wendy for reasons as yet unknown, but obviously adding to Wendy's discomfort. Wendy had lost her husband to her daughter Una. In 1965 Una had, generously or otherwise, given her mother a thirty-five year tenancy; taken it neatly to the millennium, no doubt, as people tend to do; not thinking "but mother might still be alive! What then?" What then, indeed? She had not in the past shown much mercy to her mother.

'Gerald Catterwall, who had drawn up various of these transactions, deserved to die. He was a perfectly dreadful solicitor. Nowhere in the Rice Estate schedule of assets, which I know by heart, observing, fascinated, the mechanisms by which Sir Edwin's interests are protected from Inland Revenue and wives alike, is there any mention of Lodestar. The property has simply dropped from sight, as is the fate of many large old houses in a state of disrepair, when lived in by the elderly and administered by incompetent lawyers.

'The more I perused the documents in my lonely room at The Claremont, "News at Ten" on with the volume right down, silent images of war, famine and disease reproaching me for my self pity, the more convinced I was that Tully had less time than he thought to get his hands on the tenancy. This would not revert back to the freeholder, the Rice Estate, in four years' time: no, by rights it would go to the leaseholder in a mere two years: whoever that leaseholder might now be: the heirs of the heirs of Sir Oscar Musgrave. Some taxi-driver, perhaps, or artist in a garret, who had no idea of his legal rights, and never would unless I called the matter to his attention. I would refrain from doing so, but enjoyed knowing a secret of such significance.'

7

Closer To Congo

'Keep your fingers on the keyboard, keep your eye on the screen, and keep your disapproval till it counts,' sang Jelly Lamb to herself, to the tune of 'Seven little girls a-sitting in the back seat, a-kissing and a-hugging with Fred', dabbing her Ram-roughened cheek with a damp tissue. This morning there was a scrawled letter from Congo Warby in the post, the decrepit but valiant husband of Tully Toffener's even more decrepit, even more valiant grandmother-in-law Wendy, once Lady Musgrave, now Mrs Warby.

Jelly opened the letter which was marked 'Personal and Private'.

Dear Moss, it read, in a quavery hand.
My wife and I are puzzled by your letter. We have no intention of going into a home, certainly while I have life and limb left to fight the ghosts. I am sorry to hear of Mr and Mrs Toffener's difficulties in finding suitable accommodation. As he is, I believe, a Minister of the Crown, albeit a junior one, couldn't the Crown provide? As he is well aware, Wendy and I are Republicans. We don't see that Lodestar House

would be a suitable residence for the Toffeners, if that's what they're after. Sara always told Wendy that she hated the place, and you have to have a clear mind and a good heart to fight the ghosts, and Tully has neither, as the poor people of this country know to their cost. From the look of him on TV, the fact that Lodestar Avenue is within walking distance of Westminster would not be helpful to him – two yards at a brisk walking pace would kill him. Does he think we're senile? Sara was always a greedy, heartless little bitch, worse even than her mother – it seems she's married a man just like herself. Please stop bothering us; we are old now and need some peace.

Jelly copied the letter for the file she would later take home to The Claremont for deeper perusal, and put the original in the 'Today's Post' folder for Mr Moss.

'I'm tempted just to pass Warby's letter to Tully,' said Brian Moss as Jelly sat poised with her shorthand pad. 'Not bother to construe tactfully.' Most middle management these days, including solicitors, compose their letters and memos directly on to the word processor and have them checked over by others for compromising statements, but Catterwall & Moss still preferred to work in the old way. 'Then Toffener would have apoplexy and we'd be free of him.'

Dear Tully, continued Brian Moss,
We've received a letter from Mr Warby. He and Mrs Warby are apparently reluctant to vacate the premises. Mr Warby is seeing ghosts, and is demonstrably not of sound mind. Under the 1983 Mental Health Act he would need to display this mental

unsoundness in a public place. He could then be taken by police or social workers to a place of safety; and thereafter, should Mr Warby be certified in that place by a doctor as being what we call incapable, a Document of Protection could be activated. Mr Warby's nearest and dearest would then take control of the old man's property, and for his own safety place him in a residential home. Perhaps he could be persuaded to pursue his so-called 'ghosts' out into the street?

In the sad event of Wendy Warby's death, Lodestar House would then not pass to Mr Warby but to your wife Sara. Mr Warby could argue his entitlement as 'a family member' but not if already declared incompetent. The provenance of the property is complicated, as you realise. There are two years of the original tenancy agreement to run, and under new legislation the long-term tenants have the right to sell the freehold at will. Mr and Mrs Warby show no interest in selling, though this unusual, prime property would fetch in the region of one-and-a-quarter million.

My best regards to your wife.
Brian Moss.

Jelly White put the letter to Tully Toffener, which seemed to her to amount to incitement to murder and false imprisonment, into the computer, printed it out, had the printout checked through by Brian Moss and signed by him; then, in his presence, she slipped the letter into a stamped, addressed envelope and sealed it. And then left it to Angelica to go down into the powder room and tear envelope and letter into little pieces and flush them down the lavatory pan. It took three flushes before all the shreds were gone. Angelica did not see why Tully Toffener should be given information it was better he did not have. Atmospheres come off letters. She liked Congo Warby: his scratchy, impetuous letters, his spidery but definite handwriting. The Toffener file exuded something sour and seedy. Angelica was happy to take a risk on Congo's behalf: she did not have the scruples Jelly did.

Sometimes Jelly felt she was the only moral person left in the world. 'I don't know what came over me,' she could always say, if challenged.

8

At Livermore Gate

'I don't know about Brian Moss any more,' said Tully Toffener to Sara. He drank neat whisky from a chunky crystal glass. She drank gin and tonic from a fluted goblet. A fire burned in the grate although the day was warm. The crimson velvet curtains at the grand, ungainly windows had faded to a thin pinky colour: the furniture was mahogany and too large: the leather sofa, purchased by Sara on a rash day, had been a mistake. It was a hideous room. 'He never seems to answer letters.'

'I expect he knows what he's doing,' said Sara. She was as thin and scraggy as Tully was tightly stuffed: the piece of crumpled, browny skin around the chicken's leg when it comes out of the oven, as opposed to the plump moist thigh. She was not unattractive: men liked her. She was often under attack, and in need of defence: she would engage attractive men at parties with long tales of woe and hardship; it would occur to them that the only way to stop all this would be to bed her. But she was true to Tully most of the time and he was true to her: a redeeming feature in both.

'I bloody hope so,' said Tully. 'I get the feeling his mind isn't on the job.'

And they had their usual pre-dinner discussion about the appalling state of the nation – the way the law protected the insane at the expense of the sane, the poor at the expense of the rich, the unhealthy at the expense of the healthy. Then Ayla the Philippine maid served the steak and kidney pie, and Tully and Sara sat at either end of the dark shiny table and toasted each other in the 1983 Saint Estèphe, opened three hours earlier. But he had to hurry over the apple pie because he had to get back to the House of Commons for a late night debate on the rights or otherwise of the handicapped, in which he was speaking, arguing for a stricter definition of what constituted handicap. His government maintained that whereas 'disablement' was not sufficient cause for state benefit, 'handicap', at least in some categories, might so do. The apartment at Livermore Gate was a forty-minute taxi drive from the House: were he and Sara to live at Lodestar House a mere ten minutes would do it.

Tully had dropped gravy on his tie. He went to the bedroom to find another. Sara followed him. They embraced and, full of dinner as they were, had what they liked to refer to as a 'quickie' on the floor of the walk-in wardrobe. Ayla, coming in to turn down the bed, disturbed them. She was standing transfixed when Tully, on top of Sara, looked sideways to see her stolid, sandalled feet just by him. She came from a peasant background: her face was broad and her look was sullen. Neither liked her.

'Fire that woman,' said Tully, as Sara knotted his fresh,

pink silk tie for him. 'Don't tell me she has nowhere to go, and four children to keep –'

'If she couldn't support them,' said Sara, 'she shouldn't have had them in the first place –'

'My, you're tough,' said Tully, admiringly. 'She's ugly, she has no tact, she's obviously an illegal, she can't cook, and we could get someone better than her at half what she has the nerve to ask. Thank God there's no legislation yet to protect the rights of incompetent servants, and if I have my way there never will be.'

And off he went to the House of Commons, and Sara fired Ayla.

'I not do it again,' said Ayla. 'More careful next time.'

'I want you out of the house,' said Sara, 'within the hour. You are simply not fit to work in a civilised household. It's not your fault: you come from a primitive background and you simply don't understand how things are done over here. My diamond ring is missing. Think yourself lucky I don't press charges.'

Ayla cried, and said she had nowhere to go, and just stood helplessly, so Sara went into the small box room where Ayla slept on a camp bed, and packed up her few belongings into a black plastic sack and put them on the front steps, and held the door open until Ayla gave in and joined her possessions.

'I come to collect my letters?' begged Ayla. 'Letters for me from my children?'

'Certainly not,' said Sara. 'I am not a forwarding agency.' And she slammed the front door.

She had another gin and tonic and then noticed that

the dinner things were still uncleared. She rang up the twenty-four hour 'At Your Service' agency.

'What, again, Mrs Toffener?' asked the dismal voice at the other end of the phone. 'What happened this time?'

'This time,' said Sara, 'you sent me a thief and a voyeur. I need someone else within the hour. Someone honest, reliable and not physically deformed, if it's not beyond your competence. The apartment is a tip. My husband is a Minister of the Crown; some standards are expected.'

'Mrs Toffener,' said Marty Walker, ex-social worker, on duty that night, responding to the urgent calls of the great, the famous, and the wealthy in one kind of domestic distress or another, 'when you say Ayla is a thief, do you have any proof of that? You shouldn't make these allegations otherwise. And did you pay her wages in lieu –?'

'Good God,' said Sara, 'the woman's an illegal: she has no rights.'

She slammed the phone down and started to cry. Sometimes she wondered why she was so disagreeable but could find no answer. Perhaps if she'd had children she would have developed some nicer, kinder side of her nature? But she doubted it. They being small and helpless, she'd have merely bullied them too. And the children would have added Tully's genes to hers to create themselves, and would probably just bully back: grow up to commit patricide, matricide.

Sara went out to collect Ayla and her black bag from the step. Ayla was waiting there, as Sara knew she would be. She had nowhere else to go. This kind of incident happened every few months or so.

9

Sara Attempts To Visit
Her Grandmother

Companies are reluctant to offer flood insurance for properties in Lodestar Avenue. It is too near the River Thames and every year the level of the water rises as new embankments and levels contain and speed its flow. Besides, the river is tidal, and though there are great new flood barriers at the river's mouth, the seas are rising, are they not, and once or twice a year the city's newspapers panic and say this time we are finally out of luck. The moon is full, a swollen tide, the wind is strong and from the East, nothing can save us now. Why, in such a climate, should insurers take a risk? They, whose ambition in life is not to take risks though their function is to do so.

Gerald Catterwall engaged Sun Life in a long correspondence on the subject of their refusal to offer Wendy Musgrave flood cover, and they relented; sensibly, since I notice from the files no claim has ever been made in this respect.

But I like to think of Sara Toffener, beating upon the side door of Lodestar House – the front door is all but hidden by ivy, and has obviously not been opened for a decade or more – in her attempt to gain admittance, looking behind her to make sure that black flood water was not trickling down the steps after her.

The side door was below ground level. To get to it you had first to pass through a kind of lych gate in the high grey brick wall which enclosed the property, using the rusty iron ring handle which left reddish-black marks on the hand, and down a short flight of stone steps, through much vaulted and pillared masonry which oozed water (or so one hoped it was: perhaps it was sewage, from some fractured pipe or other) in slow drops upon the head. The flight of steps which rose above were these days decorative, not functional, leading nowhere but to stone patterns inset into brick. Someone along the decades, probably Una, Sara's mother, the trouble-maker, had seen fit to block up the original front door: or perhaps the structure had suffered bomb damage, and a temporary measure had drifted into permanence.

Tully Toffener felt, rightly, that to live in Lodestar House – especially as the Heritage Department would pay for the house's repairs and modernisation – would reflect well upon his status and standing. The garden could be sold off for development, for yet further millions. Or he could be bold and do the developing himself. Nothing wrong with an apartment block or so at the bottom of the garden. But Lodestar! – a house which had been in the in-laws' family for generations – Good Lord, how naturally a title would then come. And Tully twisted Sara's moral arm to persuade her of it. Poor little Sara, sent away from home at three, and none the nicer for it.

Victims are seldom nice: that is the effect of victimisation. Evil is not easily rectified. It is as infectious as measles: it has a knock-on effect: ripples as smoothly as dominoes will, each one tipping the next, falling one after another.

'Let's just get the Lodestar matter settled,' Tully would say, 'then we'll have children.' And Sara hardly liked to say she did not particularly want children for fear they would inherit Tully's genes, as if they would not be bad enough without, but took the point well enough that he was wielding an axe above her head, though only he believed that axe had substance.

To have children, if you were Sara, you had to have servants, nannies, and Sara's files at Catterwall & Moss were already thick with correspondence about staff who had robbed her, or were demanding unreasonable compensation for dismissal; enquiries about the penalties for illegal entry into the country and so forth. She had learned from Tully the gift of hanging axes.

'When we finally get possession of Lodestar,' Sara had once said crossly to Tully, having temporarily just got rid of a girl who'd worn Sara's best shoes to go to a wedding and thought she wouldn't be discovered, 'I'm as likely to burn it down as restore it, and build some nice new labour-saving bungalow in its place, and live without servants altogether,' and Tully had looked at her admiringly, for he loved everything that was drastic in her nature, and when she was pink with anger looked almost pretty, and said, 'Over my dead body, so it's suttee for you, my girl. Lodestar will stand and you will be Lady Toffener and London's premiere hostess, or it will be the worse for you.'

And he wished he had the nerve to ask Sara to wear her high-heeled shoes to bed and to tie him up to the bedposts, but he never quite could.

10

Scenes From Wendy's Life

Sara comes to visit Wendy, claiming to be her grand-child, but Wendy sees this as some kind of time-slip, some spacewarp reversal, some peculiar anomaly of sequential logic. She herself is the child. She can see herself now, in this very room, at the age of six, standing transfixed in front of a mirror, in a white dress, all folds and flounces, calf length, snugly belted, and with stout lace-up boots.

'Is this me? Is this who I am?' she asks.

The mirror answers 'Yes, and always will be.'

'How did it happen?' she asks. 'How did I come about?' but this is beyond even the mirror to explain, not that Wendy cares. Wendy can tell she is no bad thing to be – pretty, wilful, bright, temperamental. A yell from her can bring the adult world to its heels: a smile and a toss of her head brings its attention. She puts on her mother Violet's shoes and clatters about the room. In her mother's footsteps. She will be a bohemian like her mother, and have lovers like her mother, and be in charge of this house, and hummingbirds will fly about its vaulted ceilings. She kisses the mirror. Life is all future.

'Congo,' murmurs Wendy. 'Don't sell the mirror. I can see the mark where I kissed it. Let's sell the mirror last of all.'

The mirror is a cheval glass, mounted on stout Victorian legs, practical but not beautiful. Wendy can change the angle of the glass with her walking stick. Then it shows her other scenes.

Wendy runs out of the house into the garden; her brother Theo follows. They look like the children in an E. Nesbit story book. Or has Wendy got memory and the book illustrations confused? It scarcely matters. Theo's wearing loose knickerbockers, as loose and unrestricting as Wendy's dress. The Musgraves are a family of free thinkers, progressives; Violet is a member of the Fabian Society – 'Fabian, my dear, was a Roman General who was proud of conquering little by little.' Little by little, the Fabians believe, socialism will triumph, and all mankind be glad and free. Cure ignorance, poverty and disease and you will cure all human ills, because mankind is good except where these three evils make it bad. It was a plausible enough belief at the time: though World War I made a nasty dent in the smooth surface of burgeoning human aspiration, the expectation of progress.

Both Wendy and Theo are handsome, well cared for, and much loved children. They are both illegitimate; that is to say, born out of wedlock; purposely produced according to current theories of free love. George Bernard Shaw, a frequent visitor to Lodestar, maintains that marriage is a form of friendship blessed by governments: H.G. Wells, who also often dines with Violet, thinks it is the duty of any superior male (as he most evidently is) to propagate his genes.

Violet had listened, and worshipped, and believed, and some said Wendy was Shaw's daughter, and Theo was H.G. Wells's son, but Violet said no, both children were fathered by her friend and lover Oscar, who loved her deeply, but being married already was not in a position to marry her, even had she consented to marry him.

Marriage was all about property anyway, said Violet, whose eyes were enormous and the colour of the flower after which she was named; she had soft brown massy hair which could be piled on top of her head after the fashion of the day, and a long, elegant neck and a very white skin against which pendants and ear-rings always looked good. She had a high plump bosom; she went without corsets, being a progressive and a bohemian. She was a fine painter, mostly of portraits, occasionally of landscapes, which earned her the respect of her circle, and had a temperament and intelligence as refined and interesting as her work. She had started life as an artists' model, and everyone knew what that meant – a girl from nowhere. She had been fortunate enough at the age of eighteen to get an actual nude modelling job at the Slade School of Art, where kindly and concerned people had looked over her and then after her; had discovered talent in her and, what is more, had developed it, and where she met Oscar Rice Musgrave, then Professor of Fine Art, who, hopelessly enamoured of her, had installed her in Lodestar and taught her the social graces as well as theories of art and politics. After Wendy's birth, he made over the property to Violet, to his wife Alice's distress. But a man must follow the Life Force: Free Love is a principle as well as a justification. What can Alice do?

It's 1914. In spite of Violet's socialist principles, Wendy and Theo have never been allowed to play in the street, as urchins do. One day they are peering into the forbidden world from between the bars of the castellated lych gate, when one of the forbidden urchins runs by blowing a whistle and crying, 'Take cover, take cover!' And they see he is wearing a sandwich-board bearing the same notice, which they can read but he quite probably cannot. The child points skywards as he runs whenever he can, between whistles.

Violet comes running out of the house, a waft of oil paint and turpentine following. Her apron is streaked with bright artists' colours. She is permitted by society, by virtue of her talent, to be a little messy. Her children adore her: so do all the great men of her day, many of them other women's husbands. The wives will look sideways at Wendy and Theo searching for resemblances. In summer, Violet loves to give dinner parties on the lawn. There are a couple of sandstone Gaudier-Brzeska sculptures stuck casually in the flowerbeds. Sandstone is barely durable or waterproof, but never mind. Art is everywhere and sculptures two a penny, and the artist off at the Front so can't protest anyway. A casual mother-and-child fresco in the garden wall is a gift from Epstein; dustbins are thrust up against it. Inside the house, proudly presented but carelessly regarded, are Mucha etchings, William Morris tiles and furniture, a couple of Holman Hunts, Wyndham Lewis drawings. Alice, Oscar's wife, charms no one and receives no homage, no gifts, but has the advantage of respectability.

'What is that terrible noise?' Violet cries, and looks out the gate, and perceives the scurrying, shoeless child. 'What is that poor child thinking of? He's disturbing the whole neighbourhood!'

And there is a bang and a crash as a black object falls from out a dirigible balloon, which has been drifting casually down along the river alarming no one. The object lands on the new Thames embankment – that strong brown God, as T.S. Eliot was later to call it, with its alarming propensity to flooding. The high wall of Lodestar House has a noticeable water line some two feet up from the ground, and there is a closable hatch across the lower part of the barred gate to keep the flood tides out.

The bomb, such as it is, makes a hole in the embankment and uproots new trees and flowers. The hole fills instantly with filthy water – London's sewage system is nowhere near completed yet – which trickles across the road towards Wendy, Theo and Violet. The urchin is blown along the street but amazingly is unhurt, and reappears a couple of hours later wearing a placard saying 'All Clear' and blowing his whistle again. By that time they are still shivering and shuddering inside the house.

'What's cover?' asks Theo. 'And why should we take it?' And Violet weeps: it is the end of the magic days; she can see it. She has a presage of disaster.

Wendy hastily shifts the mirror.

Now she sees herself marrying Congo: it's her third marriage. How did she ever get to be so old? First Leon, then Mogens Larsen, now Congo and she are marrying in the French Consulate in Cairo because it's the only place there's air-conditioning and the season has been so terrifyingly hot and humid. Congo is twenty years younger than she and works for the British Council. She's come to Cairo with an exhibition of Violet's paintings, but there is some kind of political trouble and the French Institute have taken over British affairs. She's wearing a gauzy kind of dress and Congo is wearing flares.

Wendy recovers her courage and tips the mirror back to her younger days. She was right: the gauzy dress was not sufficient to disguise flabby upper arms. Her spirit was thirty, her flesh double that, and you can't disguise it and shouldn't try. Though Congo never seemed to mind.

'A penny for your thoughts,' says Congo now. But Wendy shakes her head. The world opens out like a flower into calm or stormy weather, closes down at the end of the day. What use are words? What happened to the Epstein fresco? Perhaps it's still there, under creeper. If she could walk, she would go and see. She can't be bothered asking Congo. The past is more interesting than the present. When she has run through it, assessed it and assembled it, she will die.

Wendy and Theo are playing in the garden with the Rice 'cousins', Leon, Georgina and Bridget. Their mother Alice hates their coming, but Oscar insists. Light dapples through the leaves of the red beech tree. Leeks are growing amongst the roses, and tomato plants as well. They spring unheralded, because for three hundred years the ground hereabouts served as a market garden, and also, though no one will admit it, Lodestar House has a cess pit and some of its old lead feeders are cracked and household waste escapes into the soil. The garden is certainly very fertile and, these being the days before detergent when soda was the only cleaning agent available, household waste, both kitchen and bathroom, could do nothing but good. Once sewage flowed directly into the Thames, but after the Chelsea embankment was built, it found its way blocked and seeped up wherever it could, between paving stones, into cellars, into gardens.

Wendy thinks, 'This is probably the prettiest place in the world, and I am probably the luckiest girl in all the world,' when her cousin Leon, who is four years older than she, says, 'When your mother dies, this house will belong to my father, and I'm going to inherit it because you lot are bastards and I'm the only son,' and Wendy is conscious of a pang of apprehension, a foretaste of an uncertain future. Usually she discounts what Leon says. His name means lion, but he is, in her eyes, a pitiful, wretched, stammering creature whose father fails to love him. Violet has told Wendy so. In Violet's eyes all human misery is due to failure to love and be loved. Wendy can see that she might have to take Leon seriously. His back is straightening, his chin firming: the need to survive is toughening him up. Soon he will be big enough to strike his father dead, if he so chooses, and he may well so choose. Leon has learned early how not to forgive; how not to be a nice person.
'Don't be silly,' says Wendy, throwing Leon a ball he can't possibly catch. 'Butterfingers, anyway!' she calls out as he drops it. Leon looks at Wendy spitefully: his little finger is bending at an odd angle. Wendy's broken

it, and she already knows he won't forgive her. She wishes now she had thrown it properly.

Another push at the mirror but there's no getting rid of certain scenes: they are part and parcel of the dreadful past.

Now they're in the big living room with its acres of green Morris curtaining, the pewter mugs on the medieval refectory table, its tiled and vaulted ceilings. Violet is crying. Oscar, oddly supportive of Leon, wants Wendy punished for breaking Leon's finger, or that's how Wendy construes it. Oscar is saying that Wendy is ill-mannered, violent and tomboyish, and needs proper discipline and to go to school.

'You don't love me any more!' weeps Violet, and Oscar huffs and puffs. Men don't like talk of love, not once their sweethearts are mothers, as Violet says to Wendy.

Wendy is made to go to school, which she hates. She attends Marshall Hall, a progressive girls' school in Fulham.

These days Wendy is careful not to be alone with Leon, who has taken to putting his hand up her skirt if he possibly can, saying that if she doesn't let him he'll have her turned out of her house the minute her father dies, so she has to stand still and let him do what he wants, though why he should want to she cannot understand. She wishes her clothes were less advanced, like every-one's thinking, so he had more of a problem getting inside them. Wendy understands that Leon might very well kill Oscar quite early on, but Oscar becomes a war artist, goes to the Front and dies before Leon is old enough to do it. Wendy tries to cry about Oscar's death, but can't: Violet weeps enough for a whole street-full of war widows, which annoys Wendy, for some reason. Violet has a house, a small annuity and friends. Oscar was Alice's to grieve for: mourning is surely a luxury reserved for official wives and current mistresses.

Miss Reynolds, the Classics mistress at Marshall Hall, looms large in Wendy's life. Miss Reynolds has a habit of stroking Wendy's hair and holding her hand tight; kissing her when she gets Latin verbs right, slapping her when she construes them badly. Wendy finds it imposs- ible to talk to Violet about any of it: Violet still believes that the world is a beautiful place. It's why Violet is so popular with the men around her, Wendy can see that. Violet even in the end grants Oscar eternal life in her head: she will, she knows, meet up with him in heaven. Violet becomes a spiritualist and holds séances in the dining room: curtains are pulled, hands stretched and touched around the table. Ectoplasm forms and frightens Wendy out of her wits, but the medium employed, as a laundress might be, to attend the sessions turns out to be a fraud. Yet Violet remains, as she describes it, a spiritualist socialist.

Who can Wendy consult about her problems? What exactly is Leon's now long-healed little finger doing, still pressing up beneath her bloomers, longer and more enquiring now and most insistent? What are Miss Reynolds' tear-filled eyes and moist warm mouth about? Ask Violet and she'd have it that they were the mere expression of free thought, free love and the energies of the life force.

No, there is no one for Wendy to talk to. Judy the maid,

Mrs Bates the cook, are not suitable confidantes. The circumstances of the servants' lives are too different from her own. Judy has an out-of-wedlock baby and Violet employs her in the same spirit as she takes in stray kittens. Because others are so unkind, she, Violet, must make up the balance. Mrs Bates lives in, and is a respectable widow. Theo is a boy and her brother; Wendy would be far too embarrassed to speak to him. Leon grows two feet in six months. Wendy remains petite. 'A pocket Venus', Violet calls her, but Wendy knows she's being kind. What she really means is 'dwarfish'.

Push the mirror again.

Wendy's fifteen. Violet goes to visit Lady Annette Columbia, who wears flowing oriental robes and has fluffy blonde hair; who, with her daughter Cynthia, is giving a party in a house in Bayswater. Violet takes Wendy along. It's Wendy's first dance: there's an ebony floor, a wind-up gramophone to supplement a string quartet. Violet dances with, amongst others, Aleister Crowley, later known as The Beast 666. Cynthia Columbia has cropped hair and wears a tie and dances with other girls. Violet's good friend Nina Hamnett, an artist, warns Wendy that Cynthia is probably a lesbian and suggests Wendy keeps out of her way.
'A lesbian? What's that?' asks Wendy.
'Darling,' says Nina, 'a lesbian is a girl who likes girls, not boys,' but Wendy still doesn't understand. Babies get born when married men and women share beds, or so she has been led to understand; though how to explain herself away is difficult. Perhaps she was an immaculate conception? Further enquiry could only lead her into the dark, forbidden and attractive territory which no one

talks about. Nevertheless, at this stage Wendy trusts her mother to have done the right thing by the rules of the bohemian society to which she clearly belongs. Only no one has told Wendy quite what the rules are. They seem mostly to consist of saying one thing and doing another. Wendy is becoming anxious, argumentative and critical, and Violet doesn't like it.

Nina warns Wendy off Aleister Crowley, saying not only is he a common little conman with no breeding, but is also in touch with The Devil. Go to his apartment, as Nina had recently done, and discover that fires would mysteriously break out in corners of the room. 'At first I tried dousing them with water from the flower vases,' said Nina, 'until I discovered that water didn't quench the flames. But then the flames didn't burn my hand either, so I learned to put up with them. I expect they were all in my head.'

Later in the evening, Wendy observed Nina dancing with Cynthia Columbia; they pressed their bodies together and looked into each other's eyes. Wendy did not enjoy her first dance. She felt clumsy and that the guests were not loveable, serene and artistic as she had expected, but as troubled and complicated as the parents of her friends at school. She would have danced with The Beast 666, but he didn't ask her. He was dancing a rather clumsy waltz with Violet. Later they disappeared together, without a thought for Wendy.

'You poor dear,' said Berta Ruck, the novelist. 'I expect she just forgot she'd brought you along.'

It is left to Berta and her husband, Oliver Onions, to take Wendy home to Lodestar.

'What a monstrosity,' observes Mr Onions, peering up at the great grey turrets. 'You poor little thing!'

Wendy cries; she does not like to have her home insulted, nor does she like to be so humiliated by her mother. Forgotten! Bertha assures her that Violet hasn't done it on purpose; that Mr Crowley has strange and secret powers to control others, especially beautiful women, and make them do his will. Berta and Mr Onions drive off, leaving Wendy at the gate. She can't wake the cook, and she hasn't got a key, so she has to break in the cloakroom window, which is easy enough – she has been doing it since she was little – but she manages to hurt her ankle. Now see what you've done, Mother!

Wendy finds herself alone in Lodestar House for the first time in her life. She imagines it is haunted. She wonders what dark and secret things are happening to her mother. She sleeps. When she wakes it's morning and her mother is in her room, apologising. But Violet looks rather pale and sleepless and her mouth is swollen.
'I completely forgot you; how can I forgive myself? My poor little darling! What a wonderful man. Do what you will shall be all of the law! What a revelation!' There are sweet odours on Violet's breath: Mother sways, Mother sings; she stretches her arms, draped with gauzy scarves, to heaven. The arms are not as young as they used to be, Wendy notices. 'With all my being: all of it, every little corner of it, I must consent.'

What is Mother talking about now? Wendy decides to be a Marxist, not a Fabian. She needs something with a little harshness in it, a little discipline.

Later the newspapers reveal that Lady Columbia, 'society hostess', has no right to her title, and is a trumped-up nouvelle riche. There are a succession of scandals relating to Aleister Crowley, and his relationship with very young girls. Violet stops swaying around the house, sweetly breathing, and weeps and breaks things.

'All he wanted was to get to you through me,' she snarls at Wendy. Somehow hope and love are vanishing. It's as if the tidal estuaries of the Thames, the strong brown God, now suck in blood from the killing fields of coastal France. Wars are never as far away as anyone hopes. Fear, hate, blood flow uncalled for, unlooked for, in a tidal backsurge. Wendy has no idea what her mother is talking about: but finds herself freezing in the violence of Violet's response. Adorable has become difficult to adore: it is too violent, angry: whim has turned into dangerous unpredictability. Theo is away at school: he mutters and murmurs over the holidays about the public disgrace of being his mother's son. An artists' model, now notorious whore: 'Fancy Woman to the Beast', as the papers put it, in a divorce case.

'What do you mean?' begs Wendy. 'What do you *mean*, Theo?', but he won't say. She beats her fists against the lych gate, wanting to get out into the forbidden land, frightened to go. 'Take cover, take cover!'

'You've been meeting Aleister secretly,' says Violet. 'I know you have, you nasty little creature. That's why he doesn't want me any more.'

The cook leaves, the maid leaves. Friends don't call.

Wendy is too distressed even to cry. One night, Violet crawls and screams on the stone floor.

Leon, bold and brave in flannels, almost handsome, now almost calling-up age, calls to visit his father's other family. Wendy, for once, is glad to see him. Leon takes over and summons the doctor. Leon 'steals a kiss' as he calls it. Violet is diagnosed as having 'a nervous breakdown', and is taken away to a clinic. Leon pays: he tells Wendy he'll allow her to live in Lodestar, and Wendy doesn't even have the sense to ask to see documents, assumes Leon would not tell lies of enormous stature. For some reason, Violet going off to a 'clinic' seems the grubbiest thing of all that's happened. School is Wendy's only comfort. She lives in Lodestar House alone for a month or so; Mrs Bates the cook has pity and comes back for a time. Now at least Wendy has company, but she gets head lice. Mrs Bates takes paintings and sculptures to Portobello Market and sells them for food. Oh, it is the worst of times.

Leon asks Wendy to marry him and she agrees. No one forbids the marriage. There's no one to forbid it. Violet's raving away in a padded cell somewhere. Theo won't come to the wedding. No one has ever said anything openly about a shared father: 'cousins' pleases everyone better. The lost girl Wendy will now, thank God, be Leon's responsibility. And Leon's mother Alice, Oscar's widow, cuts Leon out of her life on the grounds that her son, in marrying H.G. Wells's by-blow, is no longer worthy of the family name.

Lodestar House becomes heavy with secrets that later generations would think of no consequence, but are nonetheless oppressive: the sheer weight of them could kill the soul. The vaulted ceilings, the curving staircases, which an architect saw as springing heavenward, a paean of praise to love and laughter, light and freedom, the new spirit of the coming egalitarian century, become echoey, horrid, sinister; Lodestar is the forgotten dungeon beneath the palace: foul water seeps from the walls, as blood would seep from the earthen walls of the trenches where young men by the million died. But people will make their own individual wars; manufacture their own griefs. Those were the days when to be mad was to bring shame, the word cancer was not spoken aloud, to have a child out of wedlock was a disgrace, to have an illegitimate child enough to get a woman locked up in an asylum as a moral imbecile, and the penalty for attempted suicide was death by hanging. Enough, indeed, to kill the questing soul, the enquiring intellect. But houses recover as people recover: Lodestar was one day to come into its own again.

11

A Property Worth Having

Jelly was not unhappy. The more files she brought home to The Claremont, the more concentration she applied to them, the quieter Angelica, Angel and Lady Rice remained. She found herself without personal history or active sexuality; a woman without sorrow, recreated every day. Sometimes in the evenings she had a headache, which she suspected was created by her other selves, hammering away for head-time, airtime, but she denied it to them. She needed a rest. Besides, she was a moral entity – it seemed to her the others were not.

She became studiedly virtuous: she could see that Angel was the worst threat. She no longer employed Ram to take her to the office. She would see the Volvo hovering, but would shake her head and walk briskly, head held high, to Bond Street Underground, while he attempted to follow her, against the flow of the traffic. She slapped Brian Moss down: literally, aiming a blow at his well-suited crotch, which quietened him considerably. If Lady Rice rocked nightly in her sea of sorrow, if Angelica went to Fenwicks on Saturdays or for late-night shopping, Jelly at least did not know about it.

Nightly Jelly filled her notebooks: scraps of fact, fiction, essay. She kept them hidden at the back of the clothes cupboard, amongst her shoes. The number of pairs, she noticed, were increasing: shoes and boots she would never, as Jelly, wear: platform-soled, absurdly pointed or brutishly squared – nothing at all to do with convenience or the shape of the human foot.

She summoned Angelica to reproach her.

'Why do you do this?' Jelly demanded. 'Why do you waste so much time, energy and money buying absurd things you never need and don't wear?'

'I need them,' said Angelica crossly. 'I like them and I'd wear them tomorrow if only you'd put them on.'

'What these?' inquired Jelly, picking up a black suede thigh boot jangling with chains, with six-inch platforms. Jelly was sitting on the bed, facing the gold-framed mirror. 'You're insane.'

'You're so safe and boring,' sneered Angelica. 'Mummy's little small-town girl.'

'I really like those boots,' said Angel, finding her voice. 'I helped Angelica pick them. I'm glad she bought them. If you'd put them on now we could go down to the bar.'

'You're ridiculous,' said Jelly, shutting them off and out, as these days it seemed simpler to do.

'Give them to charity,' murmured Lady Rice, who was swimming around in there somehow. 'Get the alter egos to counselling. You need to find a support group for compulsive shoppers. Thank God it's nothing to do with me.'

Jelly picked a mound of useless clothes out of the wardrobe and shelves: see-through blouses, metal belts,
leather trews, purple velvet leggings, cloche hats with
flowers, absurd knickers, crotchless tights, lacy suspender belts – unused, unworn mostly, with the price
labels still on them – masses of cheap jewellery, expensive
face creams gone sour and caked because they'd been
inspected, not used, and the lid left off; cheap and cheerful cosmetics, hair curlers, wigs. She gave them all to the
corridor maid, who did not seem particularly grateful.

With these out of the way, and nothing but the sensible
skirts, pastel jumpers and warm coats left, she felt more
herself.

She had to pay for the junk out of her earnings as Jelly
– her mother forwarded credit card accounts – only pur-
chases from the hotel boutique being chargeable to
Edwin. She hoped Angelica and Angel would have
the grace to be ashamed of themselves, but didn't stir
them to ask them. She investigated Lodestar House
further.

She found a mention of the house in a book called *Walks
in Old Chelsea*. '1–3 Lodestar Avenue, Lodestar House,
is a solidly built house dating from 1874, of what is
known as Tuscan-Gothic design, set in a quarter acre of
land on the slopes of the River Thames where Belgravia
eases into Chelsea.'

On Sundays Jelly would walk down to the Embankment,
passing the high grey brick walls of Lodestar House: once
even standing on a dustbin to see over into the garden,
and later wrote this in her notebook.

'The city has nudged up around the property and contrived to steal some of its original land so that it now occupies a mere corner site. It's an ungainly giant of a house, castellated and turreted, Grade One listed, high-walled in dark grey brick, where Lodestar Avenue and Terrace meet. Once you could walk from the back door down the long garden to the river, through orchards. No longer. A main road and an embankment bar the way, though the high walls cut off sound and fumes. All around there are agreeable, well-built Georgian terraces. In return for a strip of land for the embankment, in 1888 Number 3 Lodestar Avenue was demolished by the authorities and that land given back to the freeholders: the Musgrave family.

'Tuscan-Gothic is, I know, a contradiction in terms, but then so is the house, built to defy and annoy, the subject of interminable legal wrangles, passionately loved and hopelessly hated, a focus of that struggle to keep in balance the world of emotion and the world of financial and practical representation of that emotion, the spiritual and the material. 1–3 Lodestar Avenue is a brilliantly reflecting yet blighted planet which any sensible traveller would do well to avoid.'

Reading it later, she thought that perhaps Lady Rice, with her obsession with the scales of justice, had had a hand in the writing.

12

Edwin's Offer

Edwin writes to Brian Moss that he feels his wife Angelica is entitled to nothing at all. She betrayed him, insulted him, humiliated him in front of his friends, turned out to be a different person than the one he married – couldn't he seek an annulment rather than a divorce, on this account? And then strip her of her apparent right to keep a title she had obtained by deception? Her use of the title shows her contempt for all things decent. And shouldn't she be compelled to disclose her whereabouts?

Brian Moss writes back to say that the Courts are not likely to allow Angelica to go completely unmaintained. If he offers her a small apartment and £1,000 a month, as a starting offer, it is likely that his wife will withdraw her counter-petition, and his divorce can go quietly ahead and he can anticipate being married to Anthea before the year is out.

Jelly puts an extra zero on the £1,000, changes 'small apartment' to 'substantial house on the Rice Estate'; prints out the letter, wipes out the changes on the computer and re-enters the original. When Edwin writes back saying that he will offer her half that sum and that he does not want his ex-wife living anywhere near him, she destroys the letter and substitutes for it one requesting Brian Moss offer his wife £5,000 a month, signs it, and gives it to Brian Moss to read. She changes Brian's reply, omitting his expressions of surprise, but suggesting that if he doesn't want Lady Rice living close by he should perhaps offer her, in final settlement, a semi-derelict house in Lodestar Avenue, presently coming back, upon expiry of leasehold, into the Rice Estate: Brian Moss has reason to believe Lady Angelica is prepared to withdraw her counter-petition if this is done.

At this point, Jelly allows the natural correspondence to flow untampered with. Any inconsistencies she can iron out as she goes along. She is good at Edwin's signature, has Rice Estate letterheads to hand: she keeps in her desk drawer sheets hand-signed by Brian Moss a-plenty. The important thing is that she is not late, or ill, so that Brian Moss doesn't get to open his own mail.

Jelly speaks by telephone to Barney Evans, refraining from saying that if she had taken his advice and declined to counter-petition, she would not now be in so strong a position, and asks him to write to Brian Moss saying the financial offer made is ludicrously small, considering the length of the marriage, and Sir Edwin's conduct; how about £7,500 a month. Brian Moss passes the message back to Sir Edwin.

Jelly kisses the back of the envelope before dropping it into the letter box. She is not sure why she does it. Perhaps Lady Rice surfaced again, stirred up by this almost-contact with Edwin? Jelly fears it may be because the entity still loves Edwin, rather than that the several personae have this one thing in common, the need for money and comfort; but can't be sure. Jelly doesn't think for long about matters like that, so it was as well it was she, not Angelica or Angel, who did the posting. Or the letter would have stayed in the back of a drawer while she made up her mind. Or thus she persuades herself. She is quite a Polyanna.

All is looking well for Jelly until a letter arrives from Edwin asking Brian Moss to hurry the whole thing up, get everything settled, he wants to marry Anthea, they want to have babies.

Jelly, opening this bombshell first thing in the morning, begins to cry. She cries and cries and has to tell Brian Moss when he comes in that she's allergic to the poppies on her desk. He flings open the window and tosses poppies, vase and all out, in a gesture which reminds her of Edwin, so she cries some more. Brian Moss clasps her and tells her tears in a woman always affect him: he'd like to make love to her there and then.

Jelly pushes him away, and says certainly not, this is appalling sexual harassment. He says that weeping is its own form of harassment, but goes into his office and sulks for the rest of the day. Lady Rice is back in control: much weeping always revives her. Jelly has to go into hiding, keep the company of Angelica and Angel. With Jelly there to control her, at least Angelica doesn't spend so much time in the shops, and money is saved. And Angel is cheered up: Lady Rice gives

Angel some opportunity to take over from time to time.

One of the first things Lady Rice does is to reinstate Ram's morning journeys to work. They stop off in the car park, but Lady Rice is nervous, afraid of being seen, worrying that her husband might find out, and Ram puts an end to the relationship. Lady Rice is relieved, and Ram says to his friends he doesn't understand women one bit: they lack consistency.

13

Lady Rice On Her Alter Egos

It is not that I dislike Jelly: she just doesn't inspire me. It's she who makes me the boring company I think I sometimes am. Edwin certainly thought so, or he wouldn't have preferred Anthea to me.

Jelly is the kind of woman who has few friends: who gets up in the morning, enjoys a solitary breakfast, feels the satisfaction of a good day's work, buys the cat food and goes home on public transport. She is not a compulsive telephone talker: she does not like sharing and caring with just anyone; she enjoys a flirtation because she can see that sooner or later she will need to get married and have children, and anyone likes to be admired and to be in control. But Jelly does not particularly need or enjoy the running commentary on life that friends require and provide: the oohs and ahs and guess what she said, and he didn't, did he, the bastard; how could she, the bitch! that others seem to enjoy: she is not, frankly, interested in very much or curious about others. She likes to look neat and sweet, and she is certainly not above spying and prying because this too gives her power: she likes to have secrets, she is secretive; she likes to know secrets, to have them in her possession but not pass them on.

But she has learned her lesson about friends. They can and will betray you, and though you offer loyalty, loyalty is not necessarily offered in return. Judas Iscariot didn't care about the money: he just wanted Jesus up there on the cross. The closer you nurture the worm to your bosom, the more likely it is to bite.

Seek solitude, thinks Jelly. Jelly doesn't feel all that much: she prefers to think.

Angelica had friends. When she became Lady Rice, she gathered around her all the bohemians in the area; such writers, painters, sculptors, weavers, cookery experts, TV directors there were to be found. All she needed, after her years as a pop star amongst people whose favourite phrase was 'Know what I mean' – because passion and puzzlement so outstripped their command of the language – was a dinner table. Over eleven years these bohemians became her old friends. Edwin found the conversation of the non-gentry around his dinner table interesting, and would come home saying 'Who's coming to dinner tonight? Well? Well?' rather than just 'What's for dinner?' The talk would be about books, films, reviews, politics, the world of the imagination: not horses, dogs, weather and crops, and required more keeping up with, but Edwin did not complain. Edwin read books, he read poems – though he found his legs too long for theatre seats, and his knees twitched at the cinema.

Edwin was to revert later, of course, to type, to his original state; was to put the Jaguar behind him to go back to the Range Rover: to the wuff-wuffing insolence of the hunt, the tearing to pieces of hungry beasts: the pop-popping of shotguns, the bringing of the soaring spirit dead or dying back to earth, if only to show who's who round here. We, the hunting/shooting/landowning gentry.

Imagination hurt: that was why sensible people discouraged it. Speculation unsettled: certainty helped you sleep at night. If you shot wild creatures, you were less likely to shoot your wife, less likely to lose her in the first place. For these changes in Edwin, this regression, Lady Rice blamed Susan and Lambert almost more than she blamed Anthea: Anthea at least acknowledged herself as an enemy; Susan posed as a friend.

Angelica had only by accident been a pop star, Edwin would explain to everyone, trustingly, in the warm bright days when others were still to be trusted. A teenage girl of wit and temperament which far exceeded that of her parents, a rarity, a talent; her father dying, herself led astray (not sexually, of course; she wasn't like that): discrimination was Angelica's middle name. 'Discrimination is Angie's middle name,' he'd say, and Susan would nod her ever so slightly patronising head, with its bell of heavy blonde hair: or turn her bright bird eyes on Angelica and smile sweetly and say, 'Oh me, I'm hopeless; anything at all makes me happy' and all the men around would wish they'd be the anyone to make her happy, their things the anything; and sometimes Angelica wondered if Edwin should be included in 'all the men', but surely not, Susan was her best friend. Best friends were not like that.

Lady Rice, in The Claremont, refrained from calling room service to say her club sandwich was horrid, would they take it away and replace the smoked bacon with unsmoked, but controlled herself and Angelica slipped back into limbo.

14

A Curse From The Past

'Verbal assault,' Edwin had claimed. That she had verbally assaulted him. What can he have meant? Lady Rice thought and thought. She was, truth to tell, no longer so much concerned with the matter of alimony as she had been. For all her fine words, for all the apparent finality of her opinions on the subject – as if she had reached some mountain peak of truth and there was no going down again; you were obliged to spin for ever around your conclusions – the subject had ceased to be obsessional. She would leave all that legal stuff for Jelly to get on with: she would leave Angelica with the burden of looking up old friends, and the attempt to restore the integrity of the self before marriage – a silly slip of a girl in a leather jacket with rings in her nose – and get on with the task of considering her guilt, her possible contribution to the break-up of the marriage: not that she believes she can have had any part in that: no, it is just that remorse, or the appearance of remorse, might win her husband back – not that she wants that either, no, never –

In the Velcro Club, where the hearts and souls of those sundered or about to be put asunder, are understood, it

is well known that obsessions are as changeable as the weather: and that the change is as painful as if the Velcro were alive, a million nerve endings twanging, and the shift from one obsession to the next hurts terribly as the stuff goes skew-whiff, and a screaming fills the air, too high-pitched to be quite heard, but there, there –
Verbal assault. Was she ever rude to Edwin? Did she ever berate him, insult him? Surely not.

'Flop and wobble,' she'd once said to him, and he'd taken that amiss. Flop and wobble.

'Flop and wobble,' Angelica's mother would say, surveying the jellies her little daughter loved so much. Mrs White, nee Lamb, would often make such a hopeless desert, incompetently if devotedly, for Saturday tea – alternately soft red, acid green. 'Flop and wobble,' she'd complain. 'How does it happen?' A rhetorical question her little daughter saw fit to answer one day:
'You don't put enough of the packet in,' Angelica said. 'It's obvious, silly.'
She was her father's little girl and had his casual habit of diminishing her mother: not that she ever seemed to mind.
'I follow the instructions exactly,' said her mother. 'It would be a wicked waste to do otherwise. One half packet to one pint of water – as I am instructed, so I do.'
Stephen White, coming back from choir practice, would survey the shaky structure of the family dessert and say, 'Flop and wobble again, my dear,' in kind affection and jump up and down to shake the room and make the confection collapse totally. Of such detail, it seemed to Angelica, good marriages were made. Those were the

days when Angelica was called Jelly, her given name proving too long a word for easy saying.

But even blessings can turn out to be curses; landmines laid in a long-forgotten war.

'Flop and wobble,' said Lady Rice aloud one early morning as she lay in her marriage bed beside Sir Edwin Rice. 'Flop and wobble,' and indeed she was thinking of nothing but family tea and happy times, pre-adolescence, but Edwin took it as a slight, turned abruptly away from her, removed his enfolding arm, lay with his back to her for a little and then climbed out of bed and dressed. They had been married for ten years: the days of misunderstandings and makings-up were long past. Lady Rice could not think why he chose to take offence. Later she realised her husband was at this time 'seeing' his cousin Anthea.

Unfaithful husbands divide into two kinds: the one who feels guilty, brings flowers, baths babies, tries not to hurt: though later spoils things by confessing all. The other who feels guilty but looks for justification in his wife's behaviour: see, everyone, how she fails to look after me properly, has grown fat, or undermines my self esteem, whatever, wherever her weakness lies: but when the affair has ended – should it ever end – he keeps the secret to himself: refrains from burdening his wife with it: she has paid in advance, as it were, for his blow against the marriage politic.

This particular morning Lady Rice did what she could to explain: 'flop and wobble', she pleaded, was not a slur upon her husband's prowess. How could he think such a thing? But indeed he had not lately been as moved by his wife as once he was, but Lady Rice supposed that to be a normal fluctuation in his sexual energies. Worries at work, perhaps. But Edwin would have none of her excuses, though Angelica prattled on. Edwin, usually so easily entertained, so happy to hear tales of his wife's childhood, remained for once obdurate, unfascinated, profoundly offended.

'It's no use,' said Edwin, when finally he spoke, 'trying to deny your own words. What is spoken is what is meant, consciously or not. What you were doing is wishing impotence upon me. You're trying to undermine my confidence again.'
'You just want to take offence,' she had wept. 'Why are we having this dreadful time? What is the matter with you?'
He gave her no clue. And being, as Edwin would have it, unobservant, or, as she would say, innocent, Lady Rice failed to connect her husband's claim to martyrdom at her hands with his guilt. She was to be blamed for the crime against her. To put it bluntly, Edwin had fallen out of love with his wife and was inclined to blame her for this loss. He felt it, oddly enough, keenly, and the more keenly he felt it, the more he blamed her. What a mess!

Flop and wobble, verbal assault. Lady Rice could see what Edwin meant. No such thing as an accident; no unmeant, casual remark, however unconscious the impulse to deride.

15

An Unbelievable Narrator

I know what my problem is. Call my problem X and solve it. Too many Xs for a simple equation: quadruple equation either.

Ex-virgin, ex-pop star, ex-wife, ex-socialite, ex-convent girl, ex-everything, ex-everyone, that's me: primarily ex-daughter of a radio ham. Daddy, Daddy, speak to me! I can't, my darling, my angel, I'm saving ships at sea. What ships, Daddy, what sea? I don't know, my darling, my angel, but sooner or later, if I search the airwaves long enough, I'll rescue someone, somewhere, and you'll be proud of me. In the meantime, sweetheart, just leave Daddy in peace.

Are you Daddy's darling or Mother's little helper? God knows.

I feel as Zeus must have before Athena burst out of the top of his head. The pressure on poor Lady Rice, trying to contain so many different natures inside her, is tremendous. Velociraptors, velcro-raptors prowl within. A black band as if the head itself were a hat, confines and tightens. The whole bulging swarm of identities is getting a terrible headache. Something has to give.

I repeat: I can't live for ever in an hotel room, under a false name, growing alternative personalities as if they were pot plants, feeding them, nurturing them for lack of anything else to do, while I wait for my husband to commit my sins to paper: my fantastical adultery with my best friend Susan's husband Lambert. Lies, all lies!

Or look at it another way: I am the twisted cord of a telephone wire: dangle it and watch the rapidity with which it untwists itself; so rapidly indeed that it then twists the other way, almost as badly, and who then has the patience to wait for it to settle? Not me, whoever I may be. I'd rather wrench the whole thing from the wall and go cordless.

Too much unravelling can't be good for you. Of course I have a headache.

A bath, I think, may soothe me. The baths at The Claremont are deep, wide and marble. They are also, I notice, difficult to clean. I take the scouring powder from the cupboard beneath the basin, and with the help of a damp face cloth, stretch to reach the section the maid has failed to clean and, when I straighten up, catch my head on the shower fitment.

I stagger to the bed. I lie down. My headache is worse.

16

Ajax Is Born

Lady Rice has a real headache: aspirin won't touch it: it's the kind she got before the internal amoeboid first began to split: she had it before the conversations in her head began, before Angelica and Jelly separated out. There is something important going on here, she senses. This time it's something male, something magnificent: something, someone bursting out perforce, who has to be in charge, to be in control: to take a clear-eyed over-view of herself. Some hero who knows everything, and understands what's going on, who can tell a friend from a foe, and slay the foe. And even as Lady Rice came to this conclusion, gave permission to herself to think such incorrect thoughts, (these chattering women, that noble man), lo! I, myself, Ajax, was born.

The purifier, the scourer of thought; the hero of old; the banisher of the bath-ring of guilt.

Look at it this way: Angelica, Jelly and Angel, as the single Lady Rice unit they still tried to be, were perforated but not quite split. Now, traumatised and persecuted by an attack from within, from the internalised love object himself, Edwin, and sent screaming in all directions – Angelica cheating, spying, lying; Jelly typing, earning, office-serving; Angel fucking, sucking, wailing, howling for all of them – they spawned between them one further personality: one male to three parts female; that's Lady Rice's special recipe. Ajax.

Ajax it is who knows everything there is to know about Angelica, Jelly and Angel; by their initials let them be known: AJA. Then add an extra X for maleness. AJAX. Ajax who reports on these perforated-to-the-point-of-split personalities: Ajax, writer, rider, hero of the aether, Lord of all narrative, Lord of all joy, Lord of all grief, and all stages in between. Ajax, not the sleeping sentinel of the past, but the fierce and waking Guardian of the present. I, Ajax the Hero, before his disgrace, before his fall. Ajax is to be the only I round here, from now on.

If the chaos is extreme enough, words form, God forms. If the pressure of black is sufficient. Light dawns: if the tumult in the female head is dire enough, Man is born. Oh, I'm a fine Fellow-ess indeed! I, Ajax. I too shall write a novel.

PART THREE

Ajax's Aga Saga

1

Angelica First Brings Edwin Home

'Mum,' said Angelica from a phone box, 'I've met this man. I'm bringing him home.'

The phone box was probably the prettiest in the country. Special permission had been obtained by environmentalists to paint it green, avoiding the traditionalist's scarlet, so that the box did not disturb an eye adjusted to the delights of its surroundings. For home was the village of Barley, on three successive years awarded a prize as the most charming in the country – with its well-tended, cosily-gardened stone cottages, all hollyhocks and buzzing bees in the summer, its white-painted, brown-beamed medieval houses, leaning into one another for support; its central copper-spired church: the village green, the ducking pond, its ancient market, and its coach park just beyond the village limits for the tourists. And even these latter did not disturb too much, for the Parish Council allowed only one souvenir shop, and made few amenities available for the tourists' convenience, so news got round and the coach parties, on the whole, stayed away.

Angelica's mother lived with her new husband on a small new estate, discreetly surrounded by trees, a mile or so from the market, Barley's epicentre, just outside the village proper. Here teachers and social workers lived, and others with good hearts and low incomes. Barley proper was these days noticeably occupied by the wealthy, people who needed to travel to the city only a couple of times a week, if that, for Directors' meetings, and a few 'originals' – the old men who gave local colour in the pub, and applauded the incomers' dart matches: their wives cleaned others' houses, or staffed the few village shops. It was a happy village: everyone agreed, and so of course an artists' colony flourished here, in buildings converted from their original use, since current generations had no need of them. Former schoolhouses, chapels, a dozen barns, the old railway station now gave the space and style required by the creative spirit: writers, potters, weavers, sculptors, architects came to Barley in the hope of encouraging and supporting one another, to have 'someone to talk to': that is, as it transpired, to swap spouses, the group eventually to collapse beneath a weight of bitter gossip, spite and envy, and rise again, talent and hope renewed.

For this purpose, for this rebirth, a sacrifice is required: Angelica was to find herself this sacrifice, but that was in the future. This was now. Barley dreamt in the sun: Angelica was bringing Edwin home to meet her mother. And Edwin, by chance, was scion of Barley's dilapidated great house, Rice Court, five miles away, and its even greater stately home, a further two miles deeper into the Great Park, into the Green Forest, Cowarth Castle, where Lord Cowarth, Edwin's father, lived. Or perhaps not quite by chance, for how many people do not travel far and wide in search of adventure and distraction to discover that the one they set their hat at, the one who so occupies the erotic imagination, in fact comes from the same town, the next street, the house next door even: escape from one's origins, it often seems, is out of the question, barred by fate. Like calls to like.

'You're too young,' replied Angelica's mother, understanding at once the import of the words – 'I've met this man. I'm bringing him home' – from a daughter she hadn't seen or heard from in six months, other than in press cuttings: glad enough to have the girl report in, alarmed by what was going to happen next. Angelica was seventeen. As it happened, Edwin was a mere twenty-one, a stripling, not even in the music scene: this mother was lucky.

'You don't trust me,' said Angelica. 'You never have. You treat me like a child.' How easily and quickly the two of them resumed their normal relationship. Angelica had been saying that since she was twelve, when a film company had moved into the village to make Hardy's *Tess of the D'Urbervilles*. Nothing had been the same after that.

'You are a child!' said Mrs White. 'For all the rings you have in your nose.' Angelica at that time had twelve in each ear as well, but Mrs White had got used to that. 'If it interests you, I've met a man, too, just like you.'

'But Dad's only been dead a year,' said Angelica, upset.

Widows are meant to fade away; they should keep a low profile for the sake of their kids. That way everyone knows who's where.

153

'Your father wouldn't mind,' said Mrs White, pleasantly.
'He always wanted me to be happy.' The man she was
meeting was married, the father of Angelica's school-
friend Mary. His name was Gerald Haverley. He'd once
been on the PTA with Mr White, now in his grave. They
had got on well enough, it was true, during his lifetime,
before he had left his wife a widow.

'I don't believe this,' said Angelica. No one likes to be
upstaged. Here the daughter was, bringing home what
she'd thought was the catch of the season, only to find
the mother already sporting with dolphins.

Edwin and Angelica, having warned Mrs White, came
on round to see her. They drove up in a red MG; two
bright young things. Edwin wore a tweed jacket and a
knotted scarf. She wore leather.
'That's a nice car,' said Mrs White.

Mrs White was wearing a red miniskirt. She had been
married to a man twenty-seven years her senior for
twenty years. Now she was free.

'It's a red MG,' said Edwin defensively. 'A lot of chaps
have them.'
'Most chaps aren't as well-built as you,' Mrs White
remarked. Edwin was six-foot-four and weighed two
hundred and ten pounds. Angelica's mother looked him
up and down appreciatively.
Angelica nudged Edwin and tried to explain that in their
circle 'everyone' had Ford Fiestas or got on the bus.
Edwin looked puzzled and said he could remember
Angelica very well driving a Lamborghini, what was she
talking about? Angelica said that was different and Mrs

White said she could see they had a stormy relationship, and Edwin said on the contrary. Mrs White said trust Angelica to bring home an argumentative man.

'Is this all some kind of character test?' Edwin asked.
'Yes,' Mrs White said promptly. 'If you mean to marry my daughter you'll have to go through one or two.'
'I never said I was going to marry her,' he said, alarmed.

Angelica burst into tears and went and sat in her father's study, where her mother had never gone. Now her mother followed her in.
'Don't embarrass me,' said Mrs White.
'But you embarrassed me,' said Angelica, accustomed to having the moral upper hand in these family matters.
'And you're supposed to be so tough,' said Mrs White, looking her daughter up and down. Angelica wore boots up to her thighs and a fringed leather shirt down to her knees, and her hair was canary yellow. If she couldn't look after herself by now it was time she did.

'No one's said anything about marriage,' said Angelica. 'We haven't even been to bed together.'

Mrs White had been to bed with Gerald Haverley, and his wife was now divorcing him: that was different: they were grown-up people. These two were children: Angelica was having a difficult adolescence; Billy Bunter, the fat schoolboy, still looked out of Sir Edwin's eyes, and Alice in Wonderland out of Angelica's, for all she'd earned two thirds of a million pounds from a record called 'Kinky Virgin', sensibly put away in a Building Society.

'Then stay out of it,' said Mrs White.

'You don't think I'm some sort of pervert?' asked Angelica. 'I just don't like the thought of sex. I'd much rather just sing about it.'

'I'm sure it's not my fault,' said Mrs White. 'I never put that idea into your head. I can't have.'

Angelica stayed out of Edwin's bed, and presently he asked her to marry him, on the old-fashioned premise that that was the only way he'd get her into it.

2

How They Told
Edwin's Father

'We're going to get married,' said Edwin to Lord
Cowarth, his father. His mother had drunk herself to
death long ago. Edwin was the youngest son so no one
took much notice of him. He was allowed to live in Rice
Court to keep the damp and moths away.

Lord Cowarth looked Angelica up and down. At Edwin's
request, she was wearing a white sweater and a black
wool skirt. Her hair was dyed brown, and she had
removed the rings from her nose. The scars were healing,
the holes filling in. She looked thoroughly conventional
and easily shocked and spoke with the slapdash incoher-
ence of her generation. Lord Cowarth wore a dressing
gown thin with age which fell apart to show skinny
shanks and a tiny member.

'Has she got any money?' he asked. He carried a cleaver
wherever he went. He was short, rubicund and savage;
thin in parts, fat in others.
'A few hundred thousand,' said Edwin proudly.
Lord Cowarth grunted.
'I always thought you had your eye on that bint Anthea,'

he said. 'Plain as a pikestaff but just right for you, the
fat boy of the form. Can't abide a fat child,' he said, and
Angelica thought she saw Edwin wince. Mostly Edwin
kept his face friendly and still, accustomed as he was to
parental rebuffs and insults. 'Most of my children were
thin. Perhaps you're not my child at all. When I think
of that tart of a woman I married –' Lord Cowarth's eyes
narrowed – 'it wouldn't surprise me.' He spun Angelica
round with fingers which clawed into her neck. 'What's
your game?' he asked. 'What are you after? A title, a
house, or an education for your children?'

Angelica took hold of Edwin's hand, but her fiancé
seemed incapable of helping her get free. All the strength
had drained from him. So much old stags can always do
to such progeny as rashly stay around.

Lord Cowarth balanced the cleaver in his hand, letting
go of Angelica the better to do so. The cleaver was made
of rusty old iron, solid old wood.

'I think he likes you,' said Edwin softly.

'What are you whispering about? What are you plotting?'
The old man had a front tooth missing. He struck the
blunt back of the hasp against his lips. Presently the next
tooth would go. There would be blood in his mouth next
time he opened it. A useful trick. When he went to the
House of Lords, for a Coronation or the investment of a
relative, he would dress in finery: otherwise he kept to
his dressing gown, and liked to have a bloody mouth.
He seldom left his apartments: he could run the Rice
Estate well enough from there.

'I love him,' said Angelica. 'That's what I'm saying. Sweet nothings, you know?'

That silenced him.

At least he did not forbid the wedding. Edwin could not have stood out against his father, and Angelica would not have expected him to. But now she had a chance to save him, build up his self-confidence, help him recognise and accept himself; she was brimming with good intentions.

'Will your brothers come to the wedding?' asked Angelica.
'Doubt it,' said Edwin, stoically. He and she would marry quietly. She wanted to make him happy. She had not understood how anxious family life could make a man, riddling him with the expectation of rejection, of failure. His elder brothers, twins, twenty years older than he, now lived in warmer climes, in the Southern Seas; they had beautiful brown wives. One twin kept a restaurant; the other a marina. The Rice Estate kept both businesses in efficient managers: fish swam up, the yachts slid in: money flowed: titles entranced everyone. The languid tones of the English upper class travel well, though these days they grate upon the domestic ear.

The Kinky Virgin band would, of course, have none of Edwin: of his tweed jacket and knotted scarf, so Angelica would now have none of them.
'I'm giving music up,' she said. 'All that was only a flash in the pan. I haven't any real talent.'
Now she'd seen her mother in a miniskirt, she'd lost her

appetite for excess. Now she'd perceived the depths of Edwin's woes, the sorrow and the exhilaration of the rock stadium seemed distasteful. Besides, her father had died and who was there left to shock? Her mother had become unshockable; family friends had come to appreciate her, since she put their own young into a better light.

Angelica's arms were so skinny Edwin could close his hand right round where her biceps would be, were she to body-build. He liked that. Who these days could win a virgin bride? He felt marrying such a one would make the crops grow, and the dry rot recede: his breaking of the hymen, his staining of the marriage sheets, would bring good fortune and sanity to a land ruled by that mad old man, his father.

Someone had to be responsible: his twin brothers had left him behind to be just that; had run out on him. He had seen his life as a sacrifice: terrible girls had wooed him in spite of his looks, in spite of the veil of fat which protected him in his early years, making his penis seem tiny, his sufferings absurd; they had wooed him and bedded him for the sake of his title, his landed state, his patrician accents, forget he would never properly inherit wealth, only a fearful responsibility and rejection: would, like as not, inherit madness from his father, but without his father's power. Little by little Lord Cowarth had devolved that power to Robert Jellico, his Land Agent, and Robert Jellico, as well as being unerringly competent, was a powerful, sensible man, not given to evident emotion or the recognition of the financial duty that kinship imposes. Edwin complained Robert Jellico looked at him strangely.

'He's gay,' said Angelica innocently. 'That's all. That's why he looks at you the way he does. He's going to hate me. He's a man who rises at seven and doesn't understand the way you stay in bed till noon.'

Edwin loved Angelica because she reduced terrible and complex things to such simple and graceful components, and seemed threatened by no one, except her mother, who could make her cry. But those tears were the tears of the child, confident of love and the eventual pleasures of consolation.

3

The Wedding

Everyone came to the wedding, including the ghost of Edwin's mother. She was seen at the top of the narrow, ugly Jacobean stairs in a white dress, angrily waving a bottle, with a kind of miasmic mist floating from her: it left a damp coating on the bannisters which Mrs Mac-Arthur, the housekeeper, said was mould. Staff scrubbed and rubbed away at it but it kept returning; you couldn't get a shine to it, no matter what.

'She's not angry with you,' said Angelica to Edwin, 'but I expect she's angry with your father. I'm sure she loved you very much.'

'Why?' he asked, gloomily.

'Because you're loveable,' she replied, and he looked at her in gratified astonishment, and kissed her chastely. He had got accustomed to that. He didn't quite see how on a marriage night the habit of chastity was meant to change to the habit of uxorious sexuality, but if it had for his forefathers – as Angelica had assured him was the case – no doubt it would for him.

'Why should my mother be angry with my father?' he asked. He took his father's behaviour for granted, as sons will; as the father sees the world to be, so it is: daughters are often more critical.

'Your father is a monster,' Angelica explained to Edwin and Edwin seemed quite surprised.

'That's just how he is,' said Edwin, and only reluctantly conceded what his mother had come to know so clearly: that his father was unpleasant beyond normality, even for the upper classes.

Pippi and Harry, Kinky Virgin's violinist and drummer, had seen the apparition.

'A cloud of fucking sperm,' Pippi complained, 'floating down the stairs. This old lady, following behind, waving a bottle. Was that your mother-in-law?'

None of Angelica's friends wanted her to marry Edwin: snobby twerp, nerd, cunt: from the posh end of yuppie-dom, who'd given the band, with its foul-mouthed, intelligent cacophony, a passing popularity and been the more resented for it. And rightly, Sloaning and boning its drugs; drawling through the early hours, slamming car doors in the dawn to wake up the babies of the boring, toiling classes, the ones who worried about mortgages and children who failed exams and how to crawl out of the pit of necessity, the miasma of need, which shortened lives and narrowed hope; the steady, frightened classes who included Kinky Virgin in the things most wrong with the world today. Thus the careless and the crude, the wealthy and the wilfully distressed, joined forces in the clubs, each despising the other, but despising the rest more.

Edwin and Angelica married, joined hands across a chasm, and the phantom dogs of hate leapt up out of the depths to snap and snarl and make them break apart if they could, but at the time the lovers, or lovers-in-waiting, scarcely noticed their enemies; just felt surprised their match was so unpopular. All the world, which was meant to love a lover, plainly didn't.

'Is it wise to marry for money, darling?' enquired Boffy Dee of Edwin at the wedding. Boffy Dee had bedded Edwin once or twice, he later found for a dare; she'd reported back to his circle, for reasons best known to herself, that his member was minuscule. He had found himself hurt and humiliated by this: he'd had much comfort from Boffy Dee, in a warmly dark and confident way; he'd believed in her affection, trusted her pleasure and his own. Boffy Dee was wearing a tight orange dress and a cartwheel hat, which made her ugly: he hated her.

'I'm marrying Angelica because I love her,' said Edwin, with the simplicity for which he was scorned. It was his bulk made them believe he was slow-witted. Rice Court was a mass of small, dark rooms and twisted staircases, alternating with large, panelled halls, mostly open to the public and therefore not home; if you moved quickly or impulsively you'd break some piece of wooden carving off something, as like as not, and cause hysterics: he'd got quite accustomed to moving around with caution, and what Angelica saw as a kind of grace but others interpreted as nervous obtuseness.

Anthea Box, his cousin, was wearing Laura Ashley sprigs which did nothing for her horsey looks, but made him feel affectionate towards her. She was the only one who seemed to have a good word to say for Angelica.
'I expect the holes in her nose will heal up with time,' said Anthea.

4

Lady Rice, One Year Into
Her Marriage

'I'm not interested in money,' said Lady Rice. 'I'm not one bit materialistic.'

She and Edwin lived quietly in Rice Court; they spent a great deal of time entwined in bed; not with great passion, but with considerable affection, secure in each other's commitment. She didn't see her friends: he didn't see his. They smoked a great deal of dope. They went into the town for lunch and dinner, often to McDonald's. They relived, and recovered from, their childhood. Within weeks of the wedding, Robert Jellico suggested Angelica use her funds to buy into the Rice Estate: with the money so released, Rice Court could be refurbished. The place had been closed to the public of late: an ornate plaster ceiling had fallen and injured a visitor. Insurance had paid but everyone had had a nasty shock. Robert Jellico's perfect shirt had been seen awry and his smooth skin had sweated slightly. Money was being lost while the young couple idled and slept. Even Mrs MacArthur, housekeeper, who acted as their nanny, seemed vengeful, changing the sheets on the four-poster bed once a day, practically shaking the couple out of it; rattling empty

Coke tins into black plastic sacks, hoovering roaches and snipped bits of this and that, broken matches, throwing out baked beans on plates cracked because Edwin had stepped on them by mistake.

'She gets paid, doesn't she?' said Edwin. 'Why does she get in such a state?'

Lady Rice wrote Robert Jellico a cheque for the amount the cash machine said she had in her current account, minus one thousand pounds. £234,000.00.

'That has been in your current account,' said Robert Jellico, dazedly. 'Not a high interest account, not even a building society? What was your mother thinking about?'

Mrs White was busy thinking about Gerald Haverley mostly, and wondering why his wife Audrey was being so difficult, and why Mary, who once was such a good friend of Angelica's, cut her dead on the street. It seemed strange to Mrs White, as it had to her daughter, that the world was so full of people who didn't want you to be happy.

'Take the money,' said Angelica grandly. 'Money is of no importance. Invest it in Rice Court, if that's what you want. The Rice family is my family now, and that includes you, Robert.' And indeed Robert Jellico, with his flat face, his overhanging eyelids, his cardinal's mien, his grey eminence, seemed the old-worldly yet contemporary expression of the determined Rice soul. He it was who kept the balls of the whole business juggling in the air. For all his complicated love for Edwin, his weary disparagement of Angelica, they knew Robert Jellico was trustworthy enough. He knew money and property must be looked after. If Angelica's money went into the tenderest, most vulnerable, most simply sacrificed, last-in-first-out enterprises of the Rice Estate, the crumple zone of the juggernaut, then that was the tax Angelica had to pay because she had no presentable family, and no social status; only money and a recent marriage. Robert Jellico made sure Angelica's money did not go directly towards the rebuilding of Rice Court, in case of future litigation, and any claim that might be made alleging the place to be the matrimonial home. He was not so stupid and she did not notice. Who, lately married, ever anticipates divorce?

The day the money disappeared into Rice Estate coffers, Angelica sat up in bed and said, 'Edwin, we have to stop this now. We've recovered from the past, which was an illness. I shall smoke no more dope.'

And nor did she, and presently he lost the habit too. They looked around and saw what they had, and it seemed full of promise.

5

Lady Rice, Three Years Into Her Marriage

– spent a lot of time trying to get pregnant. That is to say, now in bed with Edwin only some twelve hours out of every twenty-four, she failed to take contraceptive precautions. She could see it would be nice to be two people enclosed in one and carry that one around inside her: the thought made her dozy and warm. If there was a baby, the twelve waking, walking hours would flow easily and naturally: unedgily, undriven. The warm, milky smell and soft feel of babies, the slippery, honey scent of Johnson's Baby Oil would drift the days together, make day like night, summer like winter, bed and waking hours the same: she would be universally approved: her mother would think of her, not of Gerald Haverley and The Divorce: The *Tatler* would come and take photographs of her and Edwin together and a baby in a long, white Christening robe in her arms – Angelica herself had never been christened: her name had always been some kind of variable. With her baby's christening, she would find herself shriven and finally named herself.

'Very nice,' said Edwin, 'but the camera would get dust in it. The photos wouldn't come out. Everything's crumbling.' Edwin, they agreed, tended to look on the gloomy side of things; to expect very little of the material world. If he was disappointed before he began, then failure could be interpreted as success in at least one thing – that he had been right all along. But Angelica encouraged him in good cheer.

Edwin began cautiously to take up his axe, to chop down a rotten tree or so on the Estate; to tear away the odd beam made flaky by woodworm before it actually fell, whether on to the dining room table or the bed; he learned to trace the tap-tap-tap of the deathwatch beetle, to pare away wood and reach the devouring little insect family, remove them carefully to one of the stables where they would do less harm. Such was her power over him, at the beginning. Angelica, who was tender-hearted towards all living creatures, though they demolish her house, eat away at her inheritance.

Every month with the moon, Angelica bled. Dr Bleasdale said it took a long time for marihuana to clear itself out of the system, and the drug, even though they scarcely used it now, impaired fertility.

'It's not a drug,' said Edwin, 'it's a leaf. And I don't believe him.'

After a year, the doctor went further and attributed Angelica's inability to conceive to Edwin's sperm count, lowered, he claimed, by drug-taking in the past. Edwin refused a test and Angelica did not blame him. The process involved sounded disgusting to both of them.

'Jealous of a simple jar!' said Edwin. 'Fancy you!'
'Yes,' said Angelica. 'I am. Fancy me!'

They started going to the younger, female partner at the surgery, a Dr Rosamund Plaidy, who said there was lots of time. Babies came when parents were ready for them. That felt better. Angelica became less sure that she was ready to be a parent. The convictions of youth diminished; the doubts of maturity strengthened.

These days Lady Rice would follow her husband out into the fields to watch him sawing branches, lighting bonfires. Edwin was developing muscles: a broad shoulder, a strong back. She hadn't wanted a baby desperately, Angelica told Boffy Dee; it had been a mood, that was all. She would wait until she was older. If she had a baby now, Mrs MacArthur would just take it away on the pretence of looking after it. One day Lady Rice, Angelica confided in Boffy Dee, would do without Mrs MacArthur: it was just that in the meantime she had Rice Court to look after; she didn't want her white hands to become rough, in case Edwin would not love them any more, would not suck her fingers one by one, as he did now, as if he'd been dealt a handful of lollipops by the Great Gambler in the sky, and wanted to show his appreciation and gratitude. Things were pretty good, thought Angelica, and, if she did nothing in particular, would stay that way.

Robert Jellico reported back to Lord Cowarth, at Cowarth Castle, five miles up the road, that his youngest son was showing signs of reformation; that, surprisingly, the marriage was holding. Angelica's money had now been taken by the official Receivers of Rice Estate Fungi (Continental) – which had served as the year's most effective tax loss for Rice Estates. Jellico took some credit for the unexpected durability of the youngest son's marriage. Women without funds made better wives than women with funds, being more dependent.

Robert Jellico had started a steady relationship with one Andy Pack, a jockey, and these days was prepared to exchange a non-acrimonious word with Angelica, and an un-neurotic one with Edwin. He even, in a flush of generosity, inflation-indexed the young couple's allowance. The Estate paid staff wages and household bills; Edwin and Angelica had to pay only for food and entertainment, and since their entertainment was by and large each other, they could even make savings on what came in. Angelica saw fit to send her mother fifty pounds a week: Gerald Haverley was retired now and it was difficult for the couple to pay so much as their heating bills.

'Don't you have each other to keep each other warm?' Angelica asked when her mother complained, but clearly everyone's habits were different. The younger generation kept to its bed, if it possibly could: the older you got the easier you felt out of it, until old age set in, when there you'd be, under the covers again.

Robert Jellico felt it was unreasonable that Rice Estate money should go to Edwin's mother-in-law, whose husband's duty it surely was to provide for her, and said as much to Edwin. And Edwin said to Angelica words to this effect – 'The fifty pounds a week you give your mother would be better spent on the fabric of this house, on Rentokil and rat catchers. The medieval drains are collapsing, and you don't even seem to notice.'

'You should never have let that archaeologist in,' said Angelica. 'I knew he'd be trouble.'

A representative from the University of Birmingham's Department of Medieval Studies had turned up to photograph the brick sewer system and, though asked to touch nothing, had removed for study some critical piece of figured brickwork and thereby started a general collapse of a system which otherwise would have lasted another couple of hundred years. If Lord Cowarth fired shotguns at all comers, whether vagrants, gypsies, academics or social workers, Edwin began to understand why.

'There you go again,' said Edwin, 'trying to blame me for a failing in yourself. Your heart's too kind.'
'But my mother needs the money,' said Angelica. 'She'll be cold and hungry without it,' and Edwin, after complaining that she overstated her case, fretted and frowned and put it to his wife that surely she saw the importance of the present. That surely it was time she put her old life behind her: why should Angelica help Gerald Haverley, the betrayer of Angelica's one-time best friend Mary's mother, out of a fix? Why not? enquired Angelica. The difference caused a slight coldness between them: a frisson, perhaps, of differences to come, like wind tinged with ice because it's passed over the snow of a mountain range, chilling the slumbering foothills.

'And think of all that money I gave the Rice Estate,' said Angelica. 'Surely something's due to me from that?' But one of the rules of the Rice Estate was that money swallowed was money swallowed, buried in earth, as hillsides were moved at Lord Cowarth's direction; roads were driven; river courses changed; estates developed and others torn down to make way for artificial grouse moors or ski slopes: mud everywhere, and gaping holes all around, grand canyons, yawning to receive the gift of other people's money: endless diversification, from mushroom farms (bind, bind, the crumbling soil with rhizomorphs) to sewage purification plants (drink, drink and profit us, it's good for you!). In exchange for all this frantic, destructive energy, the Rice organism spewed out money neatly and in deliberate fashion, all but unobserved, to interested parties in whom it did not include a youngest son's first wife. The Rice Estate knew when to waste, and when to save. Robert Jellico saw to all that: saw to it that the Estate sucked up millions, shat out tidy, tax-resistant cash pellets. The more that trust was put in Robert Jellico, the more smoothly the operation would run: that was the general understanding.

'I don't even have a receipt,' Angelica would worry sometimes. 'And work hasn't even started here; what *happened* to the money?'

And she wondered why it was that water still drained from the hand basin before she even had time to wash her hands, so badly had it cracked; why there was so little comfort in her daily life. Mrs MacArthur, who enjoyed the threadbare character of her job, who liked nothing better than a domestic emergency, who loved making do and mending, just said, 'Four inches of water is more than enough for anyone to wash their hands in, my girl. The crack starts four and a quarter inches up. Don't be so greedy.'

'This place is a disaster area,' said Angelica to Edwin one day. 'Couldn't we move out of it?'
'You don't love me any more,' said Edwin. 'You never

used to notice,' so she gave up mentioning it. Money gone is money gone, like water.

They were lying in the sun on a grassy mound where Cromwell the Protector was reputed to have single-handedly chopped down a maypole. Lord Cowarth's ancestor, Cromwell's friend, had been of an ascetic nature and grudging temperament, and had welcomed the coming of Roundhead politics; his descendants since had specialised in debauchery, excess and dramatics, as if to make up for the sheer meanness of the man who had founded their fortune by personally shaving the ringlets off Royalist neighbours and seizing their estates.

Even as Sir Edwin and Lady Rice lay on the grass hand in hand, bodies touching, they watched a bird alight gracefully on a chimney. They saw the high brick erection crumble and fall through the tiled roof, heard the debris rumble down through the attic floor, the bedroom floor, to the library below, whence a puff of dust blew out through open latticed windows and dispersed. Of such events are the memories of marriage made.

Ashes to dust.

Lord Cowarth's disposition had improved over the previous three years. Infections had given him abscesses under his remaining teeth – six left from a once full set, mostly towards the back – and pain had finally driven him to the doctor. He had been given Prozac, a new anti-depressant, still undergoing clinical trials, by Dr Rosamund Plaidy. He had even signed the consent forms, in a sudden rush to the head of social spiritedness.

Lord Cowarth had married, within six weeks of the first dose, a blonde and leather-booted woman in her mid-fifties, Ventura, Lady Cowarth. The wife of a mere youngest son and the wife of a full-blooded, propertied Earl are accorded the same title, so Mrs White, now Mrs Haverley, told her daughter: 'Lady' covers all degrees of honour, saving only 'Princess', 'Countess', 'Duchess' and 'Queen'. Ventura drank a great deal of whisky, but was kind, buxom and efficient, and liked Angelica, with whom she shared a common taste for leather; though Lady Rice, little by little, was taking to jeans and sweaters, neat skirts, little collars and long sleeves buttoned at the wrist.

'She may be a bit "other ranks", said Ventura to her husband, 'but at least she's a local and at least she's on hand!' Unlike, by inference, Edwin's elder brothers, the twins who had simply run out on the whole caboodle.

Lord Cowarth had lately found the tie to his dressing gown. If it did still occasionally fall apart, it was to reveal skinny parts more robust than heretofore, and fleshy parts less hideous.

'Rice Court does need money spent on it, dear,' Ventura said to her husband, 'in fact as well as theory: brick by brick, not just a business plan!' and her husband had a word with Robert Jellico, who released half a million pounds to that end. The falling of the chimney had impressed everyone. A further half million, it was inferred, would follow when Angelica produced a child.

'I had no idea,' said Angelica, distressed, as Edwin made constant efforts, night and day, to impregnate her, she by now having completely gone off the idea of babies, 'that there were families left who behaved like this. Your father's worse sane than he was mad.'

'There is no such thing,' said Edwin, his great, consoling bulk heaving over her, 'as a free title,' and Angelica laughed, but she was hurt. Edwin would do this for money, but not for love? For Rice Court, not for her?

If Edwin wanted a baby for his family's sake, not for hers, not as a celebration of their love, she would rather not have one at all, or at any rate not yet. Better to live in a rose-covered cottage, however humble, abrim with domestic love, to have children as an outcome of that love, clustering around the knee, than to live in a mansion, have nannies, and be expected to breed for the sake of a line, in the interests of a family who thought themselves better than others for no good reason, especially since, so far as Angelica could see, that line was now more connected to commerce than to the land. And supposing the baby inherited its grandfather's madness? Its grandmother's alcoholism, its father's idleness? She loved Edwin dearly, but without a doubt he was idle. And had not the early Rice forbears been robber barons, the criminals of the Middle Ages? The more she thought about it, the worse it seemed. Her side of the family might be mildly eccentric, but surely dwelt within the bounds of decent ordinariness: what could truly be said of the humble was that they tried to be *good*, if only from lack of energy to be otherwise. The Rice family had no problem being bad.

If Edwin showed signs of wanting a baby for his wife's sake or, better still, saw a baby as the natural outcome of a great and enduring love, no doubt these worries would be quickly swept away in a wave of wanting – but until this happened, until Edwin grew up a bit, stopped trying to placate and gratify his awful family, she would not risk the change in status that the having of a baby entailed. Better and safer to be the wife Edwin insanely loved, than the mother of a Rice child. Through history they'd found themselves driven to drink, or pushed downstairs, or walled up, or just left at home and thoroughly neglected, once their purpose was served. They'd been allowed to dress up in their tiaras and produced at coronations, or state funerals, or victory parades to keep them quiet, but that was all. She dug out forgotten family portraits from the cellars and brought down monographs from the attic: restored, dusted, framed them all, and found in the family history more than enough proof for her suppositions.

And so to everyone's surprise Angelica didn't get pregnant. In fact, she had prudently asked at the surgery, before it was too late, for a contraceptive implant, one of a new kind which lasted for a whole five years, and young Dr Rosamund Plaidy had obliged, tucked it under the skin of Angelica's buttocks with a deft incision of knife and needle. Gently, day by day, the implant leaked oestrogen into her system, keeping her rounded and placid and gentle. The more fertile she looked, the less fertile she was, and no giveaway card of pills either, hanging around to be found.

Dr Rosamund Plaidy was thirty-four, wholesome, pleasant and well-informed, and was married to Lambert Plaidy, the writer. She had had her own first child at twenty-six and naturally believed that to be the optimum age for such activity. Angelica, at twenty-one, had lots of time. Angelica agreed.

6

Lady Rice, Eight Years Into Her Marriage

– gave dinner parties. Lady Rice had made a circle of friends. Rice Court was open to the public again, and the Great Hall and bedrooms had been roped and annotated – here Oliver Cromwell dined; on this spot the first Lord Cowarth fell, poisoned; here the bed in which he recovered, alas; see here the priest-hole in which the priest was walled-up alive and died; this the Chinese vase presented by Queen Victoria; here the love couch on which Edward sat entwined with Mrs Simpson, and so forth – but the back of the house, which faced south in any case and caught the last light, could be run as the more ordinary but still splendid home of a comparatively ordinary young couple. Ceilings and chimneys no longer collapsed, doors fitted, windows opened: in the kitchens ancient iron pots had been replaced with stainless steel saucepans; ceramic hobs now ran on electricity rather than hotplates on coal and coke. Mrs MacArthur seemed ten years younger than once she had. Her hair had been permed, and ringed her dour face in girlish fashion. Mr MacArthur had been made redundant from his work as a bodywork welder up at the auto factory. His wife was now the family breadwinner and there was no hope of

Angelica firing her. But she allowed her employer her head when it came to running the visitor trade.

It was acknowledged, even by Lord Cowarth, that Lady Rice was efficient when she put her mind to it: had a gift for knowing what took the visitors' fancy, why they would prefer cream to butter on their scones, why they would buy fudge but not mints, why they gawped at Mrs Simpson's love seat but didn't care for Lord Cowarth's collection of arrowheads.

And after the last visitor had gone, when the money had been accounted for and sent off to swell the Rice Estate coffers, and she had earned the approval of Robert Jellico, what could be more pleasant than to have friends round? To prepare meals, using the cookery books brought home by Edwin, who shared the cooking with her, trying out dishes from everywhere, from Afghanistan to Georgia to Iran – places at that time not so riven by violence, cruelty and war as to make their very food suspect, too potentially full of grief for enjoyment.

Edwin and Angelica, Rosamund and Lambert, Susan and Humphrey, were the central couples: others around, espoused or as singles, performed a dance of delicate social balance; creating their own precise etiquette. Friends, acquaintances, colleagues flitted in and out of focus round the table; each knowing their place; smiling faces breaking bread, providing advice, entertainment, common cause. Edwin and Angelica offered the most eccentric yet the grandest table of the group. Though the power and prestige Rice Court represented was now seen as fit only for tourists, even peasant food tasted good on a refectory table large enough to seat twelve and with lots of elbow room.

Rosamund, the doctor, responsible, kindly and steady, and Lambert her husband, a writer, wild-eyed, wild-haired, made up in skills and talent for anything they lacked in style: a double act and a crowded table in a book-lined room, down the corridor from the kitchen. Susan, the potter from Minnesota, rosy, exotic and sexy, with her bubbling enthusiasms, her fair shiny hair, her attractive naivety, a basket-full of English garden flowers or chutneys, Easter gifts or winter comforts somehow always on her arm, for ever bearing gifts, her adoring, plump, good, mournful, clumsy husband Humphrey, the architect, served food Japanese fashion, on the carpeted floor, amongst cushions.
Rosamund had two children, Susan had one, Angelica had none. Edwin still took that amiss.

'Perhaps I should have had a sperm count,' said Edwin one night at Susan's. 'What do men *do* when they're not fathers?'
And everyone laughed.
'Love their wives,' said Angelica, and realised with alarm to what degree she counted on Rosamund not to tell about the implant. Too late to tell Edwin herself: why had she not when first Rosamund tucked it under her skin? She could hardly remember. Time enough, time enough, as Rosamund averred. A five per cent increase in visitors this season: there was so much for Angelica to do, and Edwin too if he wanted, but he didn't. Edwin merely seemed to potter and brood; he began to have a puzzled look, as did Humphrey, whose architectural practice was failing. It is a terrible thing to have to look

for occupation. Lambert, too, was in financial difficulty. His publishers dropped him from their list; his agent was too busy to speak to him. He was misunderstood. He spent more time with the children, leaving Rosamund free to do night duty; indeed obliged to do so, if bills were to be met.

Angelica, the youngest in the group, saw her task as learning, and learn she did; over the dinner table. She could talk now about abstract matters: what justice was, and injustice; understood better when to confide, when to stay quiet; had opinions about what art was, who really ran the country and so on. Whether *agents provocateurs* let off bombs, or terrorists.

From Susan she learned a kind of sophisticated feminine response; things her mother had never taught her. She learned that flowers need to be arranged, not just plonked in a vase; that their leaves had to be stripped, stems crushed. Sensual pleasures, Susan implied, were the same. The more you postponed, the more you enjoyed. This apparently went for sex, too, and suited Angelica very well. Or, as Susan said, 'Gosh, your English men are so bad at important things like wooing. This is certainly no red rose culture you have over here!' Though, heaven knew, Humphrey circled Susan with bouquets, took her for romantic weekends to Vienna, had her portrait painted, personally manicured her strong potter's hands in a manner most un-English.

Susan took it as her due. She had previously been married to Alan Adliss, the now famous landscape painter. She'd run off with Humphrey, taking him away from Helen, his fat, faithless and insensitive wife – or so everyone described her, taking Susan's word for it. No one in the circle had actually ever met Helen, of course, nor wished to – she belonged to some other world layered behind this one, its sufferings incomprehensible, irrelevant: whining voices on answerphones demanding consideration, remembrance, the money second wives saw as their due. Unloved women, those in the past, should simply fade away, as should widowed mothers. At least there was no one like this in Edwin's past: she was his first wife, his only wife. These emotional and marital difficulties were for others, not for Angelica. She was conceited.

The voices in Angelica's head had not yet powered-up, splitting and dividing her, offering alternatives on the path to heaven or hell. As it was, she assumed she was the nicest person in the world: there was not even any internal discussion about the possibility of this not necessarily being the case. How could there be? She was the heroine of her own life. Her lack of response to her father's death puzzled her. The event had scarcely marked her otherwise. Why? It was as if he had been some kind of prop, not a person at all. Surely this must be a failing in him, not in her? All the same, she could see her non-grief at his death as being some kind of time bomb somewhere in her persona, as the oestrogen implant was a time bomb in her body, antipathetical to the very origins of life.

Sometimes these days Angelica turned away from Edwin in bed; fastidiousness could tire you out: sleep could become the greater desire. Or was it that the potential of pregnancy, framing sex with light, was what kept sex interesting, as the sun behind a dark cloud will frill it with brilliance? She could almost believe now, in any case, that the implant was imaginary. The Rosamund she'd met for the first time in the surgery had been a stranger: now she was a friend. Everything was different, why not this too? Better not to enquire. Perhaps anyway such implants had been proved not to work: how could anything keep working for so long; and who was to say whether it was actually this pellet of artificially deposited hormone which kept Edwin's and her destined child out of the world, or an act of God? Perhaps she was infertile anyway? If Rosamund had made no mention of the implant the first time Edwin had said over dinner, 'We're not too hot in the fertility stakes, Angelica and I', or however he'd put it, in his offhand, English way, perhaps it was because there was indeed nothing to mention. Years drifted by and the events of one year were lost in the dramas of the next.

She wished Edwin was more like Humphrey; more adoring, more romantic, less companionable.

She made herself go and sit by her father's grave: the Rice Estate was digging up the churchyard cemetery overflow, where her father's body lay, to build an extension to a new sports centre. She knew if she didn't visit now she never could, and even this sense of his corporeal, albeit disintegrating reality, be lost to her. But still she could not bring Stephen White properly to mind: he had been too elderly, too amiable, too vague to be quite real. Someone who had failed to elicit strong passions in her, who had lived in the past, but whose time had overlapped hers; whose enthusiasms had been alien to hers, making her feel a changeling.

She felt dull. Edwin's former clubbing friends would turn up at the new, improved Rice Court from time to time, or from the ex-hunting and shooting, now property-developing, junk-bonding set, observe just how very, very dull country life could be, and depart. Angelica's ex-music-biz friends would arrive to gaze at the country moon under the influence of one substance or another, deplore what marriage and maturity could do to a girl, even leaving babies out of it, and depart.

Sometimes Anthea came to dinner, and Edwin would yawn and say, 'She thinks of nothing but horses: keep her away from me, though she is my cousin. Do you realise, if I'd been a girl and she'd been a boy, she'd have had my title.'

Or Boffy Dee would turn up for a heart to heart and a glass of gin. She was marrying a racing driver who'd had so many knocks to the head he couldn't speak without slurring, but Boffy Dee did not see brain damage as an impediment to marital happiness. On the contrary.

7

Trouble In The Group

Rosamund called Angelica one evening and said, 'Angelica, this is terrible: we have to *do* something. I think Susan is having an affair with Clive Rappaport. I keep seeing his car and hers parked in strange places when I'm out on my calls, and nobody in either of them.' It was summer and the grass was green.

Clive Rappaport was a solicitor, one of the outer circle of friends: quiet, serious, romantic; very much married to Natalie, plump, dark, effervescent.

'That's completely out of the question,' said Angelica.
'Why?' demanded Rosamund. And Angelica reminded her that only a couple of weeks back, at a picnic on the old railway track – Susan and Humphrey lived in a charmingly converted railway station – Natalie had confided, half-joking, half-serious, as women will amongst friends, that Clive had gone off her, lost sexual interest.
'What do I do?' Natalie had asked. 'We've never had trouble like this before.'
'Wear black lingerie,' Susan had replied. 'Lace and garters, high heels. Parade up and down. That always

works.' And everyone had laughed, a little awkwardly. Because it had seemed a strange thing to say, in a group so dedicated to the notion that sex was to do with love, not lust.

'If Susan was having an affair with Clive,' said Angelica to Rosamund now, 'she couldn't possibly have said a thing like that.'

Which just showed, in retrospect, how little Angelica knew about anything.

'Oh yes she could,' said Rosamund, 'if she was secure enough, conceited enough, knew absolutely certainly that no amount of black underwear could ever get Clive happy in bed with Natalie again and was trying to cover her tracks.'
'She's not like that,' said Angelica, shocked. 'Not Susan.'

At least until now she had supposed not. It was true men became animated when Susan came into a room: with her bony, slightly gawky figure, the thick bell of blonde hair swinging; but then so did women: it was obvious Humphrey adored Susan, Susan adored Humphrey. Angelica gave the matter minimal thought and put it out of her mind. Rosamund was overworked: mildly paranoid. She was having a hard time with Lambert, who would put her down in company, lament the minimal size of her breasts, her concern for everyone in the world but him, and Rosamund responded, no doubt, by seeing trouble everywhere but at home. She reported to Edwin what Rosamund had said and Edwin replied, 'What on earth would Susan see in Clive Rappaport: he's dull as ditch water,' which was not quite the response Angelica would have expected, but then more and more things these days were unexpected.

Unexpected, too, when the next week Lambert, Rosamund's husband, came to Angelica and said, 'Angelica, I think Susan and Edwin are having an affair,' and Angelica said, 'Lambert, you are absurd, and what would it have to do with you if they were, anyway, which they aren't? Are you having a breakdown? Why do you look so dreadful?' Lambert did: he wore tracksuit bottoms, an old army shirt untucked in, and had not had a shave for a week or a haircut for three months.

'You should never have had that contraceptive implant,' said Lambert. 'Rosamund told you so at the time but you wouldn't listen. Look at the trouble it got everyone into. You're Edwin's wife. You should have given him a baby.'
'What?' enquired Angelica. 'What? Who said I wouldn't give Edwin a baby?'
'It's in your file at the surgery,' said Lambert, and declined to say more. Angelica's concerns were none of his. But *if* Lambert told Susan, and Susan told Edwin – no, it was beyond belief. Lambert was, in any case, out of his mind.

'Rosamund,' said Angelica, going round after surgery, finding Rosamund rubber-gloved amongst blood samples and card indices, busy with the tragedies of others, 'Rosamund, what are we to do about Lambert?'
'We?' enquired Rosamund. Her hair was curlier than ever with sweat and exhaustion. Her honest, bright face was pale: her freckles stood out. She was loveable,

Angelica realised, and admirable, but she was worthy, and would never be glamorous.

'Friends,' said Angelica. 'We're all friends,' and Angelica gave Rosamund the gist of Lambert's lament, as one would relate the tale of a madman to those most concerned with his welfare.

'There is all kind of stuff here,' said Angelica, 'that could really upset people. Doesn't Lambert realise that?'

'Angelica,' said Rosamund, 'of course he does. It is naive of you to suppose that people will avoid doing harm if they understand what harm is. Some people like doing harm.'

'But not Lambert,' said Angelica. 'Not anyone we *know*.'

Rosamund raised her eyebrows and busied herself emptying test tubes down the sink.

'Isn't there anyone else to do that?' asked Angelica.

'If I pay them,' said Rosamund, shortly.

'Rosamund,' said Angelica, 'this is important.'

'It's not life and death,' said Rosamund. 'Mrs Anna Wesley has too much protein in her urine. That's important. Lambert has told me that Susan's little Roland is his child, that Humphrey isn't the father. I've looked in their files. The blood types correlate. Humphrey has a really low sperm count, as it happens.'

'Lambert's insane,' said Angelica.

'Lambert's been in love with Susan for years, apparently,' said Rosamund. 'He stayed with me for the children's sake – not mine, he tells me: I don't somehow enter into the equation. Poor Susan. Poor Humphrey. Poor Lambert. Me, I just do the work round here and earn the living. And now Susan says she's pregnant, so Lambert's convinced it's Edwin's.'

'But why?'

'Because you won't give Edwin a baby, and Susan's so kind and soft-hearted,' said Rosamund, adding, with savagery, 'fucking little slut.'

Angelica stared.

'You can't keep implants secret,' said Rosamund. 'Lambert looks through the files for material for his stories. Everyone knows, except you. You did know but you seem to have forgotten. You're very peculiar, Angelica. Sometimes I think you sleepwalk through your life. I'd never suggest Prozac for you: you're enough of a Pollyanna as it is, rising cheerful and positive to each day.'

'I don't believe any of this,' said Angelica. But when she thought about it, it was true that Lambert and Roland had the same wide-spaced, prominent, wild blue eyes: now the thought was in the head, the evidence was there. Just as the understanding that the continents have drifted apart, over the aeons, from the one original land mass, became evident and obvious to anyone who looked at a globe after 1926, when the notion was first floated, but simply didn't occur to the generations before.

'I don't believe Lambert's in love with Susan,' said Angelica, hopelessly. 'You two are too good together. You go together. Why should Lambert love Susan when he's got you?'

'Because I'm boring,' observed Rosamund calmly, 'and Susan's not. I only speak when I've something to say and Susan babbles ceaselessly on. I work regular hours and wear myself out toiling for humanity, while Susan is full of artistic sensibility. Lambert's a writer, Susan's a potter. Creative, you know? They need the likes of Humphrey and myself to earn their livings, but we're not exactly sources of powerful emotion, are we? We can't expect to stay the course.'

'And if Susan's having an affair with anyone,' said Angelica, 'it's Clive Rappaport, not Edwin. You said so yourself. And Susan would never do a thing like that to me. I'm her best friend. Lambert must stop saying these things. He's insane.'

'I'd rather it was Edwin than Clive,' said Rosamund. 'Because if it's Clive, poor Natalie will have to get to know, and poor Humphrey as well –'

'Well, thank you very much,' said Angelica. 'You don't think it matters about poor me?'

'Oh, Angelica,' said Rosamund in dismissal, 'you're like me, you can look after yourself,' which surprised Angelica very much. It had never been her intention to turn out sensible, good-natured and enduring: the kind of woman who would put up with a husband's infidelities for the sake of the greater good.

'And, anyway,' Rosamund added, 'you don't have any children so it's hardly important.' Which made Angelica see why Lambert might well have set his face against Rosamund, might well prefer Susan. Angelica was almost convinced, but not quite. As for Edwin fathering some putative child of Susan's, that was simply not possible. Edwin was too responsible, too serious, ever to take Susan seriously. They liked her, but she was lightweight.

Angelica rang up Susan to say perhaps she'd better come round and talk a few things over: Humphrey picked up the telephone; someone tried to snatch it away. All kinds of noises came from the other end of the line: bangings, batterings, little Roland crying, then finally screaming; an unknown voice saying, 'Humphrey, don't speak to anyone. I forbid it. See a solicitor first.' More breathings, and then Humphrey was in charge of the instrument.

Humphrey said, with unwonted passion, 'Is that you, Angelica? You bitch! You've been conniving with Susan; you knew all about it; she took her lead from you; she's told me about you and Lambert.' And Humphrey put the phone down.

Angelica laughed. She could not help it. Edwin came into the room.

'What's funny?' asked Edwin.

'Susan's having an affair with (a) Clive Rappaport, (b) Lambert, (c) you. I'm having an affair with Lambert: you and/or Clive Rappaport are fathering Susan's baby.'

'I don't think that's funny,' said Edwin, but he seemed unsurprised. 'Why do you laugh at other people's troubles?'

'Well,' said Angelica, 'if it was true, it would be my trouble, too.'

'So you're denying it?' asked Edwin. 'Susan says it's true.'

Angelica cannot believe it of Susan, that she should tell such lies to get out of trouble, as if everyone were back at school. A clear sky is suddenly swept by clouds: black ones, layering, level upon level, and a different storm swells up between each layer, each feeding upon its fellows. Lightning cracks the sky: thunder blasts; the tempest pours. Angelica no longer stands pure, untroubled, shone upon by the sun of love and good fortune. The ground she stands upon trembles. The best she can hope for now is not to be utterly cast down. It is all too sudden.

Edwin turns on the television as if nothing is happening. 'Edwin,' says Angelica to her husband, 'something extraordinary is going on at Railway Cottage. Aren't you interested?'

'No,' says Edwin, 'it really has very little to do with us.' He has found a documentary on Northern Ireland. He does not take his eyes from the screen.

'I think it has,' says Angelica.

'I knew you'd try to make a meal of it,' said Edwin. 'It's not a good idea to turn private matters into public gossip.'

'But Susan is my friend,' says Angelica. 'She's in trouble –'

'You have hardly behaved like a friend to her,' says Edwin.

'If she's telling lies about Rosamund's husband and myself –' says Angelica.

'I think she worries about your plans for her own husband, forget Rosamund's.'

'This is bizarre,' says Angelica.

She would shake her husband, except he has turned into a stranger, and a hostile one at that.

'Do you have no loyalty to me?' asks Angelica. 'You'll listen to any old gossip.'

'You're the one who asked it into the house,' remarks Edwin. 'You're the one who wanted a social life. Susan rang me yesterday. She wanted my advice.'

And he told Angelica that Susan had been on the phone to Clive, discussing some work project. Natalie had picked up the extension, listened in, misunderstood and become hysterical.

'Though Natalie's own conduct,' says Edwin, 'scarcely gives her leave to object to whatever Clive chooses or does not choose to do, but when were women ever reasonable? Their idea of justice is very one-sided. Susan was afraid Natalie might cause trouble by calling Humphrey, so she rang me. That's all.'

'Why you?' asks Angelica.

'I suppose,' says Edwin, 'because I'm her friend and the only one she can rely on not to gossip or make a drama and a meal of something so important. Could all this wait till the programme has ended?'

'I think not,' says Angelica, and switches the TV off. Edwin sighs.

'I do not believe Susan has ever had the slightest suspicion about me and Humphrey,' says Angelica. 'Humphrey is old enough to be my father. Shouldn't we investigate this? Perhaps it's Humphrey's fantasy? That I'm after him?'

'I expect Susan is over-sensitive,' says Edwin. 'She worries so about growing old. I told her she was being silly.'

'How do you know?' asks Angelica. 'How do you know things about Susan I don't?'

'When you're busy with the Heritage Shop,' says Edwin, 'Susan and I sometimes go for walks. She's interested in all kinds of things you aren't. English wild flowers, for example.'

'The bitch!' says Angelica finally.

'Sometimes I think there's a lesbian element in your make-up,' says Edwin. 'Susan says she senses an erotic element in yours and her relationship. It makes her uneasy.'

Angelica paced, and thought, and thought, and paced, while Edwin stroked and patted the dogs, labradors, one of whom lay on his lap and the other over his feet, large, soothing, fleshy golden creatures. Edwin turned the television back on. The programme on Northern Ireland was finished.

'What advice did you give Susan?' Angelica asked, finally. It was as if she were allowed only one question, as in some child's game, so that question had better be good.

'I pointed out that Natalie was a vindictive and possessive woman and was almost bound to tell Humphrey her suspicions. Better for Susan to tell Humphrey herself what had happened. She said she would.'

'Edwin,' said Angelica, 'that was very strange advice. What are you trying to do? Blow things apart? The only thing Susan should have done was to deny everything, everything.'

'My dear,' said Edwin, 'she consulted me, not you.'

There was a kind of scraping at the door, a sound halfway between a scrabble and a tap, and Edwin opened the door to Susan, weeping, swollen-faced, shivering with cold and barefooted. There was snow on the ground outside. Her toes were blue. Susan sat in an armchair while Angelica fetched blankets and Edwin took Susan's feet in his hands and rubbed and patted to restore their blood supply.

'He threw me out of the house,' wept Susan. 'My own husband. My own house. I did everything you told me, Edwin. I confessed to Humphrey. I admitted I'd been silly and stupid over Clive: I told him it meant nothing. I told him Natalie was over-reacting. I told him the last thing on my mind was to hurt Natalie. I explained that he'd had been so caught up lately with business matters, he shouldn't really be surprised if some other man attracted my attention. I explained that Clive and I have an intellectual and artistic rapport – sex hardly enters into it at all. We just sometimes meet on our own, the way you and I do, Edwin. Edwin and I go on nature walks sometimes, Angelica. I told Humphrey he should learn from this incident and realise his marriage might be in danger so he'd better try harder at it; neglecting me wasn't going to work. And all he did was turn into a primitive Victorian in front of my eyes. Oh shit! He threw me out of the house without giving me time even to put on my shoes, and locked the door so I couldn't get back in. I called Clive from the neighbour's but he said Natalie had just taken an overdose of sleeping pills and he was waiting for the doctor. He called her 'his wife' as if it were a kind of magic. She has him totally under her thumb. She is such a bully. She'll do no matter what to hurt my poor Clive.' Susan caught Angelica's arm. 'This is an appalling time for me! You won't let me down, will you, Angelica?'

'Of course not,' said Angelica.

'Because you're civilised and you understand these things. You and Lambert, after all. And Edwin doesn't make a stupid fuss, let alone lock you out in the snow. Humphrey is not a sane person. And he would never have had the guts to do it if his parents weren't coming to stay tomorrow so they can look after him.'

Angelica unhooked herself from Susan's grasp. Edwin went on massaging Susan's feet. Whether or not he had caught the gist of Susan's remark regarding Lambert Angelica could not be sure. Perhaps these insane statements just washed over him: he wasn't even listening.

'Susan,' Angelica said, all the same, 'because you go round having affairs with your best friends' husbands, does not mean everyone does. I certainly don't.'

Susan laughed harshly and said that all she ever got from the English were pious platitudes and no understanding at all of love or its imperatives. All the subtlety of her relationship with Clive, all the power, the passion, the throbbing soul of it, reduced to the glibness of Angelica's phrase – 'having an affair'.

To which Angelica said, 'Bet you didn't say all that "throbbing soul" bit to Humphrey, unless of course you're sick of Humphrey, which I would understand.'

'Why?' enquired Susan rashly, displaying a sudden and mean vulgarity. 'Because you'd like to get your sticky little fingers on him?'

Angelica laughed.

Edwin said, Susan's cold foot now pressed against his cheek, 'Angelica, don't be nasty to poor Susan. She's in a terrible state, and she's pregnant, too. We have to look after her.'

To which Angelica replied, inanely enough, 'Don't call me Angelica, call me Lady Rice.'

And having said it, Angelica, that young woman of many parts, fled without warning, as abruptly and rashly as people flee to escape rocket attack, earthquake, forest fire, in the interest of survival itself, leaving Lady Rice behind, to cope as best she could.

Lady Rice, that masochistic, loving, drooping creature, afflicted by a hopeless obsession for justice which could only make her miserable, so little of it is there in the world – one could search for ever to find either a just or a merciful God – now stood alone: like some eighteenth-century face mask, the kind worn at balls, behind which a series of others hid; some blonde, some dark; some young, some old; all deathly still, all terrified – only Jelly, perhaps, craning a little this way or that, just visible, showed flickers of life, of intent. None of the other souls had yet, of course, introduced themselves to Lady Rice. She perceived no difference in herself.

Lady Rice fainted. As she fell into the black and sickly swirl of a consciousness deprived suddenly not just of oxygen but of familiar identity, she thought she heard Edwin say:
'Poor Susan. But it was the best thing to do.'

Lady Rice had to ease herself to sit against the edge of the sofa, had to scramble to her feet unaided. Edwin was helping poor, shook-up Susan to the one spare bedroom available, at the top of the house. The decorators were in all but this one.

Thus it was that the personality of Lady Rice perforated, allowing Angelica to resign, if only temporarily, from life. Just simply and suddenly resigned, subject as she was to too much upset. It could happen to everyone. A trauma, a shock, a faint, a bang on the head – who's to know who you'll be when you recover?

Lady Rice went to bed, where Edwin presently followed her. He said he hoped she was feeling better but she should try not to steal Susan's limelight. It had been absurd, pretending to faint like that. Everyone knew she was as strong as a horse.

Haltingly, Lady Rice tried to persuade her husband it was simply not so about herself and Humphrey, not so about her and Lambert, but all Edwin said was do be quiet, what does any of that matter, women always deny everything anyway, you told me that yourself only this evening. Lady Rice thought she'd better be quiet.

'Poor me, poor me, poor me,' sighed Susan, now a house guest, through Rice Court. Poor Susan, all echoed. Locked out of her house, separated from her child. Those few in the Humphrey party – his parents, Rosamund, and a handful of comparative strangers: for example, the man in the Post Office who hated all women, the hedger and ditcher who believed in UFOs – urged Humphrey to go to his rival's house and beat Clive up, but Humphrey, though he raged against women, against Susan, Natalie, Rosamund and Lady Rice, as all in one way or another party to the legitimisation of his wife's whorishness – they'd encouraged it, sanctioned it – did not ever meet his cuckolder face to face. Even in such circumstances, Rosamund complained, men stick together. The faithless wife gets murdered: her lover is left unharmed.

'Get that woman out of here,' said Mrs MacArthur. 'She's trouble!' but the new Lady Rice was somehow vague in her dealings with the world, and forgetful; perhaps she'd bumped her head when she fell, and only imagined the horrors of false accusation. Susan was being sweet, and tearful, and full of confidences; Lady Rice took her to the Rice lawyers – four weeks later Susan was still locked out, still separated from her little Roland, Humphrey still holed up in Railway Cottage; if you tried to get him on the phone you heard this terrible, harsh voice saying 'Bitch! Cunt!' over and over. He had taken leave of his senses. He was going through some kind of fugue. It was assumed he would recover. Rosamund said he might if she could keep the psychiatrists off his back. She thought little Roland was in no danger: Humphrey's parents Molly and Jack were there with their son, sometimes gently removing the receiver from his hand, replacing it, with a 'Sorry, caller.'

But the Rice lawyers, summoned by Edwin, were clever: injunctions were served, Humphrey was given no time to recover: he was ejected from the home, Susan re-installed, with little Roland back in her care, within six weeks. Clive and Natalie attempted a reconciliation but Natalie could not stop crying: not even Rosamund's Prozac helped.

The upset had lost Susan her baby (though Mrs Mac-Arthur claimed it was too much gin and a purposefully too hot bath that did it). Humphrey was blamed by nearly everyone for his insane jealousy, for murdering the child by upsetting the mother. No one blamed Susan. It was clear to everyone that Humphrey had driven Susan to infidelity. He was obviously unstable. Susan was too open, too innocent, too charming, too impetuous to have the marriage-breaking instincts which Natalie, Rosamund and Humphrey claimed she had; they regarded her as an obsessive hater of wives, rather than a lover of men. Natalie, on the contrary, was said by everyone, except Rosamund, to have a long history of infidelity, culminating in her current affair with a colleague at work. Clive was to be pitied, not blamed. If only Clive and Susan could get together. Possessive Natalie stood in the way of true love.

Before Susan left Rice Court, she said to Lady Rice, earnestly, 'Don't ever think Edwin isn't safe with me: you are my friend, after all,' but there was a look behind a look, a smile behind a smile which made Lady Rice then say to Edwin –

'Did you and Susan ever –?'
And Edwin looked astonished and said, 'Good heavens, Susan's like some kind of sister to me. I'm very fond of her.'
Nevertheless, Edwin reported that encountering Humphrey in the street, Humphrey spat at him. Spat! In the circles in which Edwin had been reared, infidelities were commonplace, but no one *spat*. Lady Rice felt herself to be included in, indeed responsible for, Edwin's distaste for the world his wife had created around him: people now scarcely worth the candle of his acquaintance.

And of course it didn't stop there. Once sexual betrayal splits a community of apparently like minds, the evil's never over. Households fall, writs fly, children and adults weep alike. Sometimes one could almost believe that if a war, an earthquake or a famine doesn't come along and get in first, people will set out to destroy their own households, their own families, their own communities. As if we build only to break down, as if the human race can't abide the boredom of happiness. As if truly the devil is in them. The fireworks of Bonfire Night are a burnt offering to the Gods of War, to appease them, but no one really wants those Gods appeased for long. Peace is boring, war is fun. Non-event is a terrible thing.

8

More

So there was Susan living righteously at Railway Cottage, the snows of winter past, the hollyhocks of summer beginning to burst into purples and mauves and pinks. She was beginning to look quite pink and healthy again, people said: she had recovered from the miscarriage, though not yet from what was seen as Humphrey's mistreatment.

Susan herself said very little about the events of the past months, as if by ignoring them they would cease to exist. She lived quietly, though it was known that she had changed her solicitor and her doctor. She was divorcing Humphrey for unreasonable behaviour, and Humphrey had decided not to resist it, for Roland's sake.

'I suppose I should be grateful,' was all Susan had to say, 'but so typical of poor Humphrey! He has these passions but he can never persist in them. Of course he's a Gemini. You never know which twin you're kissing.'

It was obvious that Clive, so much and publicly in love with Susan, could hardly handle the legalities of the divorce; and apparently Dr Rosamund Plaidy no longer suited her as a medical advisor. Rosamund did rather gossip, Susan murmured to one or two friends, about her patients. And had not Rosamund treated her own husband for low spirits, and thus tipped him over into real depression? Had she not stood between Humphrey and the psychiatrists when it was obvious that Humphrey was raving? Was such behaviour ethical?

One day Natalie came across Clive weeping into his rose bushes when he should have been at work.
'I suppose you're weeping for love of Susan,' observed Natalie.
'I am,' said Clive.
'Not for the grief and trouble you've caused myself and the children, but for yourself? Because you'd rather be with her, not me?'
'Yes,' said Clive. 'I wish it wasn't true, but it is.'
'You under-rate me,' said Natalie. 'You wait!'
Natalie went upstairs and threw Clive's clothes and papers out of the windows, out of the house, into the garden, into the street. There went his school photographs, his early letters to Natalie, his secret porn videos, his cigarette lighters, his compact discs. Clive packed what was left of his belongings after Natalie had finished into cardboard boxes and put the boxes in the back of the car. The children watched. Daddy was leaving home. They were too stunned to cry. Natalie opened the bonnet of the car and took out plug leads and threw them into the brook which ran so prettily through the English country garden.
'I want the car,' she said. 'It's mine by right. I need it to take the children to school.'
Clive called a taxi, and left home in that. It had begun to rain. Taxi tyres drove the mementoes of a happier

past further into mud. Later Natalie went out and retrieved what she could.

Clive went to Susan and said,

'I know you don't love me. But aren't you lonely in Railway Cottage? You and little Roland need looking after. Let me move in with you. Please?'

'No,' said Susan.

'But I love you,' said Clive. 'I've given everything up for you. Home, wife, family. All for you! I'm losing my clients; my business is failing. When you left me, so did others. You're all I have!'

It was true that Clive was losing the confident, well-fed look a successful lawyer needs to have. His little moustache had turned grey.

'Clive,' chided Susan, 'don't be absurd! We had a certain *rapprochement* for a time. It was wonderful and I don't regret it and I don't want you to. But it wasn't the stuff of which futures are made. Can't you get back together with Natalie? I'm sure she loves you. It's all such a great fuss about nothing. You have your children to think about.' When Clive wouldn't go, she became plaintive and reproachful. 'Please don't pester me like this. It's thanks to you I've lost Humphrey. Poor little Roland has to make do without his father. I've been treated so badly and I'm behaving so well. I don't know why I bother!'

Clive took a bedsitting room in town and hung about in the supermarket, hoping to catch sight of Susan. But Susan changed shops, and blamed Clive for that too. She had to pay more.

'It's really hard to take men with moustaches seriously!'

said Susan to Lady Rice, meeting her in the green-grocer's. Sometimes boredom would drive Lady Rice to shop in the village. 'Natalie is being so horrible to me: she just cut me dead in the street. It's not my fault her husband's the way he is about me. She ought to look after him better. I thought she was my friend but when it comes to it she's as cold as the rest of you. You'd all rather have a grievance than a friend. Why doesn't she just ask him back and be nice to him? He'd soon get over it. Women round here make such a fuss about this kind of thing. If I go to a party and Natalie's there, Natalie just walks out. It's kind of stupid of her: people will stop inviting her if she keeps making scenes.'

And Susan was of course right. Susan got asked out. Natalie didn't. The wronged make depressing companions.

'And Rosamund's another one,' said Susan. 'She acts strangely towards me, too. It's unprofessional of her.'
'But you're no longer her patient, Susan,' said Lady Rice. Susan enthused over the quality and colour of local apples, and the greengrocer's wife, with adoring eyes, offered her a bagful free. Susan accepted.
'But you still are,' said Susan, 'and I am rather surprised. She's such a gossip: all that silly stuff about your having an oestrogen implant, when we all know how much Edwin wants a baby. Remember how he wept when I lost mine? You and Edwin were so good to me, I'll never forget that. You're like sister and brother to me. But Rosamund – why is she the way she is about me?'
'I think she thinks Roland is Lambert's,' said Lady Rice.

Susan turned pale. The colour drained from her face.

She looked quite gaunt and nearer forty than thirty. She left the shop. Lady Rice followed.

'You will tell everyone that's ridiculous,' said Susan. 'It's obvious, just to look at him that he's Humphrey's. And he has all Humphrey's talents and qualities. Poor Humphrey; he could be such a wonderful companion sometimes, but he just never understood what marriage entails. He can't face any really close relationship. He's emotionally crippled, like so many English men of his generation. But that leaves his genes okay, doesn't it? So that's what Lambert's saying. Good Lord! Men get so obsessional, don't they! And full of fantasies. They'll always claim you've been to bed with them when you haven't; actually what's happened is they've tried but you said no. No wonder Rosamund is paranoid. It's not just me, it's you as well, Angelica. Well, I guess that's solved. What a problem village life can be!'

And, quite recovered, she went on down the village street, basket over arm, strong stride, fair hair shining, exotic yet domestic; with all the confidence of her own goodness, likeability.

Lady Rice called in upon Rosamund. It seemed prudent. 'You and Lambert? I never said any such thing,' said Rosamund to Lady Rice. 'Susan, or the Great Adulteress of Barley, as some call her, just enjoys stirring up mischief. Roland is indeed in all probability Lambert's child, but Lambert has gone right off Susan since she had her affair with your husband. I'm not saying for one moment Susan actually did, just that Lambert, who is paranoid, believes she did, so what's the difference?'

Lambert was back home again with Rosamund. Susan-damage, as Rosamund observed, had so far been restricted to three households, four children – two of hers, two of Natalie's, and one baby, who never got born. The village had calmed: gossip was stilled. Rosamund was beginning to build up her medical practice again. When one patient goes, others do.

'Angelica,' said Rosamund, 'I'm pregnant again. Don't you think it's time you and Edwin began?'
'I don't think so,' said Lady Rice quickly. Angelica might well have said yes, what a good idea. But the new Lady Rice found herself frightened of change, of sex, of pain, of swelling up, of sharing her body with another personality. As well grow a monster as a baby. Lady Rice was a little person, with narrow hips. Edwin was big. If the baby inherited Edwin's size, how would it get out? These things hadn't occurred to her before. Maternity, to Lady Rice in her discouraged state, seemed a very bad idea indeed.

How quickly time passed. Rice Court went on the Heritage brochure as a three-starred family outing.

'Do come to Roland's birthday party!' said Susan to Sir Edwin and Lady Rice. He'll be four on Saturday. I've asked Rosamund and Lambert to come. They can't keep up this silly quarrel with me. I asked Humphrey but he won't come. So uncivilised. You'd think, even if he can't do it for my sake, he'd do it for his son's, but no.'

Susan made the garden pretty for the party. It was her gift to make things pretty. Ropes of coloured lights twisted through the flower beds. Little iced cakes were prettily arranged; there was champagne. Susan had forgotten to provide additive-free fruit drinks for the children so they made do with water. Lady Rice observed to her husband that it didn't seem so much a children's party as one to celebrate Susan's childhood.

'You women are so catty about poor Susan,' said Edwin. 'You must have your scapegoat, I suppose.'

Rosamund declined to come to the party, though all those of note and influence in the neighbourhood did: it seemed ungenerous of her to stay away. Lambert came without his wife. He wore a shirt unbuttoned to the waist. A piece of string held his trousers up. His shoes were unlaced. But the disorder seemed born of triumph, not tragedy. His eyes sparkled. He was animated.

'Are you okay, Lambert?' asked Lady Rice, startled.

'I'm more than okay,' said Lambert. 'I left home today.' And he held Lady Rice by her two shoulders, and stared into her eyes. 'Everyone deserves happiness.'
Everyone agreed that Rosamund tried to pressurise Lambert into respectability, made him look and act like a husband and father when actually he was a creative artist.
'I'm never going back to Rosamund,' said Lambert. 'She's destroying me. I'm moving in with Susan today. Susan can't cope here on her own; she gets lonely and frightened.'

Susan was laughing and chattering amongst her guests. She held Roland's hand. She had dressed him in the party attire of a hundred years ago – white broderie anglaise flounces, leggings, black patent-leather shoes.

He was a quiet, passive child. Angelica didn't think that much would frighten Susan, but she didn't say so. Lambert would have his own view.

'What about Rosamund?' asked Angelica.

'I want you to break this to her, Angelica,' said Lambert. 'You're her friend. Rosamund will get over losing me very quickly, I promise you. She doesn't like me; she just wants to own me. But Susan loves me.'

And indeed, when Susan looked at Lambert, her eyes did seem to soften, just a little. She came over now to stand next to him.

'Wild man,' Susan said, running her finger over his stubbly chin. 'Wild man! Wild animal! I can see I'll have to tame you, groom you a little.'

Lambert roared like a lion. People stared. Lambert was certainly livelier in Susan's company than in Rosamund's. Little Roland was frightened and cried. Susan squeezed the child's hand to allay his fears. Perhaps she squeezed too hard because he cried louder. Lambert picked him up and tossed him in the air and caught him. 'Don't cry!' he said. 'Don't cry. Daddy's here!' But the child just howled louder.

'Don't!' said Susan. 'You're not his father!' And such was the force of her protest that Lambert's wildness drained. 'Sorry,' he said, quite mildly.

When Lady Rice had recovered a little, she trailed Lambert into the wooded area where once the railway track ran. Susan was attending to her guests.

'Lambert,' said Lady Rice, 'what about your children? Had you thought? And isn't Rosamund pregnant?'

'When you speak to my wife,' said Lambert, 'tell her I advise her to get an abortion. That is if she thinks she can't cope. It's her decision. But really Rosamund can cope with anything. It's a daunting prospect for a man. Susan's such a feminine person – she can raise a real family. I'm going to make up for all the unhappiness of the past. I already have. Keep it a secret, Angelica, but Susan's pregnant.'

'Well,' said Lady Rice, 'I'm not going to tell Rosamund, and that's that. Do it yourself.'

> 'Hi, Lady Rice,' said Jelly. 'Let me introduce myself. My name is Jelly White. That might have been a rude thing to say but you have my total support. Indeed, you can hold me responsible for saying it.'

'Are you okay?' asked Lambert. They walked together back into the garden. Lambert held her elbow.

'I thought I heard voices in my head,' said Lady Rice. 'I expect it's the hot weather.'

Edwin came up and said, 'You two seem to be having an intense conversation.'

Lady Rice said, boldly, 'Don't you "you two" me, Edwin.'

> 'That's right,' said Jelly White. 'Stand up to him!'

Lambert said, 'For a gentleman you can be very ungentlemanly, Edwin.'

Edwin said, 'You could make her pregnant too, only fortunately your wife's made her sterile.'

Lambert said, 'I never saw you as a family man, Edwin. Too many drugs. But you need an heir.'

Edwin said, 'At least I have something to be inherited,' but by that time Lady Rice, unaccustomed to such open hostility in a social setting, had fainted again. Lambert had told Susan who had told Edwin. How else? It was too much.

English country garden flowers are tall: delphiniums, hollyhocks, lilies. Lady Rice simply fell amongst them, breaking blooms and stems. Shorter flowers might have survived better. Susan blamed Lady Rice for that, too: ruining the flowerbeds! Lady Rice felt so bad about the damage she'd done that she agreed to tell Rosamund that Lambert had left, having made Susan pregnant. The shock of the fall seemed to have blotted Jelly White out. There was no help there.

'Four households and six children,' was all Rosamund said. 'Susan is doing well. Natalie and her two, add Humphrey and his one – or so he thought – me and my two, and another on the way. I shan't go through with this pregnancy. Though I daresay Lambert will return when he has to change a nappy or put up with a tantrum. Susan is very bad with little children. She tends to smack them when no one's looking. In the meantime, I have patients to see.'

Word got round. A few concerned voices were raised. The man in the Post Office refused to sell Susan a stamp and told her she was a marriage-breaking trollop. Edwin had a word with Robert Jellico about this and the man in the Post Office lost his job. He was told he was not sufficiently customer-friendly for the post. Now so many visitors came to Barley, to admire the church, the old village pump and the quaint country cottages, someone more up to date was needed. Susan was upset by the incident. 'Why do people say unkind things about me?' she asked. 'The worst I've ever done is love not wisely but too well. Aren't I meant to look after my own happiness? I can't be responsible for other people's, surely?'

Rosamund had an abortion and made no attempt to hide the fact. The village was censorious. Sympathy returned to Susan, and Lambert. Poor Lambert, everyone said; what a dreadful wife. Killing her own baby as an act of revenge! And Susan so charming, so lively, so bright; so much in love. Rosamund had never *loved* Lambert. Career women made bad wives, everyone knew that.

Susan gave birth to a little girl, Serena, with the same prominent eyes as her brother. Lambert's eyes: people nodded and smiled and wished them well. A family reunited at last! Roland was a quiet child, and Lambert, installed in Railway Cottage, had at first been able to write in more peace than he had ever enjoyed in the rooms above the Health Centre. He had almost finished a commissioned stage play. But after Serena's birth, alas, that was out of the question. Serena cried, wept, stormed, shivered: her health demanded constant medical attention: the running of sudden high fevers, the swelling of infant eyelids, the clenching of scarlet baby hands made this unavoidable.

Susan would march into Lambert's study (once Humphrey's), and thrust Serena into his paternal arms. 'Your baby,' she'd say. 'You're the father, you look after it; you call the doctor; don't leave everything to me.' Lambert would do his best, but there was a certain problem getting doctors to call: Rosamund's colleagues proved more loyal than expected. Nothing for it but for Lambert to abandon his stage play mid-sentence and take little Serena to the Emergency hospital twenty miles away.

She was always well enough when she got there: symptoms of concussion – Roland suffered from sibling rivalry and tended to lash out at his little sister – disappeared, fevers fell and breathing difficulties evaporated at the first smell and sight of a regular medical establishment, a green or white coat, a kindly and enquiring stethoscope. You would almost have thought doctoring ran in the child's blood, she and the medical profession had some special relationship – yet how could that be? Word got round that Rosamund's spirit hovered like an unsatisfied ghost in Railway Cottage, for all her physical self remained in the Health Centre, head high, defying the world's strictures.

One day Natalie called to see Lady Rice, who was often now at home alone in the evenings. Rice Estate business kept Edwin away: he had been to visit his brothers on tropical islands and had not taken his wife with him. 'We are too much in each other's pockets,' Edwin said, and Lady Rice believed him. Besides, how would the Rice Court visitors get on without her constant attention? The cream for the cream teas – now a favourite line – might sour; the floors stay unpolished, the accounts not get done; and the visitors liked to get a glimpse of anyone titled, albeit an upstart: just the whirl of a headscarf behind a pillar, the flick of a sensible skirt. No, Lady Rice would not evade her responsibilities.
'No such thing,' Edwin would laugh, his favourite joke. 'No such thing as a free title!'

Natalie said that day to Lady Rice, 'I used to be a really nice person. Now I'm not. That's what betrayal does to you. Let us hope you never learn. My lawyer has access to all Clive's bills: part of my ongoing argument that I should receive more alimony; Clive being perfectly well able to manage on less. It's not over between Clive and Susan. He calls her every weekday at twenty past nine. That's when Lambert's taking Roland to school. They talk until a minute before a quarter to ten, which is when Lambert gets back. My belief is that Susan only wanted Lambert as a babysitter, and thought because he had a stage play commissioned by the National Theatre it was a good bet he'd amount to something. Clive makes a good adulterous lover, but as a live in partner he'd be hopeless; Susan could see that. Me, I liked Clive. I loved him even. He was my husband. I have no objection to boring and practical men. But you show Susan a happy marriage and she'll be in there, breaking it up, which meant ours had to go. Should I tell Lambert Susan's getting bored with him? What do you think?'

'Yes,' said Jelly White, back again. 'Tell her. A good idea.'

'Yes, a good idea,' said Lady Rice.
'Mind you,' said Natalie, 'I can see anyone might need Clive as an antidote to Lambert. Lambert's got big feet, damp and smelly: he's fleshy: you'd have this great white belly bumping up and down on you every night. He's not one, they say, to let an opportunity go by. He quite exhausted Rosamund. Whereas Clive – he's so neat and contained, and he never smells, and he hardly breathes, and he has this little piston thing, deadly accurate. I loved him: now there's no one.'

Natalie started to cry. Doing without familiar sex, when you've been married for years and never thought you'd lose it, can be hard.

Lady Rice obligingly told Edwin, who naturally told
Lambert, who then left Susan and went back to
Rosamund, leaving a vacancy in Railway Cottage. This
vacancy was filled by Clive, which Natalie had not
anticipated.

'If only I had a rewind button for my life,' she mourned
to Lady Rice, 'I'd wind it back to when I came across
Clive weeping in the rose garden. I'd have made him a
cup of tea and resisted the drama of throwing him out.
Now I have to put up with the kids spending Sundays
at Railway Cottage. I think I'll die.'

'See what you did?' said Lady Rice to Jelly White.

'Sorry,' said Jelly. 'Poor Natalie!'

'Better poor Natalie than poor us,' said another
voice. 'You ought to rejoice. If it hadn't been
Clive, it might have been Edwin.'

'That is just absurd,' said Lady Rice. 'And who
are you, anyway? How dare you even think things
like that!'

'Just call me Angelique,' said the new entity. 'I'm
what you might have been.'

'Then get the fuck out of here,' said Lady Rice,
with unaccustomed vigour. 'You'll only depress
me.'

Angelique said, 'Okay, okay, but don't say I
didn't warn you,' and went.

'It wasn't working out between Lambert and me,' Susan
explained to Lady Rice at the chemist's. 'It was becoming a destructive relationship. It's difficult for two
creative artists to live under the same roof; and once his
play was turned down by the National, Lambert was
impossible. Jealous, possessive, even violent! If Rosamund can cope, she's welcome. Clive's taken his old

study as an office. He's the lodger. I'm glad to have someone sharing, especially at night. Sometimes I get the feeling the place is haunted. But I guess I'm just being the over-imaginative artist!'

'I guess,' said Lady Rice.

'Is that Natalie over there?' asked Susan, her bony arm on Lady Rice's, and Lady Rice looked and said, 'No. Just someone who looks rather like her.'

'I keep thinking I see Natalie,' said Susan. 'Not that I want to. She hasn't been much of a friend. What a dance she led poor Clive. People see sex in everything. Clive moving into Railway Cottage isn't a sex thing. I hope people realise that. You will tell them?'

'Of course,' said Lady Rice.

In and out, in and out, like a piston through the night, blotting out ghosts, blotting out Natalie.

9

Dinner Party

Lady Rice was busy. Ventura Lady Cowarth had a bad back – she'd had a fall from her horse and, though to be hopelessly drunk is meant to protect a rider from injury, had disabled herself badly. She could barely wash, though she got herself hoisted on to horseback to follow the Hunt and managed that. 'I can't fuck,' she told Lady Rice, 'but I can still hunt.'

Lord Cowarth was upset and knocking away again at his teeth, such few as were left, and they were mostly at the back so he had to open his mouth wide to do it.

Lady Rice was up at Cowarth Castle four or five times a week, nursing, shopping, answering the phone, parrying Milord's insults and oddities, preparing for the visit of the twins, back from the Caribbean for business reasons but unaccountably laggardly in visiting their ancestral home. If only I had a baby thought Lady Rice, I'd be allowed to focus my family responsibilities in my own home. I wouldn't be so tired. But too late for that now. These days Edwin said he didn't want children. He didn't want the family insanity passed on.

Rosamund Plaidy was no help: she declined, these days, or so it was said, to give anyone Prozac. In fact she was giving up medicine altogether, the better to look after her children.

Rosamund, Lambert told anyone who would listen, was on a masochistic binge; she was doing it on purpose to mortify him, but he declined to be mortified. He was living at home again, but Rosamund refused to speak to him, other than when entirely necessary. She encouraged the children in the same behaviour. He was, she said, only a temporary kind of husband and father, there today, gone tomorrow, best not to get too close to him, if only because closeness was what drove him away. He was emotionally immature, she said, as if definition somehow improved matters. Lambert claimed to like the surrounding silence: it allowed him to get on with his work. Oddly, they all seemed to enjoy their lives together and when a social researcher, enquiring into the domestic lives of doctors, asked them to rate their 'happiness', all replied 'good'.

'Let's ask Susan and Clive to dinner one night,' said Edwin. 'We never get to see them these days. Let's try and get the social scene round here going again. It's up to us. Noblesse oblige.'
He'd been reclusive lately, and had put on weight. He stayed in bed till late in the morning, and went to bed later than Angelica. He snapped at her and found fault. But now suddenly he had his arms round her, and seemed full of resolution and she was happy. She remembered what times past had been like, and saw they could be good again. Skies could cloud so gradually you

hardly noticed as bright turned to overcast, until suddenly there was the sun again.

'We'll upset quite a lot of people if we do,' said Angelica,
and they counted them up between them: those to whom
the social acceptance or otherwise of disturbed and disturbing, shifting and changing couples mattered.

> Humphrey.
> Rosamund, Lambert and their two chil-
> dren Matty and Pierre.
> Natalie, and little Jane and little Jonathan.
> Roland, who missed Humphrey, and little
> Serena, into whom the spirit of Rosa-
> mund's aborted baby had entered, or so
> some said.
> X, the name given by Angelica to Susan's
> miscarried baby.

'You can't really lay all the responsibility at Susan's
door,' said Edwin.

'I do,' said Angelica.

'Then what a woman she is,' said Edwin. 'The femme
fatale of Barley: the Great Adulteress.'

Clive and Susan were asked to dinner, at Edwin's
request. Another mistake, to believe a social circle could
be revived.

'Darling Angelica,' said Susan. 'I thought you'd never
ask. Everyone's been so unsociable lately. Shall we just
all start over? Ask Rosamund, Natalie, Lambert, everyone? Shall I bring a chocolate mousse? Why don't you
ask that new man at the church, the Rev Hossle? We
could have a civilised dinner and a service of reconcili-

ation over coffee. People do it all the time back home. Everyone's got so horrid to everyone, and we all used to be such friends!'

Lady Rice rang round and did indeed invite other guests; neutrals, semi-strangers, but not Rosamund, Lambert or Natalie. Not yet.

Lady Rice was serving the lobster bisque when there came a ring at the great front door, not the humble side one. Unusual. Mrs MacArthur let Natalie into the house, into the dining hall. Natalie was dressed in black: hollow eyes stared from a gaunt face. Once she'd been plump, lively and smiling. It was generally felt that she liked to make the most of her misfortunes: it was even suspected that she used eye makeup to enhance the hollow-eyed look.

'Wives don't *own* husbands,' Barley society said. 'These days men and women stay together because they want to. If one of the couple no longer wants to stay, that's it. Goodbye. No obligation! And the children settle down soon enough.'

But those who spoke thus were on the whole people who hadn't married, had never joined names or property, had never been spun around in some great resultant whirlwind of sexual jealousy until their wits were gone; wholly disintegrated.

And here Natalie now was, bent apparently on justifying the suspicions of her critics, advancing upon Edwin's and Angelica's dinner table. Now she swept the very spoon out of Susan's hand. A splodge of hot lobster soup landed on Susan's brow. Edwin was on his feet at once, restraining a struggling Natalie.

'Bitch, bitch!' yelled Natalie.

Now Clive tried to rescue Natalie from Edwin's clasp.

'Leave her alone, you philandering bastard,' shouted Clive at Edwin.

Susan's eyes were wild with outrage, white gleamed on either side of the pupils, her cheeks grew pink, her chin thrust forward.

'You have burnt my skin,' she snarled at Natalie, and slapped Edwin, whereupon Clive slapped Susan back, Edwin let Natalie go and Natalie sat down in Susan's chair.

'Itemised telephone bills,' said Natalie calmly to Clive, 'continue to be a boon to domestic understanding. When you take Roland and Serena, Lambert's children – though who is to be sure about Roland? – to school and nursery, Susan's on the phone to guess who? Her first husband, Alan Adliss. She meets him once a week, on Tuesday afternoons at Roystead Station car park. Intimacy then takes place in the back of the car. Alan Adliss has a major retrospective coming at the Tate Gallery. You just do, Clive, while the Great Adulteress waits for Mr Next. I am sorry for the current Mrs Alan Adliss. What misery do you have planned for her? Perhaps she's pregnant, and you'd rather she wasn't.'

'Hell hath no fury, Natalie,' said Susan, but her words lacked gravitas, since she had nowhere to sit down. 'And everyone scorns you and laughs at you. The lies you tell! Roystead car park!'

Natalie put photographs on the table. There, in a car park setting, a car. There on the front seat Susan's head of blonde hair, buried in the famous artist's lap: he with an expression of mesmerised distraction on his face.

'Clive,' said Natalie to her ex-husband, 'please will you take me home?'
Without a further look at Susan, Clive took Natalie away. Tears came to Susan's eyes, but whether of grief, shock or outrage, who was to say? Edwin put his arm round Susan: he at any rate assumed she needed comforting. Lady Rice caught just a glimpse of a look from Susan before she buried her head in Edwin's shoulder, as Susan made sure that Lady Rice understood she was defeated, in a way she'd never known existed.
'Take me home now,' said Susan to Edwin, and Edwin excused himself to his wife, and guests, and did so.

    'This is a divorcing matter,' said Jelly.

    'It isn't,' said Lady Rice. 'Edwin is behaving as any host would.'

And she served roast lamb and rosemary purée to her depleted table. Still Edwin did not return.

All left in due course with cries of 'lovely evening, darling: nothing like a little real life drama! Give our love to Edwin when (by inference "if") he gets back', and so on, and Lady Rice became aware almost for the first time that envy and resentment interwove others' liking for her. Lady Rice was too pretty, too young, too favoured by fortune, too (once upon a time) successful and rich, too happy with Edwin – or was that in the past, she could hardly remember: how did the present become the past: at what juncture? – to enjoy the unadulterated support of others. They were happy when she was cast down.

Lady Rice wept and Mrs MacArthur helped her to bed. For once, Lady Rice was grateful for her presence.

'I told you she was trouble,' said Mrs MacArthur. 'You young women are such fools. Some women are born marriage-breakers. They ought to be stoned to death.'

'But everyone likes Susan,' moaned Lady Rice. 'Everyone likes to be in Susan's company. Why is Edwin taking so long?'

'Because I expect he likes to be in her company, too,' said Mrs MacArthur tartly. 'She comes round here too often for my liking. Especially when you're out.'

Edwin returned home just after three in the morning.

'I had to calm her down,' he said. 'But she's very angry with you, Angelica.'

'Angry with me?' Angelica was astonished.

'Presumably you told Natalie Susan was coming to Rice Court. You set the whole thing up.'

'I did no such thing,' said Angelica. 'Have you gone mad? I didn't set anything up. Susan asked me to invite Natalie. I was doing what you wanted.'

'Don't hide behind me,' said Edwin. 'Someone certainly told Natalie. You've had it in for Susan for a long time. You've even suspected me of sleeping with her. That hurts her very much. It certainly insults me. You've done untold damage to Susan and her children. What are we going to do with you, Angelica?'

Edwin undressed and slipped into bed beside his wife. His body, which should have been cold from the journey home, was warm. He lay still for a moment and then pulled her out of bed roughly, and stood her against a wall, and possessed her as if she was some girl he'd met in a pub and the master bedroom of Rice Court was an alleyway. She was too surprised to protest.

'You give yourself freely enough to other men,' he said. 'Why be so standoffish with me?'

She was too surprised to say anything: too hurt, too proud, and too alarmed to discover she had enjoyed it to the point of orgasm. She got back into bed; he lay at the far side of it without touching.

'God, you're a bitch,' he said, and then he fell asleep. To her own surprise, so did she.

Lady Rice called Susan the next day. Jelly White told her to.

'Susan, what's the matter?' she said. 'We're friends. It's ridiculous to suggest I set you up. I trust you; why can't you trust me? I don't even object if Edwin takes you home mid-dinner party and doesn't come home till three. What have I ever done to you, except be supportive, speak up for you, take your side – surely, after everything –'

'I don't know what "everything" you're talking about,' Susan said, apparently both bored and puzzled. 'I've never needed your support. But we have both changed. We all have to pick and choose in life, don't we? And some friends suit for a time, and then don't. So we have to discard them. I hope you don't think I'm being brutal. But that was no favour you did me last night.'

'So long as you discard Edwin as well,' said Angelica, 'not just me.'

'There you go again, Angelica,' said Susan. 'This is exactly what I mean. You have turned into a jealous and suspicious person. As for Edwin, men and women can be very close friends without any particularly sexual implication. But you don't seem to understand that. And these days people don't have to have friends in couples. Edwin's my friend, not you. Shall we leave it at that?

We can smile and talk if we meet in a social situation, naturally, but that's the limit of it.' And Susan put down the phone.

Lady Rice wondered if she could get a posse together to go round and burn Susan alive in Railway Cottage as a witch. Or perhaps they could stone her to death as an adulteress. She said as much to Edwin, who looked at his wife askance and asked her not to cause more trouble than she had already.

And the day after that, when Lady Rice was doing the filing in the Rice Court office, still trembling with shock, confusion and upset, and Edwin was off for the day somewhere with Robert Jellico, Anthea came in without knocking. She was looking, she said, for Edwin.
'He said he'd be up at Wellesley Hall at ten,' said Anthea. She seemed annoyed. She brought in a flurry of wind and weather with her: outdoors had suddenly taken over from indoors. Anthea was wearing green wellies, a blackish anorak, and a horsey headscarf damp with rain. Her hair fell over her eyes. She carried a riding crop, from force of habit. 'Edwin's too bad. He was meant to be looking over Henry Cabot, with a view to purchase.'
'Henry Cabot?' Angelica was bewildered.
'A horse, darling, for the new stables.'
'The new stables?'
'Darling,' said Anthea kindly, 'he says you don't notice very much, and you don't seem to. What is all this secretarial stuff?'

She drew Angelica away from the files, the computer, the fax; she led her, protesting, into the drawing room, flinging aside the ropes that kept the visitors confined to the established pathways through the house, snatching up labels and throwing them to the ground as she went. She called for Mrs MacArthur and told her to light the fire – always laid but never lit – which Mrs MacArthur meekly did.

'You're meant to be Lady Rice, not some office factotum,' Anthea said. 'And it's pissing Edwin off. I thought I should warn you. And what are these village creeps you keep mixing with? Very sordid things are happening, by all accounts. You and Edwin should stick to your own kind. Well, Edwin's kind. You started off fine, exotic and eccentric; we can do with wild cards to liven up the blood stock, but you've turned into some kind of dozy housewife and what's more you haven't even bred. So what's the point of you? That's what Edwin's beginning to wonder.'

Anthea had her boots and her anorak off; she lay back in a leather armchair, unbooted feet stuck towards the fire. Her sweater was ancient and thin. Her figure, Angelica realised, was remarkably good. Her face was too thin and dried up with outdoors and lack of face creams, but it was mobile and lively.

'And, darling,' said Anthea, 'infidelity runs in the Rice blood. A capacity to chew women up and spit them out. Women of all classes, including their own. You served your other purpose: you were basically respectable, lower-middle class; got Edwin back on the straight and narrow okay. But that's done and here you are, demoting yourself to domestic/secretarial, and he's taken the Great Barley Adulteress for his mistress while he works out who to marry next. And I'd better warn you, from a straw or two in the wind, I think he's got me in mind. He can see a future in joining my stables with Rice Court land. I'm telling you this because I like you. You're hopelessly out of your depth, but it's not your fault. You're the choirmaster's daughter, and an amateur choir at that.'

'You've been drinking,' said Angelica. 'God, how you lot drink.'
And indeed Anthea was helping herself to whisky even as she spoke, delivered her bombshell.

'You haven't even decanted this stuff, Angelica,' complained Anthea, and winced at a smeary glass. Since her hands were covered with mud and some kind of rural slime, Angelica did not take this seriously.

Lady Rice pointed out politely that since Edwin was married to her, he could hardly marry Anthea; that she, Lady Rice, knew well enough how to run her own life, and that the matter of the artist-mistress – if Anthea was referring to Susan – was nothing but mischievous rumour; that she, Lady Rice, trusted Edwin with her life; that she had to get back to her work, and retype out all the labels Anthea had destroyed, and would Anthea please leave and come back when she was sober.

Anthea said, 'My God, Edwin's right. You simply do not know how to behave. This is the end.'

Anthea left, but not before saying at least Edwin didn't intend to father children outside the family. He had taken the Adulteress to be aborted at the time she'd had domestic trouble and was staying up at Rice Court. Just as well because stray babies could lead to nasty wars of succession.

Lady Rice went back to the office and wept into her computer. Still Edwin did not return.

'I hope you weren't rude to her,' said Mrs MacArthur. 'It isn't wise to queer your pitch with people like that. They're the ones with the real power.'

Lady Rice got in her little car – a runabout fit for country roads: Edwin kept the Mercedes and the Range Rover for himself – and went down to Railway Cottage. It seemed empty. The door, usually wide open and inviting, was locked. Angelica looked in the windows and saw that everything was neat, tidy and, as usual, prettily arranged. But there were no flowers in the vases. They stood drained, polished and upside down on the sill.

Lady Rice stood indecisively in the pretty English country garden. Andrew Nellor, the retired evangelist who lived in the cottage next door to Susan, in neurotic twitchiness and rumbling disapproval of everything and everyone, came up Susan's path. He was weeping. His trousers were old, and, as were Lambert's from time to time, held up with string. His little wife looked anxiously out from the top window. She was well-kept and pretty, like Susan's garden.

'She's gone,' said Andrew Nellor, 'Susan's gone. She kissed me and said she loved me, she wouldn't forget me, and she left. I always loved her. God forgive me, I lusted after her. It was her body I wanted. She had no soul. I prayed, my wife prayed, but the lust wouldn't go away. Such a strong, vibrant person. She had no shame:

she was proud of her body. She didn't mind what I saw, what my wife saw. She'd undress with the light on, she'd lie sunbathing naked in the garden. She saw nothing wrong with nudity. She wanted to give me pleasure. I think in her heart she loved me, wanted me. I painted her, secretly. My wife didn't understand. She'd cut her dead in the street. I'm sure that's what drove Susan away. I try to forgive my wife, but I can't. I shall hang the painting in my study, I don't care what she says.'
'Who exactly did Susan leave with?' asked Lady Rice. 'I'm sure she didn't leave alone.'
'With the painter Alan Adliss,' said Andrew Nellor. 'Susan loved me but I had nothing to offer her. He's rich and famous. But nobody understood her as I did.'
'And little Roland?' asked Angelica. 'And little Serena? Did they go too?'
'She took Serena but said she was taking Roland to his father. She said a boy needed its father.'

Lady Rice went down to the surgery, which Rosamund Plaidy now opened twice a week for four hours only. It was out-of-hours: the surgery was closed: when was it ever not? Lambert and little Roland sat upon the stone wall opposite. Little Roland was snivelling, 'I want my mummy,' he sing-sang. He was not an appealing child. The wail betokened petulance, not major grief, but what did Lady Rice know? She had no children of her own.

'Just be glad,' said Jelly White, 'that the bitch has left town. And not with Edwin. Sooner or later you've got to wake up to this matter of Edwin and Susan.'
'Bitch yourself,' said Lady Rice. 'Go away.'

'Rosamund's thrown me out,' observed Lambert. 'She went away with the kids and locked the door when Roland turned up. And Roland's wet his pants and is smelling.'

'Then break the door down,' said Lady Rice.

'I don't feel like doing that,' said Lambert. He was in no fit state to be left with a child. He, like Andrew Nellor, was unwashed and unshaven. 'I haven't been feeling too good lately,' Lambert said. 'I've kept to my bed a lot. I don't blame Rosamund, I blame myself. You just don't know, do you,' he said, 'when first you fuck your neighbour's wife, the kind of thing that can happen. She took Serena round to Clive's and Natalie's. She says he's Serena's father.'

Lady Rice took Lambert and Roland home, since there seemed nowhere else for them to go. Edwin was still out. That was something.

Lady Rice put both Lambert and Roland to bed in the spare room at the top of the house and then slipped in beside them. She did this to keep them warm, no more, and provide them, and indeed herself, with some human comfort. Roland dived down to the bottom of the bed, to be further from these suddenly and unaccountably close adults. Lady Rice was fully clothed. So was Lambert. The night was cold; the spare room was at the top of the house, the one the chimney had fallen through in better days, where the heating, even though newly replaced, never quite reached.

'Where's Edwin?' asked Lambert, shivering beneath the bedclothes, only vaguely aware of his surroundings, but trying to be polite. His face was flushed and unhealthy against white linen: yellow beard springing amongst pimples. Upset made him spotty, as if he were an adolescent.

'I don't know,' said Lady Rice, 'but at least Susan is with Alan Adliss. Sometimes I worry about Edwin and Susan.'

'Susan never could get Edwin,' said Lambert. 'She tried, but she failed. She got all the men in the neighbourhood except Edwin; and he was the one she really wanted, because of the title, because of this house, because he stood out against her. She never liked you, Angelica, but she admired you. She didn't understand the power you had over Edwin.'

'I love him,' said Lady Rice, and then heard Edwin clanking and calling about the house. She was too proud to get out of bed, and too tired and cold besides, and when Edwin burst in, kicking and shouting – behaving as if the door was locked when of course it wasn't: it was just the ancient cross latch worked the way you wouldn't expect, as he ought to very well know – there she was in bed with Lambert, albeit with so many clothes on, or such was her story, she could not reasonably be supposed to be sexually motivated. But Edwin assumed she was, and Lady Rice was not going to produce little Roland from under the bedclothes as chaperon: why should she, why would she?

'Whore, bitch, slut,' shouted Edwin, yanking her out of bed, hitting her, but leaving Lambert alone, as is often the habit of men who discover their wives with other men. They beat the woman but respect their rival.

Lady Rice walked straight out and went to her mother's. The village took this as evidence of her deceit, her unfitness to be Lady of the Manor: and, besides, they had lost Susan, whom everyone liked, who ran the social scene, whose approval or disapproval counted: if Susan dropped by with a jar of marmalade, you were in; if she didn't, you failed to exist, and, if you existed or if you didn't, she took your husband as the tax you owed her.

The story went that Lady Rice, out of spite and jealousy, had driven Susan out. The finger of blame might swing wildly, but it was as if blame and Susan shared similar magnetic poles – they simply could never meet, no matter what. Come within a fraction of an inch, only to veer away.

'I can't really blame Angelica,' said Edwin later to his stepmother Ventura Lady Cowarth, who repeated it to Lady Rice. 'Her background was such that she could never live up to what is expected of her as mistress of Rice Court, or as wife and woman. And all the time Anthea was under my nose! We are entirely suited, Anthea and myself. My marriage to Angelica was a folly of youth. Somebody ought to have stopped me, really.'

And that was the end of that.

10

Morituri Te Salutant

And that was the end of that. The novel ended.

Those who are about to die salute thee. I, Ajax, have done my part. I have faced the past as Lady Rice could not, she being too busy with her disassociated personalities. Now I can retire again, my affidavit presented. I am a fine and competent fellow, and my misery it is to be thus confined in a female body. I could do all kinds of things to Lady Rice, if I chose. I could make her crow and strut about a bit; I could make her put on a collar and tie and be a lesbian; I could send her to seduce, shall we say, Anthea, or Susan – that would certainly work – but for that I'd have to elbow the harlot Angel out of the way, and I am nothing if not a gentleman; so I'll allow the harlot to have her own way for a time. Lady Rice can be all angel and no Ajax.

The differing aspects of the self, the different times at which they live, begin to gather together. The places where they co-exist discover their significance.
Lodestar House stood empty for a time. Congo's ghosts swept in and got him: one night they simply dived under his broomstick defences and nabbed him. Garotted

by pirates, guillotined by revolutionaries, starved by communards, betrayed by his own heart, what difference does it make? Humiliation and pain accompanies death or does not; to try to guarantee the manner of one's end is barely worth living this kind of life or that. Play safe as a wage slave, play fast and loose as a criminal, death ignores the justice of the matter. The wage slave can burn to death horribly on the motorway and be forgotten within the week; the evil man come to an easy end in his sleep, tucked up in bed with his wife, and the obituaries drift on and flatter, for since nothing is deserved in life, why should it be any different in death?

PART FOUR

Houses Disinhabited

1

Tensions

Sara, on another mission of mercy and self-interest both, arrived at Lodestar House to find Congo and Wendy dead. Tinkerbell finally got the old woman with her sparkler: that is to say a blood vessel had burst in Wendy's brain. The executioner had apparently put away guillotine, blade and rope and decreed that Congo should die simply of a heart attack. Which one of the couple had gone first the coroner could not tell, but clearly the end of one had precipitated the end of the other. In such cases it is assumed that the older of the two dies first, which can affect the inheritance.

Tully was on the phone to Brian Moss immediately after the inquest. He'd had a word with the Coroner but it hadn't worked. Wendy had left all her property to Congo, who had in turn left everything to his niece. As a result, Lodestar House would end up in the hands of the middle-aged, female manager of a tennis club in West London: a lesbian of the old school; a woman who kept Alsatian dogs, wore a cravat and was reputed to drink whisky from the bottle. Tully swore he would do murder rather than let this happen, and was inclined to sue Brian Moss for negligence.

'Negligent? Negligent about what?' asked Brian.

'Not murdering the poor old lady before her natural time,' said Jelly, removing his member from her mouth. 'For allowing Lodestar House to slip away, like the life of its occupants. We must do this less often. It's beginning to take up too much of your time.'

'I have to remain faithful to my wife, I have to!' moaned Brian Moss. 'If I am not careful, I will become involved with you, and what kind of man falls in love with his secretary? I despise men who do it.'

Anxiety made his erection falter and Jelly was sent to search for Wendy's will amongst dusty files. She came back to say she had just happened to come across further documents in the files relating to Lodestar House, and here they were. Brian Moss perused them, and declared that since the property had already reverted to Wendy's daughter Una, the problem was solved. He rubbed his hands together and said, 'Thank God the place won't go either to Tully or to Congo's niece. With any luck it will simply be held in probate till the end of time: no one's heard of Una for decades.'

'Shall I put an ad in *The Times*?' asked Jelly, 'asking Una to be in touch; saying she will hear something to her advantage if she contacts us?'

'You're just looking for trouble,' complained Brian Moss. 'I don't know what's got into you these days.'

'You have,' said Jelly, once again on her knees before Brian Moss. The three had capitulated to his advances, not without calculation. It suited them all. The girls afforded him the simple pleasure of fellatio at whatever office hour Brian Moss fancied – both parties seeing this as pleasant sexual gratification without profound personal obligation.

'And we won't be betraying his wife, poor woman,' said Angelica. 'Blow jobs don't really count. It's all give and no take.'

'Better than no sex at all,' said Angel. 'I like it. Put cinnamon in his coffee, if it's the taste that worries you.'

'I like to see him out of control,' said Jelly. 'It's about the only power I have. And I shall ask him for a rise.'

'That won't do any good,' said Lady Rice.

She was right.

'It would be sordid,' said Brian Moss, with the pomposity with which this normally unpompous man approached financial matters. 'Sleazy, even, to raise your wages in the light of this new relationship of ours. To do so would be to reduce you to the status of a whore. Presumably you'll want to get married one day, Jelly: I'm sure you wouldn't want to have any such blot upon your reputation. It's always such a bore to have to live with secrets from the past; time bombs waiting to explode. I have one or two myself. No, better no secrets at all. Sex must never be exchanged for money: it reflects badly upon all involved. I'll keep it to our lunch hour, if you like, so there's no suggestion of office harassment. Presumably this activity of ours gives you as much pleasure as it does me or you wouldn't be doing it.'

To which in their joint heart Angel replied, 'Of course,' Angelica replied 'Presume away; I take leave to doubt it –' and Jelly replied with some vehemence, 'This is no more than bullying and harassment,' but fortunately, their mouth being by this time occupied with Brian Moss's engorged and twitching member, which mention of money always cheered up, they were not expected to respond. Jelly had lately developed quite a stutter. Brian Moss liked to believe it was his doing, that the girl's mouth had become better adjusted to sex than to speech, and the three were content to let him believe this to be the case. Better that Brian Moss did not become aware that warring personalities battled for possession of his secretary's mouth. Jobs were hard to find: should Rice v. Rice come to court and alimony not be granted, Lady Rice would need employment. These days jobs went to the ordinary, the reliable and the sane, not to the perforated and split.

'Faster and further down,' instructed Brian Moss. 'Come along! Do you think I have all day to spare?'

He was impatient: she was at first inexperienced. He enjoyed his own masterfulness. 'Not like that! For God's sake! I have a client waiting.'

If Tully Toffener paced in the anteroom, annoyed by every wasted minute, why then all things would combine to please Brian Moss the more. But he would not take cinnamon in his coffee: he was nervous that the office cleaner would deduce his activities from his habits.

'But what are you so nervous of?' Angel would ask with Jelly's mouth.

'I love my wife. She would be so upset. I have to look after her,' said Brian Moss, but the more he said it the more his penis twitched and required satisfaction, and seemed to have little connection with the man himself. 'You've put a spell on me.'

'Where are you going?' Brian Moss would ask, adjusting his clothes when her task was done.

'To the powder room,' Jelly would say. 'To wash my mouth.'

'There isn't time for any of that,' Brian Moss would say. 'Stay here and take notes.' And she would, without further protest.

'The relationship between male employer and female employee,' Ajax once wrote in his notes, 'contains a sexual element at the best of times: he controls, she submits: he makes the running, she follows after. He is dominant, she is submissive. Should the veiled eroticism become actual, it is only natural for the relationship to drift easily into her masochism. His power can only be her pleasure. If he forbids her to use the powder room when she wants to wash the scent and feel of him away, that's that. She puts up with it. She stole his power, illegitimately: now she wants him to have it back.'

Lady Rice spent these office days in bed at The Claremont, sleeping, weeping, rocking in her sea of sorrow, or so it seemed to her: though any pursuing photographers could have tracked her physical being to Catterwall & Moss and snapped her well enough, and used the photograph as evidence of her bad character in a divorce case.

Lady Rice was interested enough to hear what Angel/Angelica/Jelly had to say about their day when they returned; they would talk her through it, but still she felt it was none of it very much to do with her. So long as they brought the body back safe and well, whatever else they did was nothing to do with her. It disappointed them, but there it was.

Angel said to Lady Rice, 'I worry about you.

You're so disconnected. Not even sex can bring you back.'

To which Lady Rice replied, plaintively, dreamily, 'For me sex is to do with love. Anything else is abhorrent to me. Try to grasp that I'm a domestic kind of creature; my aim is to be gracious. You are nothing to do with me. As for you, Angel, you are some kind of changeling, and I just wish you'd go away.'

Angelica complained to Lady Rice, taking her aside, 'I wish you'd put a little effort into being in charge. You let Angel get away with everything. She has Jelly and me on our knees there in front of Brian Moss any time of the office day he chooses, and he's a married man. Brian is right: supposing we get found out? I don't want to make poor Oriole Moss miserable. Surely it's possible to incorporate and control Angel?'

'Angelica, I am prepared to recognise,' replied Lady Rice. 'I see you as myself before I married: active, picky, bright, kind, full of certainties. I take no real exception to you, except I find you hopelessly shallow. But Angel is no part of me. No. My best plan is just hang around and look the other way, so Angel gets bored and goes back to the internal whorehouse she comes from. It was lonelier before you girls appeared, but at least I knew who I was, even though it was me sleepwalking.'

Jelly said, 'Hang on a minute, it's only thanks to Angel that we're in this relationship with Brian Moss at all. He'd have fired me long ago if I hadn't obliged. And I gave up Ram the chauffeur on your say-so. His name is Rameses, by the way. He was conceived on a trip up the Nile. The poor guy's broken-hearted, but at least drives me here and there free of charge. I know you don't like me much, Lady Rice; you think I'm vulgar, common and greedy, lower-middle class, but you need me. I'm the one who earns the money and fills in the cheque stubs. None of you others would bother. And I think you should be in there as well when we service Brian Moss, not opting out, leaving the whole thing to us. And another thing, I don't want too much said against Angel. Angel's got guts, skill and experience, and giving blow jobs requires all three.'

'Skill!' jeered Lady Rice, but Jelly explained to her how the mouth could get tired, the neck could get cricked, the tongue get chafed if a girl wasn't careful: how you had to keep your teeth out of the way, masked by the lips, but not forgotten; their existence providing an edge of danger and drama.

'I think you should think about these things,' said Jelly.

Lady Rice said she would rather not.

Angel said, 'Talk, talk, talk, the lot of you. And you're nuts, Jelly. Blow jobs don't take skill, they just take instinct. And it's a Below Job, anyway:

243

Pidgin English; it's what whores do; money the only reason they bother to do it. I'm getting bored with this hotel, with doing nothing. Brian Moss doesn't count: I want some real action. Wait and see where I take you next.'

'Where?' Lady Rice, Jelly and Angelica asked nervously, but Angel just laughed and fastened her net stockings to the little bobbles which hung from the thongs of her lacy suspender belt.

'I like the grip of the fabric round my waist,' she said, 'and the stretch of elastic down my thighs. I can't stand the way you girls wear tights, just because they're practical.'

Angelica and Jelly fell silent, allowing their wilful and drastic other self her head. Later, instead of sleeping, they all, including Lady Rice, accompanied Angel down to the bar and allowed her a triple gin, and a wink or two at an Italian couple who, being on holiday, seemed anxious for a third to join them in the bed. Angel had the knack of knowing who to wink at, and whose smiles best to respond to.

Lady Rice was so furious and miserable the next day that Angel promised to be good, on pain of Lady Rice taking an overdose of sleeping pills and putting an end to the lot of them. Jelly had to take a day off to recover from the excesses of the night, which also sobered Angel; as did Angelica's complaint that the world of forbidden sex was too full of euphemism to be safe. 'Joining a couple in bed,' sounded cosy, white-sheeted, yawny and warm, but in fact turned out to be cold, unhygienic, and a matter of strippings, whips and manacles as the wife took her symbolic revenge on the husband's notional mistresses over a decade and the husband reasserted his right to have them as, when and how he chose.

2

A Gust Of Chilly Wind

Una Musgrave answered Brian Moss's advertisement. Like an answer to a prayer, like the wild gust of wind which arrives with the God, she appeared in Brian Moss's front office. Jelly happened to be doing reception work: a replacement for Lois, who had handed in her notice. She was going at the end of the week.

'Lois is in love with me,' Brian Moss confided in Jelly. 'I think she's jealous of you. Remember when she pushed the door open – and I'd thought it was locked –'

'I think she's underpaid and overworked,' said Jelly tartly. 'Nothing whatsoever to do with me.'

Brian Moss liked her to be tart: the sharper her tongue, the more pleasure he had in silencing it, the more intimate its flavour.

Be that as it may, there Jelly was, pale and demure with a triple set of pearls from Fenwicks and a nice pale pink cashmere sweater, half-price because of a single pulled thread which Lady Rice came out of retirement to attend to, a red pleated skirt, shoes a trifle battered but well polished (The Claremont's overnight service) and sturdy tights; hair neat, an exceptionally clear complexion

(Brian Moss swore that was his doing) and a buttery little mouth.

'When suddenly the door opens,' as Jelly described it to Angelica that evening, 'and a wind blows in and papers fly everywhere, and my hair's all over the place. Such a disturbance! I knew at once it was Una. She must be over sixty, but she's one of those women who might be any age. Wide eyes, lots of bone and no wrinkles.'

'Sounds like a facelift to me,' murmured Angel, whom the others did sometimes still let out to make the servicing of Brian Moss more tolerable. But remained quite shaken and subdued, after what the three referred to as 'The Italian Job'.

'Don't be so catty,' said Jelly.

'Hoo hoo hoo,' said Angel. 'If I didn't think I'd get into trouble, I'd say you'd fallen in love with this Una.'

Lady Rice, looking in the mirror, found herself going quite pink.

'How dare you say such a thing about poor Jelly,' said Angelica. 'We've none of us ever shown the slightest lesbian tendency. Heterosexual through and through, that's us. Apologise at once, Angel.'

For once, Lady Rice initiated a statement:

'Actually, I think I was far fonder of Susan than I ought to have been,' she said. 'That's why I got so upset about all that business with Lambert and Edwin.'

'Ought schmought,' said Angel. 'Where's the ought in proclivity? Personally I don't care what gender anyone is. Some people turn me on, some situations turn me on, and that's it.'

'You're so crude,' said Angelica. 'Go away.'

The others agreed that was what they wanted. Angel went.

When her little sister had gone, Lady Rice said, 'And actually I rather liked Anthea. She always had a kind of swagger. I admired her. I wanted her to accept me as her equal, but the best I ever got from her was her being sorry for me. I think the one I was jealous over was Anthea, not Edwin. I'd gone off Edwin ages back, if the truth is to be told. I'd have had a baby by him if I'd really loved him, I expect. The fact of the matter was, when I first met up with him, Edwin was a catch. Pop star marries into aristocracy; though a mean and shoddy sort of aristocracy it turned out to be, only after the main chance itself.'

'Careful,' said Jelly, 'or you'll lose your anger and if you lose anger, you might lose alimony. Practise saying it: "Every day in every way I'm more and more Edwin's victim." '

'She's not going to say that,' said Angelica. 'Mother hen just didn't like hubby preferring Anthea to her; she was humiliated. Her feathers got all ruffled. Hell hath no fury, et cetera.'

'Stop talking about me behind my back,' said Lady Rice, and burst into tears. 'Mother hen! That's so cruel!'

So Jelly went on chattering to Angelica about the sudden appearance of the magical Una.

'You'd trust this woman with your life,' said Jelly. 'She oozes self-confidence. She was wearing leather boots up to her thighs; you could see a stretch of black stocking before a pleated miniskirt began and, waist up, it was Fifties' style: twinset and pearls and a turban. The pearls were real, tiny little uneven things. I thought for a moment she was a man in drag, but how could she be; she's Sara's mother. But it was a really stylish outfit, I can tell you.'

'You're beginning to think like a typist,' complained Angelica, 'as well as talk like one.'

'Bitch, bitch, bitch,' said Jelly. 'What makes you so special? You're just a trumped-up pop star. Fame for a day and never got over it! At least I know how to do a good day's work.'

'Can't you talk in anything but clichés?' demanded Angelica. 'You're driving me mad.'

'Please stop this,' begged Lady Rice, who was banging her head with her fists. 'I'm getting such a headache. I feel so anxious. I'm going mad. I'm too ashamed to go back to work. How can I look Brian Moss in the eye? I'll slash my wrists if you're not careful. If I order a steak from Room Service, they'll bring a steak knife and I can use that. This fruit knife's much too blunt. Can't we have Angel back? At least she makes a joke from time to time. With her we'll get a social disease, but without her I'm suicidal and you two get murderous. I'm splitting. The perforations are ripping. I can't control things any more. I thought the trauma was from outside, but it's coming from inside. Somebody help me!'

'Get Angel,' said Angelica, urgently.

'Get Angel,' said Jelly, panicky. 'Get her back now.'

Angel steadied and slowed the hand that was vainly trying to make the blunt knife, provided daily with a complimentary basket of fruit, slice through the skin of her wrists to draw blood.

> 'Satan finds work for idle mouths to do,' said Angel.

Angelica laughed, Jelly sniggered, Lady Rice stopped sawing away. It was magic.

Angel hitched up her skirt to see how her legs were doing. They were fuzzy with unshaven hair.

> 'My God,' said Angel. 'You girls need me. I'm the most important part of us; why do you keep denying me?'

She made them go round the corner to the all-night beautician in Bond Street, and had her legs waxed in the old-fashioned way, with hot beeswax, smeared over the skin with a spatula, allowed to cool, and then ripped off. The process produced a smoother and more enduring finish than the lighter, less painful, quicker drying synthetic waxes now available.

3

A Mother Returns

Sara and Tully sat at either end of their polished mahogany table. The new maid, Nawal, brought in veal escalopes, mashed potatoes, carrots and peas. She was a plump and pretty girl from Iran. The Agency had relented and allowed Sara one more chance. Ayla had left, gone to kinder, steadier employers, claimed the Agency; further justification, if any were ever needed, of her employee's delinquency. Nawal's fingers on the vegetable bowl had left a grubby mark behind. Sara said nothing. Tully sniffed at the claret before pouring the wine from the full bottle into their bleakly sparkling glasses.

'You don't think she's watered it?' asked Sara, almost eagerly.

'How could she?' said Tully. 'It's full.'

'She could have drunk some and then watered it,' observed Sara. 'If all the Cabinet are as trusting as you, Tully, I'm not surprised we've turned into a nation of scroungers. I suppose you do have to open it beforehand and then leave it? It always seems so unwise.'

'It's expensive wine,' said Tully. 'It has to air.'

They were neither of them in a good mood. Wendy's death had made Tully surprisingly sad. He had lost an enemy, and that can be hard.

'I was born in that house,' said Sara. 'Now it goes to a stranger.' She bent over her escalope, forcing knife and fork into rubbery toughness; tears fell on to the hard coating of crumbs. Tully noticed.

'You won't need salt,' he said tenderly. 'That's something.'

'Wendy was the only family I had,' said Sara. 'Now I've got no one. I never even had a mother.'

'You have me,' said Tully, hurt.

'I know, darling,' she said. 'We found each other.'

He moved from the far end of the table, taking knife, fork and plate with him, and sat close to his wife. Their knees touched.

'We shouldn't have waited for them to die,' said Sara. 'We should have moved into Lodestar and nursed them. I would have done it. There were enough rooms there for everyone, but so dark and closed up it never occurred to me. I always imagined if I opened the wrong door bats would fly out and get into my hair.'

'There are doors in the House of Commons like that,' said Tully, darkly. 'So many corridors, none of them understood: the same men scurrying down them through the centuries. Who's dead, Tweedledums, who's alive, Tweedledees, it's hard to tell. Men with tight waistcoats.' He tapped his own full belly affectionately. Sometimes they spoke like this: not often.

'But nothing would do for you or me,' said Sara, 'but we pull the place down, start over, and make a fortune.

And now we're thwarted. It isn't fair, but perhaps we deserve it.'

Sara gave up the struggle with the escalope. She had served her husband the better, more tender piece. Tully appreciated her gesture. With his superior skill, his greater dexterity, he cut up the meat on her plate as if she were a child. She ate, gratefully.

A blast of cold air filled the room and made the heavy, boring curtains shudder. Tully looked alarmed.
'It's only the front door opening,' said Sara.
'I didn't hear the bell ring,' said Tully.
'Perhaps it's the new girl letting in the burglars,' said Sara, but they both just sat and waited, leaning into one another, overwhelmed by emotions which came strangely to them, and when Una strode into the room, that was how she saw them.
'Well, well!' said Una. 'That's better than I would ever have expected back then when you were five. You actually found a man who likes you, Sara.'
'Mother!' cried Sara.

4

A Sniff Of Skin

Jelly had gone to work with not just her legs but her crotch shaved, and invited Brian Moss to put his hand up her skirt, feel and admire. Brian Moss was reluctant so to do.

'I don't want this thing between us to get too personal,' he said. 'You know that. I love Oriole very much. If she won't have sex with me it's because she's too tired, poor thing. Two children under five are a handful for anyone. We bring them up in the modern way, trying to develop their personalities, so they don't sleep much. I'm in charge by night. Elsie has nightmares, Annie gets colic. I get back into bed with Oriole: I may be cold but I'm loving, yet even in her sleep my wife rolls away from me. I seem to disgust her. She says my feet smell, and she doesn't like the texture of my skin. She claims it's clammy. But I do love her. I expect she's right about me. I'm just a hopeless sort of person.'

'Feel my skin where I've shaved it,' was all his secretary said. 'You'll find it interesting. Smooth, but with a kind of prickle just beneath the surface; a very white skin there because, when you come to think of it, between the legs very seldom meets the light of day.'

But Brian Moss was not to be tempted: not by words,

descriptions, nor open invitation as she led his hand upward, rubbed his finger against the shaven skin, tried to guide it inward into the soft damp warmth of the split.

'I don't know what's got into you,' said Brian Moss. 'You never used to be like this. Oh God, is it all my fault?'

And he lit a cigarette, finding a packet in an open drawer. 'You see!' he said. 'You've started me smoking again. Oriole made me give it up when she was pregnant. Passive smoking can do untold damage to unborn babies.'

'And to you, too,' said Angel. 'But I don't suppose your wife mentions that.'

'You don't seem to think well of wives,' said Brian Moss nervously. It seemed to him his secretary was behaving oddly. He would have to get rid of her; he had let himself get involved with a seriously disturbed young woman. He would miss her but that could not be helped.

'I certainly don't,' said Angel. She was sitting on the edge of the desk, removing her little lace-up boots Jelly had bought at Marks & Spencer's. She let them fall. First the right, then the left. She kept her eyes on Brian Moss. 'And your sort is the worst. She's a cat wife, from the sound of it.'

'What's a cat wife?' he asked, though who knew where the conversation might lead.

'A cat wife wants a home and a man to pay for it, and someone to father her children and when she's got it, she snarls and drives him away. And if she can make him feel bad, she will.'

She was unbuttoning her sweater, undoing her bra, wriggling out of her skirt.

'Don't do this,' he begged. 'Someone might come in.'

She ran over to the door, neat bosom bouncing, locked it, took the key and threw it from the open window. He heard the faint dry sound of its landing two floors below.

'I know your wife's kind well,' said Angel, undoing his belt, unfastening buttons, unzipping his zip. 'And thank God for her. One man's misfortune is any whore's good fortune.'

'Don't do this,' he begged. 'You're not well. You've been working too hard. Get dressed. Get Lois to go down and get the key and let us out of here.'

'Not till I've had my fun,' said Angel. 'I deserve some too. It's my lunch hour. You'll have to do as I say, or I'll tell Oriole about you and me.'

'There is nothing to say about you and me,' said Brian Moss, 'that I won't deny at once. I'm not afraid of blackmail.'

'I'll tell her about the mole on your thing,' said Angel, giggling. 'Sometimes it seems little and sometimes it seems big. It's a matter of proportion.'

'I'll say you saw it by accident,' said Brian Moss but, since he was by now naked to the waist and leaning against the wall, his statement lacked conviction. His belt fastened one hand to the handle of a drawer above his head; his tie fastened the other to its fellow; his penis was slowly and powerfully rising.

'What have you done to me?' he demanded. 'I'm completely helpless.'

He saw the expression on his secretary's face alter. The mild look disappeared: she was prim and herself again.

'Good Lord,' said Jelly, backing off aghast, 'I'm so sorry, Mr Moss. I don't know what came over me.'

The door handle was rattling. It was Lois.

'I can't open the door, Mr Moss,' called Lois through the keyhole. 'It seems to be locked. Lady Musgrave's here to see you. What shall I say to her?'

Tears now started to Jelly's eyes. When she spoke, it was with a clipped and rather painful gentility.

'You'll have to forgive me,' said Lady Rice to Brian Moss. 'I'm afraid I'm having a hard day. I'm not really a secretary at all, though I have excellent office skills, gained during my marriage. Sometimes I feel I've been sleepwalking for years. You know?'

The expression changed again: hardened; became determined. The voice was brisk and cold.

'Personally, Mr Moss, I think this serves you right,' said Angelica, and then she called to Lois. 'Come on in. You'll find a spare key in my right-hand drawer.'

'Miss White,' said Brian Moss, struggling with his bonds, 'you're fired.'

'Thank God for that,' said all of them at once, in the attractive timbred voice they had lately developed. Brian Moss had taken credit for that too.

5

Official Business

Una walked in through the door as Lois opened it and Jelly walked out. Una looked after Jelly, not without admiration, and moved to undo Brian Moss's bonds.

'I can't thank you enough,' said Brian Moss, re-establishing his circulation, re-arranging his clothing. 'My secretary has had some kind of fugue. A *crise*. Perhaps we should postpone this meeting?'

'On no account,' said Una. She still had Brian Moss's tie in her hand. She smoothed it out and tied it for him, pulling up the knot just a little savagely around his neck. The tie was yellow, with a pink and red pattern but did little to give the impression he hoped to achieve – that of a wild man falsely imprisoned in a grey suit.

'I think it would be better if we did,' said Brian Moss. 'This has been a most upsetting incident,' but Una was persistent.

She had been thinking the matter over, she said. She would take over Lodestar House for eighteen months, and use it at her discretion. After which she would give it to her daughter Sara, before the leasehold expired. Sara and Tully would have ample time to make the fortune they felt they deserved.

'That's very generous of you,' said Brian Moss. Lois had brought him a cup of tea.

'Poor little bitch Sara,' said Una. 'She always worried that it was her fault I left home. She was right to worry; I couldn't stand her – nobody could. She shouldn't have been born, and it showed. No charm; my stepfather's child. Wendy's second husband. These family relationships get too complicated to bear. I was only sixteen when she was born. I got her into a nursery as soon as I could, but the holidays never seemed to end, so I left her to my mother.'

Brian Moss could see Jelly packing up her desk in the outer office. She was slamming and stamping about. He tried to concentrate on what Una Musgrave was saying. 'Do feel free to confide in me,' he said, falsely. 'Solicitors have good shoulders to cry upon. So – you were a victim of child abuse? A dreadful but these days, alas, an all too familiar tale.'

Una snorted. 'I was an abusing child,' she said. 'He didn't stand a chance. I'd gone right off my mother at the time, I seem to remember. I didn't want Sara growing up to do to me what I'd done to her. A customer who was a shrink told me I was right to leave the child. If I'd stayed, she'd only have repeated my pattern.'

Brian Moss could see Lois as she bent over to help Jelly with the lower drawers. Perhaps he could persuade her to stay. It was only by comparison to Jelly that Lois appeared plain. Plain girls, in any case, were more stable, less neurotic, than the pretty ones.

'No one's drama,' said Una Musgrave, 'I can see, is of any real consequence to anyone else. You're not even listening. As it happens, Lodestar House turning up in

259

my life again is a fine example of the synchronicity which has accompanied my path through life. Ever read Jung?'

'No,' said Brian Moss.

'If you don't think a little more about me and a little less about your dick,' said Una Musgrave, 'I won't pay you for this session.'

Brian Moss paid attention.

'A house with many rooms is a wonderful thing,' said Una. 'In the house of our dreams each room represents a different aspect of the self. Did you know that?'

'I don't dream much,' said Brian Moss, 'nowadays. I'm far too tired. I have two children under five.'

On her way out of Brian Moss's office, Una stopped in her booted stride at Jelly White's desk.

'If ever you want a job,' she said, 'get in touch with me. You're just the type I like.'

'What type is that?' asked Jelly.

'Demure and devious,' said Una, 'and not what you seem. Mind you, what woman is? I see you as someone with a past that you roll up as you go, so you hardly remember what happened yesterday, let alone last night.'

'It can be a problem,' said Jelly, 'and getting worse.'

'It's always darkest before dawn. Your lipstick's smudged,' said Una, taking out a little frilled cotton handkerchief from her pocket and dabbing at the corner of Jelly's mouth. 'But it's a useful little mouth, I can tell.'

6

Angel Goes Home

'I want to see Rice Court,' said Angel to Lady Rice, erstwhile mistress of what was now described in guide books as a stately home. 'Let's ask Rameses to take us down one Saturday: I can meet Edwin face to face at last. Why not?'

'I'll tell you why not,' said Lady Rice. 'Because it would break my heart. Because I would be humiliated and ashamed. Because I am like the generality of women who, knowing they are discarded, prefer to limp away, making no claim, hoping the earth will just swallow them up.' And she had another fit of weeping, from which Jelly had to extract her, with eye-masks and a pot of tea from Room Service.

'Anyway,' said Lady Rice, 'Rameses is unreliable. Sometimes he turns up, sometimes he doesn't. I think he is two-timing us.'

'Or perhaps he sees through us,' said Jelly.

'Or is disturbed by our complexities,' said Angelica.

'Or perhaps we just plain exhaust him,' said Angel.

But Angelica and Jelly sided with Angel, feeling she needed a reward for weeks of good behaviour, over-ruling Lady Rice's reluctance, and the very next Saturday there was Angel, lounging on a street corner, waiting for Ram, wearing grunge: that is to say layers of darkish fabric alternating with snatches of lace: men's socks and heavy boots, the latter bought second-hand on a market stall. A tight satin vest beneath a torn leather jacket compressed and raised her breasts.

Ram's sleek Volvo turned into Davies Street: there was his client, leaning into a lamp-post, blowing smoke into the air, like Marlene Dietrich. The car slowed, drew in on a double-yellow line.

'Is that fashion?' he asked her. 'Or disguise?'

'Neither,' said Angel. 'I am my true self again.'

He held the door open for her. He was not wearing his uniform. Passers-by stared.

'I like a woman of many moods,' he said, as they set off for the North. 'Anyone else and I wouldn't have done it. I like to play football on Saturdays.'

'Women tend to be more than one person,' said Angel, 'at the best of times. Men get just to be the one.'

'I like all of yours,' he ventured, but she did not encourage such intimacies. It was his body she cared for, nothing else. He contented himself with saying that if he were her he wouldn't go and see an ex-husband dressed like that and she said it was fortunate then he wasn't her, and they fell silent. And when, at a service station, Angel invited him to join her in the back of the car, he refused, politely. She was clearly under considerable stress. Lately he'd caught sight of her from time to time, reflected in his mirror, gesticulating, mouthing, and murmuring to herself, sometimes slapping her own wrist.

She would speak to him in different voices, offering contradictory instructions. He had worked out that there were four of them. Angel had started things off: now he preferred Angelica: she was more of a challenge. Though Angel's instant enthusiasm, instant response, was certainly useful when time was at a premium, and privacy doubtful. He didn't like leaving his women unsatisfied: Angelica frequently was. Jelly induced a kind of guilty, heady excitement which could keep him awake at night thinking about her. Lady Rice required words of love, and he'd oblige, falsely, but then she was being false too. Offer a quarter of the self and you could hardly expect a whole self offered in return. His client could have his body and that was that, and not even that if she looked like freaking out.

Lady Rice hoped to see desolation and to hear lamentation as the Volvo approached the house, but she could see that the grounds were in good order, dreaming in the summer sun, that horses grazed tranquilly in the fields; that nature conspired against her, to say 'See how well we get on without you!'. Signposts – well-painted and placed – now pointed to Rice Stables, Kennels and Cattery, as well as to The Manor House, The Restoration Gardens, The Maze, Gift Shop, Pottery, Theme Park, Exhibition and Toilets. Oh yes, there had been progress.

Visiting families wandered around the outside of the house; well-behaved children finished their ice creams before entering, and there were enough bins everywhere to take their debris. The glaziers had been: cracked panes of fine, crisp glass, saved in Angelica's day because of their rarity – some being over two hundred years old – had been brutally replaced with young, thick, tough, even glass, but otherwise Lady Rice could find no fault with what had been done to the place. It was bitter.

Lady Rice introduced herself to the unknown woman at the ticket desk – there had been staff changes, too – and noticed that entry prices had doubled. She was a friend of the family: could she see Sir Edwin? The receptionist looked doubtful, but lifted the telephone and got through to the private wing and said to whoever answered, 'Sir Edwin has a visitor, Lady Anthea,' and Angel thought that is not fair: anyone who didn't know better would assume that Anthea was Edwin's wife, and took the title from him. She felt even that singularity had been taken from her.

Lady Rice waited. Visitors looked at her curiously. Lady Rice noticed that the price asked for cream teas had risen, too. The oak floorboards which she had hand-waxed to a deep sheen were now covered with a practical polymer sealant: a little notice even said, 'Floors at Rice Court sealed by the Polyserve Company' – no doubt the price for the job had been reduced on account of it. Anthea, she had to admit, saved money where she could, spent it where she should.

Lady Rice at that moment had an out-of-body experience. She looked down at herself from a high corner of the hall, and saw that she was at that moment wholly Angelica; she wondered, from a place of safety, at the source of Angelica's deep distress. Why did she stand here, dressed ridiculously as herself a dozen years ago, on the threshold of a house which had never been really home, in which she had gone to such great lengths not to have children by a man to whom she could so easily and quickly have become a stranger? What did she miss?

The respect of others? She had scarcely had that in the first place, she could now accept. Friends? Only the ones who had betrayed her: whose whole instinct seemed to be to use her as a scapegoat. Lady Rice perceived that Angelica suffered as a soldier defeated in a just war suffers – not merely on account of pain, loss and personal humiliation, but because the hordes of destruction seem to have won over the few valiant champions of what everyone recognised to be honourable and good.

Lady Rice was joined by Jelly and Angel, and watched from the safety of distance as Angelica faced Anthea; who now came through the green baize door that divided the house into two parts: the public and the private.

Anthea was pregnant. Angelica could not say how many months, but it was evident that she was; though it seemed not to be a matter which concerned Anthea much. She moved without the self-conscious languor which many a pregnant wife assumes: rather she was brisk and purposeful.
'Can I help you?' asked Anthea.

 'Did you hear that? She doesn't even recognise me,' mourned Lady Rice. 'I am altogether diminished, dismissed. I am something from the past, the barren wife, the one who doesn't even count.'
 'All that work in the house for nothing,' said Jelly. 'The waters just close over you and it's as if you'd never been.'
 'Pregnant!' said Angel. 'That's a real facer, a real bummer. Angelica's going to cry.'
 'I won't have that,' said Lady Rice. 'Not in front of Anthea.'

Angelica's face worked as the others joined her. The woman at the ticket desk was looking sympathetic, concerned and frightened all at once. Anthea merely looked irritated. Angelica could see herself in the mirror: a mad woman, wearing peculiar clothes, hair in a mess, face all over the place, mumbling aloud, not able to reply to a simple, formal question.

Edwin came through the green baize door, to Anthea's apparent relief. He seemed cheerful, if fresh out of bed, though it was past midday: his white linen shirt was still unbuttoned: his black chest hairs showed. He had lost weight. He began to fasten his shirt buttons even as Angelica watched. Anthea drew aside her lover, the father of her child, the better to discuss what to do with the mad-woman.

> 'He's so familiar yet so strange,' said Angelica to the others. 'I know everything and nothing about this man. That small part of him a woman could ever have, another woman has. For the rest, he's his own man. His habits will have changed: for all I know he no longer snores when he lies on his back; he eats margarine, not butter; has changed his newspaper, reads the sports' section first, the art pages last. It's as if together once we made a plum tree, but the plum tree put out suckers from the roots, and from one of them a sapling grew, and all the strength of the tree followed: so now the old tree is weak and old, and the young one flourishes. To stop that happening, gardeners ring-prune the roots of good plum trees: to forestall the plans of saplings to take over –'
> 'Angelica,' said Lady Rice, 'do be quiet. There is no escape from this.'

'He's even better looking than I remember,' said Jelly, sadly. 'And I went and lost him. He wasn't stolen, he was lost. And I don't blame Anthea. I lost him by neglect and inattention.'

'Fine clutch of masochists you lot are,' said Angel. 'If we're going to mumble, does it have to be so pitiable? Couldn't we just kill Anthea altogether? Just fall upon her and tear her to bits, gouge out her baby and gnaw its disgusting foetal heart from its body?'

'Angelica!' said Edwin. 'My God, is that you?'

Anthea peered closer at Edwin's unwanted wife, and looked quite startled.

'Don't be alarmed, my dear,' said Edwin to Anthea. 'When I first met Angelica, she looked like this a lot of the time; she'd go into mad-woman mode at the drop of a hat or a sniff of cocaine. She was ten years younger then and could get away with it, just about. Angelica always has modes – there was this one; then we went through the housewife and hostess, and then the wronged wife mode, the best of all. The getting to the real her was a long, dry path and in the end not worth the journey. And then, thank God, you came along.'

'I do exist,' said Angelica. 'I do, I do. Why do you speak about me, not to me?'

'Because you're in my past,' said Edwin, 'not my present.'

His voice, like his looks, was both familiar and strange, being now pitched in intimacy to another.

'See, he hates me,' said Jelly.

'People change according to whom they are with,' said Angelica dreamily, 'and very quickly. The way the head is held, the brusqueness or otherwise of speech; all mixes and melds between couples. To share a bed is to share a soul.'

'Only if you fuck a lot,' said Angel. 'Can we get back to business?'

'You're crazy,' said Edwin. 'A crazy woman. I'm well rid of you.'

'I am not mad,' said Angelica to her husband, 'just unhappy. You've made me unhappy, destroyed me.' But she could no longer be quite sure whether she was speaking aloud or talking to her sisters.

'Don't be unkind to her for my sake,' said Anthea to Lady Rice's husband. 'See how upset she is. She's no threat to me.'

'She is to me,' said Edwin. 'She's after my money. Do you know how I met her? An unlucky accident. A friend took me backstage after a show. Angelica Barley, she called herself, after the village. Barley. Our village. My village. She never even asked permission. She was quite someone on the pop scene, but only for a very short time. A seven-day wonder: a release called "Kinky Virgin". That's what she was, technically. A virgin. That was her stock in trade. All comers could, if you'll forgive the crudity, sodomise her senseless, suck her off rigid, do everything to her any way but straight. I joined the line for Kinky's backstage favours. In those days I was innocent and so longed for experience. I was the first one to get in there, properly, in the manner a missionary would recommend but I had to get married in order to do it.'

'I don't believe I'm hearing this,' said Jelly.

'We may not be,' said Angel. 'We may be remembering it. In fact I remember that time very well. I'm not ashamed. I loved every minute of it. I was getting my way, so I could afford to keep in the background. You lot didn't know about me, until celibacy made me surface, but I was always there.'

'You're having me on,' said Lady Rice. 'You're making this up. I was a virgin when I married, not just in fact but in thought. I was innocent and pure. Everyone knew. It was all there in my PR handouts. A virgin! Amazing in that day and age.'

'Kinky Virgin', hummed Angel. 'Was the band called after you, or after the song? Kinky Virgin. Call me Violet. Violate your Violet.'

'Shut up,' cried Angelica. 'Shut up, fucking shut up!'

'Language!' That was Jelly, sharpish.

'Kinky Virgin', sung Angel. 'Inviolate. Push me this way, push me that way; call me Violet. Shrinking Violet. Slaver me and slobber me, turn me over, cover me. Kinky Virgin Violet. Inviolate.'

'I remember nothing of any of that,' said Lady Rice. 'I'm sure those weren't the words. Just get that tune right out of my head!'

Angelica was already letting out a piercing inner howl to blot the tune, to drown this inconvenient, embarrassing and traumatic rumour, posing as actual information.

'Silly old cow, you are,' said Angel. 'I remember every detail, every word. And that is how Edwin met me; bent backwards over a soiled velvet couch which travelled everywhere with the band. Astonishing we lasted so long.'

'And you killed our father,' added Lady Rice in passing, 'from the sheer shock of it all. His little Angel.'

269

'Shall I call a doctor?' asked the woman from Information. 'She's acting so strangely.'

And indeed a kind of ethnic sing-song chant was now coming from Lady Rice's lips: some prayer to a strange God which had to be repeated and repeated, an appeal for divine intervention – Dear God, whoever and whatever you are, save me, save me! – with undertones of the strangled sound the lips actually manage to make when a dreamer wakes screaming, or so it seems to the sleeper, from a nightmare. All that passion, all that effort, to end in a little mewling sound.

'I'll speak to her,' said Edwin. 'She'll be okay. She'd get like this.'

'What a nightmare for you, darling,' said Anthea. 'What a nightmare!'

Edwin led Angelica outside to the grassy slope where in better days they'd watched the chimney fall, and thereby alter their future and fortunes: destroying one, creating the other. Edwin took out his handkerchief – a cotton handkerchief, newly washed and ironed, where once a stretch of toilet roll had done – and dabbed his wife's eyes. She could see he would make a good father, and understood it had been wrong of her to deprive him of the opportunity, over the years.

'Angelica,' said Edwin, 'stop all this. You shouldn't be here. It's bound to upset you.'

Lady Rice could see Anthea standing on the front steps, pretending not to notice, not to keep an eye on what was going on; casually calling the dogs.

'I can't help it,' said Lady Rice. 'I'm your wife and I love you.'

'Angelica,' said Edwin, 'you are divorcing me and for very good reason. Anthea is pregnant. You and I have very little in common. I'm sorry if I hurt you just now. But we have to face the facts. It was an utterly unsuitable marriage. We were far too young. We tried and it failed. Let's just part and leave it at that. It's not as if we had children to complicate matters. We can be friends, can't we?'

Lady Rice was silent. Edwin re-adjusted the buttons on her blouse and waistcoat so that she appeared more decent. His touch was more like a nursemaid's than a lover's.

'Friends! I would so like us to be friends,' said Lady Rice to her sisters. 'Wouldn't that be nice!'

'Hang on a minute,' said Angelica.

'He's cheating us,' said Jelly.

'Don't trust him,' said Angel. 'Don't fall for it. He's trying to wriggle out of his financial responsibilities. Friendship today means no alimony tomorrow.'

'Perhaps we should think about friendship less,' said Lady Rice to her husband, 'and money more? I had a whole lot of the stuff when I started with you; now I have none.'

'You have become so mercenary,' Edwin lamented. 'You never used to worry about money.'

'That was when I had some,' she replied.

'I have none to spare, Angelica,' said Edwin. 'You know what this place costs to keep up. Why are you holding up the divorce?'

'Is that what I'm doing?' asked Lady Rice.

'Actually, it is,' said Jelly. 'You're between the Nisi and the Absolute, and you won't let the Absolute go through until there's a property settlement, and quite right too. I saw to that.'

'And Edwin wants to get married because Anthea's pregnant, so you're able to hold a pistol to his head,' said Angelica.

'Why do you do this behind my back?' cried Lady Rice.

'Because you stayed home crying,' said Angelica.

'I don't believe it was behind your back,' said Angel.

'You deceitful bitch! No wonder you don't have any freinds. Edwin's quite right: you're a mercenary cow who married him for his title. You deserve what you get. I'm glad you're unhappy.'

'I'm splitting, I'm splitting!' cried Lady Rice. 'I can't keep the shreds together: the perforations are tearing. I'm sorry, everyone . . .'

'The trouble with you,' said Edwin, 'was your right hand never knew what your left hand was doing.'

'Please don't put me in the past tense,' begged Lady Rice, 'or I'll vanish altogether.'

'Then don't you spite Anthea and the baby by holding me to ransom,' said her husband, father of another's child.

'I'll think about it,' said Lady Rice. 'I feel I'm writing life as it goes along, and someone's editing out all the good bits, and leaving in the bad.'

Ram's car edged round the drive and distracted Lady

Rice. He'd said he'd give her half an hour: after that he'd come and find her.

'It's humiliating,' said Angelica savagely, 'that we should now regard a chauffeur as a friend, just because he fucked us.'

'Keep your mind on what Edwin is saying,' said Jelly, 'for God's sake. Don't get distracted now, and don't start using language, or we'll be right back where we were before we married him.'

'You never were a lady,' said Angel, 'you were only ever a kinky virgin.'

'I'm astonished,' said Edwin, thus focusing his wife's mind again, 'that you can afford a chauffeur if you're as impecunious as your lawyer claims. You've probably been putting funds away in some Swiss bank account for years. Robert Jellico thinks you have. And you could always set up business as a Kinky Divorcee.'

'It just doesn't somehow have the same ring,' said Angel, drily, 'as Kinky Virgin.'

'That's more like my Angelica,' Edwin said, gratified. 'Sometimes I'd wonder where you'd gone. You walked and talked and fucked but you'd stopped being you. You were just another role-player: Lady Rice. Cheer up. Let me have my divorce. Rice Court needs its heir. All your future lies before you. You'll meet someone, the way I did. Have kids, settle down in some suburb. You'll live to bless the day I found you and Lambert on our bed.'

'Angelica,' said Jelly, 'you were really miserable married to Edwin. Listen to him now! Spiteful? He was always spiteful.'

'In and out, in and out,' said Angel, 'missionary position, and that was it. I had more fun as a

273

virgin. I feel quite sorry for Anthea, what with the kid and all. We've lost nothing.'

'Except marriage, love and justice,' said Angelica. 'Don't forget that. Don't take these things lightly or you devalue everything that went before.'

'But if he doesn't see the connection,' said Jelly, 'what's the point of it? Takes two to keep an ideal alive, and bouncing in the air.'

'One mark up for Evil,' said Ajax, out of nowhere, 'two marks down for Good. We plead Not Guilty to a crime against human aspiration. Edwin is guilty, you are not, Lady Rice. The Court of the Mind votes, decides.'

'Angel,' said Angelica, 'was that you talking just now?'

'No,' said Angel.

'I heard a man's voice,' said Jelly.

'It's just a friend of mine,' said Angel.

'You're having a relationship with him,' said Angelica. 'When we go to sleep – how dare you, who is he?'

'He's a brother to me, to us,' said Angel, frightened by their vehemence. 'Honestly.'

'It's really disgusting, Angel,' said Angelica, 'having a he in here with us. How long has he been about? It's spooky. It's rude. I hate it.'

'Then forget it,' said Angel, and Angelica did. 'Forget he even spoke.' And Jelly did. 'He's mine to dispose of. He's the one who tells our narrative; he has to, or else it's anarchy in here. He sorts us out and splits us up: to stop her taking an overdose. It's desperate in here.'

'I don't love Edwin any more,' said Lady Rice. 'I feel so much better all of a sudden. I searched inside me just now and found no love.'

'Thank God for that,' said the others in chorus. Angel alone heard Ajax speak: the others did not. She knew better than to mention him.

'I am the narrator. I move through the centuries,' Ajax said. 'I am the original idea; you are growing too strong, you are wearing me thin. A couple of you will have to go. Without a narrator we could vanish altogether. Desperate measures, desperate times.'

'So, what do you say?' asked Edwin. 'Five-hundred pounds a month alimony is more than generous. It's not as if there was a matrimonial home to sell! Just a stately home in hock to the Government.'

'I'll think about it,' said Lady Rice.

'It's more than you'd get on the dole. Do be reasonable. I'll put it up to seven-hundred-and-fifty, to show my goodwill.'

He spoke as a driver might to another after a collision which was none of his doing, courteous but disdainful, sighing inwardly about waste of time and money, but not too inwardly, to make sure the other was aware of the extent of the forbearance. Lady Rice was satisfied. She kissed him on the cheek to seal the contract. Anthea moved towards them.

'I hear what you say,' said Lady Rice. 'I'm glad we talked.'

'Let's just get out of here before I murder some-one,' said Angel.

'Let's get out of here,' said Jelly, 'and into some proper clothes. We look a sight.'

'Let's just get out of here,' said Angelica.

Edwin said as Lady Rice left, as he courteously closed the limousine door, 'Do give my regards to your mother when you see her.'
Edwin had never much liked Mrs White, a woman without style or substance, who had so singularly failed to prevent her daughter making a disc called 'Kinky Virgin' when she was just sixteen. Edwin spoke, as these days he so often did, with a double tongue. Why had she never noticed?
'Fucking hypocrite,' said Lady Rice, surprising herself.

'You told me he was good looking,' said Ram, on the way to Mrs White's new cottage. 'He's not much of a rival. Nice place, though.'

With every mile she travelled further from Rice Court, Lady Rice suffered more. She felt light-headed; she felt faint; as if the reason for her existence had gone; as if she'd been cut out of cardboard, as if in allaying her demons, her sorrowing sea-myths, she had allayed herself away altogether as well. She became one with her sea of sorrow: a mere flurry of spume and foam, catching the light for a minute, then breaking and bursting and gone. 'I'm going,' she said. 'The sea-myths are taking me with them.' But her sisters didn't hear, didn't even remember her: never found out what a sea-myth was.

Angel changed in the back of the car, out of the layers into skirt and T-shirt. She failed to stop Rameses watching in the mirror, but otherwise allowed him no further liberties: the other two prevented her, kept her tied to the mast of her majority respectability, her majority lack of desire, other than in the pursuit of her own financial interests.

'We need a little space to ourselves for once, a little time as well,' Angelica pleaded with Angel, and Angel shrugged and let her sisters, who appeared to be united on this point, have their way. They granted they needed a little psychic space: after the encounter with Edwin, time to recover. So Ram stayed for once in the front of the car.

7

A Short Visit To Mrs White

'Mum,' said Jelly to Mrs Haverley, once Mrs White, 'I can't remember much about myself as a girl.'

'I'm not surprised,' said Mrs White. 'All those drugs, all that drink, and all that sex. I wouldn't want to remember it if I were you. Until the day you got married and became your husband's responsibility, you were a nightmare.'

'Why didn't you tell me?' asked Jelly.

Mrs White looked startled.

'I didn't know I was meant to,' said Mrs Haverley, puzzled. 'You seemed happy enough, up there in the Big House, looking down on the rest of us, employing your own school friends as servants. Nose in the air. Never even came to visit me. You were ashamed. Everyone knew it. Shouldn't you bring that young man in? The one who's driving the big car?'

'He can wait,' said her daughter, grandly. 'He's only the chauffeur. He can circle the village if he's bored.'

Mrs Haverley now lived in the house where the previous Mrs Haverley had lived with her husband Gerald throughout their marriage. The first Mrs Haverley had died of a stroke after the divorce, but before the property settlement had been made final. The house had therefore passed into her ex-husband's name. Gerald's daughter Mary, still unmarried and proud of it, now lived with her father and stepmother. She had given up protest and now just enjoyed the ex-Mrs White's cooking, and the habit she had of ironing and folding clothes before putting them into drawers, which her real mother had never done. The first Mrs Haverley would wash and dry clothes but left them for the family to pick out of the laundry basket. Sometimes they would need washing again before this happened.

'Don't you feel peculiar living here?' Jelly asked her mother. 'Using her teapot? In her bed? Doesn't she haunt you?'

But apparently not.

'It's really nice living in another woman's home,' said the new Mrs Haverley. 'Other people manage to have the light switches in all the right places, and enough sockets to go round. She didn't stint herself, I must say. Nearly drove poor Gerald to bankruptcy, but what did she care?'

Angelica hurt her teeth on a rock cake that had stayed in the oven for too long.

'Shit!' she said, and her mother raised her eyebrows and said, 'If you don't like them, don't eat them. A good rock cake's always hard.'

'Mum,' asked Angelica,' did I talk to myself a lot when I was a child?'

'All the time,' said Mrs White. 'Used to drive your father mad. We'd be woken in the morning by the sound of children playing. Different voices and all. But there'd only ever be you in there.'

'Boys voices too?'
'Oh yes,' said Mrs Haverley. 'Boys and girls. All in there together!'

She served as good a scone and as bad a jelly as ever. She was an uneven cook. But with her change of name, as it happened, she no longer seemed to Angelica to be her mother at all: Angelica saw herself as orphaned. Mrs White had transmuted into Mrs Haverley, and in the sea-change lost maternal status. She had become just another of the older generation of Barley housewives. Plump and stocky legged, with happily sagging faces and breasts; their eccentricities and individuality, though no doubt there, secrets too well kept for even their owners to perceive them. The women slumped happily into the common mass; doing themselves up for their children's weddings, for Christmas, for funerals. Only occasionally, when sexual longings, pleasures and disgusts were concerned, when there was a swapping of partners, or a divorce, or tales of incest, did they bother to separate themselves out from others, take up separate attitudes, present their opposing views.

'Yes, boys as well,' said Mrs Haverley. 'Boys and girls all in that little body together. What a marvel!'
'You didn't say anything to anybody?'
'No. It kept you quiet while we lay in of a morning. You all seemed to get on well enough. Your Dad and I would joke about it. "No only-child problems for Jelly," he'd say. And I'd say, "but when she gets to teenage, will it be decent? Supposing they get off with one another?" But by the time teenage came the voices had stopped. There was just the one of you, and not a particularly nice one either, I'm sorry to say.'

    'Bitch,' said Angel. 'God, how I hated the fat,

complacent cow. I could have killed her. Can't we go home now? I can't stand even to see her.'
'Not yet,' said Angelica.

'Mum,' said Jelly, though the word came with difficulty to her lips, 'put your mind back to when Dad died. How did it happen? What was I like when it did? Because I seem to have forgotten.'
'I'd rather not say,' said Mrs Haverley, and at that moment Mr Haverley let himself cheerfully into the hall and presently joined them for tea. He ate cheese sandwiches with his right hand, while his left encompassed one of his wife's sturdy legs. Mary, his daughter, came in and out of the room, feeding dogs, tropical fish and guinea pigs, all already more than fat enough. Mary wore a diamond engagement ring. Jelly had vague memories of standing next to her at Choral Society concerts. She'd always sung off key.
'Do let me get on, dear,' said Mrs Haverley, trapped by the leg, but her new husband felt disinclined so to do, so she stayed where she was.

'Are you engaged, Mary?' asked Jelly, to distract attention from the sight of her mother and her stepfather in erotic communication, but Mary said no, it was just a ring her father had given her on her thirtieth birthday.

'Why don't you tell your girl the truth, dear,' said Gerald Haverley. Now he had finished his sandwich, his right arm shot out and he trapped his daughter's legs as well as his wife's. They all squealed happily.
'Might as well,' said Mrs Haverley. 'Once you stopped being little, Jelly, you seemed to take no notice of your father: whether he was there or not was of little or no

mind to you. You were sixteen and you'd just made your name with that dreadful record. He could just about get used to the music but someone sent him the lyrics, and he died in minutes, sitting in his chair. I used to think it was your first wife, dear,' she said to her husband, 'who sent him the lyrics. She could be spiteful, and she never liked Jelly. Jelly used to tell Mary about sex at choir practice. She thought she was a bad influence on Mary. But I knew she was wrong. I knew Jelly was a good girl at heart.'

'I remember now,' said Jelly. 'I remember you telling me my father was dead and me saying to you "but how could you tell the difference?" and I laughed and you hit me. I can see you were right to. It was no moment to be a smartarse.'

'Well, dear,' said Mrs Haverley, 'it wasn't very nice of you,' and she squealed and laughed as Mr Haverley started tickling up and down the leg and Mary squealed 'Me, me!'

'But then again,' said Jelly's mother, 'he wasn't your real father anyway, was he?'

The cottage window opened directly on to the street. Ram drew up the limousine just outside, so he could look directly through to where Jelly stood, and at the family scene within.

'But then you knew that, didn't you?' said Mr Haverley.

'Well, no, I didn't,' said Jelly.

Mrs Haverley, once Mrs White, said, 'It seemed to matter a lot once, but it doesn't any more, does it, dear? If you don't mind, why should I?'

Jelly White felt illegitimised, as if someone with no existence at all worked for Brian Moss, wrapped a wraithful tongue around his member: no, not even that kept her in this world: not even mouthfuls of his seed could keep her nourished; she was going, she was gone. Goodbye, goodbye, she called to her sisters, but it was too late, they did not hear; she was gone and no trace left behind.

'Who was my father, then?' asked Angelica.

'I had to marry Stephen, dear. I wasn't the sort to claim Welfare. It wasn't that Stephen and I weren't happy together, we were; he was just a lot older than me. That's what we'd end up doing, unmarried mothers like us. We'd marry someone older, for the house, and the comfort. Forget the sex. All that sex had ever done, so far as we could see, was get us into trouble. Or so we thought. Of course the world's a different place now.'

'You never told me.'

'I thought you would have guessed. Leave it at that, Jelly dear. You don't want to know anything more.'

'I do. Tell me about my real father.'

'Well, Jelly, at least it wasn't someone from a sperm bank. That I would be ashamed of. I was gangbanged by a football team behind the stands, after a match. I should never have gone. I never liked sport anyway, but I thought Georgie Best was going to be playing. It wasn't a nice experience, but not as bad as they make out, and that's all I can tell you, Jelly.'

'Don't call me Jelly.'

'It was your father's idea to call you Angelica. What did he think would happen? It would split into a dozen different nicknames. I told him but he wouldn't listen.'

'Don't call him my father.'

'He was a good man, and a good father to you. I'll call him what I want. Don't insult him.'

'What was the match?' asked Mary. 'Bet it was something dreary like Norwich v. Tottenham. And second eleven, not first eleven. My God, Jelly might be anyone's! Why has she always given herself such airs?'

'Don't be spiteful, Mary: sometimes you're so like your mother,' said Mrs Haverley. 'You can tell Jelly's upset. I was right not to tell her, wasn't I? Some things are better left in the closet, surely.'

'Whatever you do is right by me, sweetheart,' said Gerald Haverley, once prime mover at the PTA, now a man enjoying his prime, his hand moving so far up his wife's skirt that she squealed and Mary said mildly, 'Oh Dad, you'll shock Jelly.'

But Jelly was gone. They were talking to no one. Only Angelica and Angel remained.

8

Dilapidation

The stairs of Lodestar House were broken; the floorboards in the turret room were rotten; the whole place stank of ammonia and damp. Windows were so dirty they scarcely let in the light. Creepers had found their way between glass and frame. Plaster flaked from walls; paper shredded by tiny rodent teeth eddied in draughts from broken doors. The roof leaked: the rooms once occupied by Wendy and Congo were cold, forlorn and wretched: dejection added up to more than its filthy parts.

Brian Moss showed Una around the property. That is to say, he ventured as far as the foot of the staircase and said, 'A tragedy, a tragedy. The place is too far gone. I'll have it condemned. If I pull a few strings, I can get a demolition order, in spite of its Grade 1 listing.'

But Una said, looking back from halfway up the stairs, that the solicitor was unnecessarily gloomy. She would do the place up: it was the house where she'd been born. It had to be 'made good', in the builders' terminology. She'd hire someone competent to do it: she had very little time herself. She needed the place for an in-house residence for her Agency team. It was good for the team's morale to bring them all together under one roof from time to time. It fostered togetherness and she found it reduced the turnover rate. Good staff were hard to find, particularly in her line of work.

Brian Moss thought that even this strong woman was nervous of going further up the stairs. She was talking too much.

'I don't believe in ghosts,' said Brian Moss, 'but this place is spooky.'

'All the better,' said Una. 'The dead can be energising. My team will soon have them exorcised, in any case. Fancy mother letting the place get into a state like this.' And, thus restored by her own words, she went on boldly up the stairs, calling, 'Mother, mother Wendy? Are you there?' At which Brian Moss shivered and went outside and stood on the step; but even there the air seemed brackish, and a drop of water fell upon his nose from the vaulted stone archway above, and startled him. He longed to be back in his office; he wished old Catterwall had never taken the Musgrave family on as clients. They were all hopeless. He waited.

Una came out smiling.

'Mother's happy for me to do up the house,' said Una. 'She always meant to get round to it some time,' and, when Brian Moss looked askance, she said, 'Only joking!' He felt she was humouring him, and was not consoled. He looked at his watch: it had stopped.

A taxi drew up and a young woman stepped out. She was a stocky little thing, with a wide, low forehead from which dark curly hair sprang profusely. She had large eyes and a little mouth. Her bosom was high and plump. Brian Moss felt cheered at once.

'This is Maria,' said Una, 'my administrative assistant.'

'And you'll be the solicitor with the shoulder for crying on,' said Maria, little hand already on his arm. 'I used to be on the team but Una moved me sideways. I'm getting used to it now, but it did upset me. I'm a psychic, and the dead just don't seem able to stay away. And Una was right: it could interfere with my work.' She put her nose inside the door of Lodestar House. 'Oh my!' said Maria.

'A lot of creaks and groans,' said Una, 'even for an old house.'

'Sounds more like *cris de joie* to me,' said Maria, 'trying to get through from the other side. This place will do wonderfully. You were really born here?'

'I lived here on and off in my youth,' said Una. 'Till my mother threw me out. But I've made my peace with her.'

'What is this team you're talking about,' asked Brian Moss, more in nervous conversation than in interest. He had gone right off Maria. He moved out of her reach.

'Una's Happy Boys and Girls,' said Maria. 'And I really miss the work, but what Una says goes. That's how she is. We all adore her.'

And Una and Maria, the older and the younger woman, went back in to Lodestar House and Brian, the man, went back to his office, where Lois, whom he had persuaded to stay, waited for him.

9

Renovation

Angelica and Angel were left in partnership, if jobless, feeling lonely but proud; addenda to the self had been stripped away, adjuncts that had mistakenly been seen to be somehow central. Lady Rice, though a person of some ten years' standing, turned out to have been a mere offshoot of Rice Court, as if the building itself and not Edwin had created her, and then discarded her; had stirred in its derelict slumber one day (woken, perhaps by the sound of its own chimney falling through its own roof), decided to pull itself out of the mire, get its damp-courses mended, its kitchens refurbished, and so on; cast its eye upon Angelica on her grassy mound and decided, well, she'll do until something better comes along, and made a quasi Lady Rice of her. She had been a bit-part player in Rice Court's drama – a stand-in. And something better had indeed come along: Anthea; a slave to breed a new line of willing slaves, and Lady Rice, un-needed, had simply melted out of existence, dissolved into her own tears.

And as for Jelly, she'd seen herself as her father's daughter; she had sprung into existence with the qualities most likely to gratify that most boring man, and, once free of his genesis, and discovering the multiplicity of her fathers, understanding the impossibility of meeting all their requirements, of ever getting it right, had faded away; a little lone voice getting squeakier and smaller until all that was left was a heap of Marks & Spencer clothes and silence.

All this Angelica and Angel agreed upon, marvelling. They had never expected to be left in joint control. At first the happenstance exhilarated them. Then it made them anxious. Trauma, which created them, might also take them away. Angelica would complain of an empty black hole whirling away inside her: everything had been too sudden for her.

> 'I don't miss the others one bit,' Angel would say, to comfort her. 'Nag, nag, nag, night and day. Party poopers. Forget them.'

And Angelica missed Brian Moss and was hurt that he had been able to let her go so easily. She had never exactly enjoyed the intimacies they shared, but had seen them as some common point of reference; a bond between them. She had felt protected. Brian Moss was the kind of man she should have married.
This made Angel whistle with derisive glee. She didn't miss Brian Moss.

> 'It's your own fault about Brian Moss. You should never have opened the door to Lois. That wasn't my doing, that was yours. I want you to promise never to do anything like that again. You just don't know how to handle delicate situations.'
> 'I don't get us into them in the first place,' said Angelica. 'It's a real worry. With four of us we could move to a majority decision. And now it's

just you and me, God knows what will happen next. I wish I could meet some nice man.'

'Are you crazy?' said Angel. '"Some nice man", in my experience, is just some boring little creep who hangs around to stop you doing what you want. If they go away, what's the problem with them not being nice? Not-nice men are better in bed. Everyone knows.'

There were practical worries, too; how were they to survive?

'We can't go on living off Edwin's charge accounts,' said Angelica. 'Lady Rice could, fairly enough. But what's Edwin got to do with us any more? So far as I'm concerned, the marriage was entirely accidental; nothing more than an interruption. We're back to where we began.'

'But you can pick up such a good class of man at The Claremont,' protested Angel. 'And the beds are so soft and comfortable.'

'We are not going to be a whore,' said Angelica. 'And that's that. We've ended up in the wrong level of society. I'm the kind of person who lives modestly and comfortably in a leafy suburb somewhere. I'm sure I am. I have excellent secretarial and management skills; I might even get married again, and stay home and have babies.'

'What's marriage but legalised prostitution?' enquired Angel. 'What are wives but domestic slaves who work in the house and in the bed for their keep and no money? If I'd been around at the time, I'd never have allowed the marriage to Edwin. All work and no wages. Madness.'

'At least in marriage you get to choose your

master,' said Angelica. 'Whoring makes me feel out of control, and really depressed the next morning. You feel yourself getting addicted to chance. Whoever walks through the door, that's it.'

'But that's what I like,' said Angel. 'That's what's exciting. The absence of choice.'

Angelica preferred to call it masochism. Personally she prided herself on a delicacy of feeling. She saw the desire to pick and choose as entirely healthy, properly female: nature's way, in fact, of leaving a woman sexually responsive only to a man whose baby she could just about bear to conceive, even though a baby was the last thing on her mind.

'Crap,' said Angel. 'Sex is nothing to do with babies any more.'

But Angelica persisted: she would not consent to a life in which what she saw as a perfectly natural fastidious-ness had daily to be defied, overruled. The effort would exhaust her, she said. She would get the debased, dead-eyed look of the whore, and her mother would notice.

'Crap again,' said Angel. 'Research proves there's no telling who is and who isn't. And, as for mother, I thought you wanted never to see her again.'

Arguments, differences of opinion, gave them headaches. They were getting through too much paracetamol, too many sleeping pills. Angel was a heavier and longer sleeper than Angelica: guilt and anxiety, emotions felt only dimly by Angel, made Angelica wake first. She used the time to get her own way. One morning she wrote to

Barney Evans saying she would put up with Edwin's modest pensioning off: she would no longer fight her husband. Let him have his divorce. She had lost her appetite for justice. She posted the letter in the foyer box.

10

Perforation

One door shuts: another opens. The harder the slam, the greater the gust of air and the more dramatic the new opening.

'There's a phone call for you, Lady Rice,' said the bell-boy, even as the letter went in the box. 'Would you care to take it in the booth? We couldn't find you in your room.'

The call was from Una. She had seen Lady Rice in The Claremont bar the night before, when drinking with friends. Una had recognised Lady Rice as Brian Moss's departing secretary, had learned that she was a guest at The Claremont and had taken the liberty of contacting her this morning. It was nothing to do with Una what was going on, but if Lady Rice, or whoever, was in need of a job, she might have one to offer her.

Angelica agreed to call on Una in her Whitehall offices. She had no recollection of being in the bar the previous evening. So far as she could remember, she'd stayed in her room watching television. On the other hand, she could not remember the programmes she'd watched.

'Angel,' said Angelica in alarm, 'we're not just perforated any longer. We've split.'

But there was no reply.

PART FIVE

Una's Happy Boys
And Girls

1

A Menu Of Permutations

This was Una's belief:

– that nature, in the beginning, had crudely divided the human race into two genders, male and female. Men had cocks, women had cunts; that was that. Go forth and multiply, was all nature had to say on the subject.

– but that the cock/cunt divide was now obsolete. Sexual desire and procreation had separated themselves out. 'Men' could no longer be defined by cock, 'women' by cunt: there was a menu of permutations in between. Being hung with a penis, being split by a vagina, was arbitrary anyway. Personality was laid down at the moment of conception, said Una, according to the happenstance of combining intertwining, inherited genes. Gender comes later, she claimed: a matter of chromosomes; a flood of oestrogen, a flood of testosterone working in that base, nothing to do with *us*. Society continues to collude with nature, which is crude and barbaric, and determined we shall continue to multiply while we are equally determined not to; people grow miserable as they try to do as expected and force their sexuality in the direction of their hung-edness or otherwise. Forget it, says Una.

– she, Una, will set things right if she can; so that anyone could be everything; everyone, anything.

Una's intention was to turn Lodestar House into a brothel. She was never one to waste an opportunity, and if that brothel was to be for the dead as well as the living, as Maria assured her it could be, so much the better. If Una's reward could only be in the afterlife, and an enigmatic one at that, for the dead had no means of handing money over, what did Una care? Money was the least of her problems. She had accumulated more than enough over the decades, from the pockets of the guilty and the grateful. Una's salvation after death was more to the point: it would be useful to have friends and influence people in the hereafter as well as here on earth. Maria did not discount it.

Though Una herself saw nothing to apologise for in her profession – and could argue well enough that she provided a useful social service, offering relief to the frustrated, mercy for wives, the saving of young women from the attacks of sex-starved strangers, and so on, the formal censure of society worried her. She wanted to make amends. She wanted, like anyone else, to be thought well of.

The living sought their contentment, their happiness, their fulfilment, their freedom from anxiety and guilt, through the ecstasies of the flesh.

'But, Maria,' protested Una, 'isn't it altogether too late

for the dead? They have no flesh but only bones, and bones rubbing together create only a squeak and some fine white powder, and no observable pleasure.'

But Maria swore it was never too late; she was in contact with the dead; they'd told her otherwise. Their pleasures were voyeuristic, but real enough. The dead were always present anyway, Maria swore, whenever the living fucked. That was their treat. The living should accordingly join in fleshly congress as much as possible; a notion that suited Una. The little death of orgasm acted as a kind of one-way presentation brothel mirror: on the one side the observers, the dead; on the other the observed, the living, at their most alive, their most powerful at the moment of orgasm, always a magnet for the dead. The air chattered with their presence at such times, but who ever noticed?

Lodestar House, Maria claimed, was alive with opportunistic ghosts. Oscar, Violet, Wendy, Congo; and Maria reported sighting a skinny man who looked like an executioner, and another who seemed to be a pirate, a Tinkerbell-lookalike – but probably vicious – little fairy; just outside the side door crouched a line of Bedouins. 'You're deranged,' said Una. 'You're over the top,' but Maria just shrugged, and said it made no difference to her whether anyone believed her or not, and it made no difference to the ghosts either.

2

Touting Talent

Una had twelve happy boys and girls on the team. This team consisted, officially, of three heterosexual females, two lesbians, one transsexual, one transvestite, two gay men and three heterosexual males – or as thus self-defined; though to work for Una required them to be able and willing to move freely between at least three other gender subdivisions without protest or personal difficulty.

'Personal difficulty' could make itself evident mid-trick, that was the problem, and difficulties came in many forms. Maria's problems with the other world were one kind – clients could be put off their stroke by ectoplasm. The man in the blond wig and high heels could have quite another. If not properly liberated for gender conditioning, he/she could upset him/herself, or worse, his clients, by suddenly shuddering, pulling back from some intimate activity and crying aloud in psychic pain, 'But what is going on here? Does this make me a lesbian, or what?' And doubt would even end in violence, as primitive, instinctive passions surfaced, with their mad insistence that seed should not be wasted, not spilt into infertile ground, making both men and women murderous. But such events, thank God, were rare. If the ambience was pleasant, the atmosphere good, civilisation and civility survived.

'It's all very well,' said Una to Maria, on their return to Whitehall, 'but it will cost the earth to convert Lodestar House, to bring it back to life, to give it back its atmosphere. I could do better renting some big house in Mayfair, converted already, the way other people do.'
'It will cost you heaven if you don't,' said Maria bleakly, and her little face was crumpled and wizened, as if she were her own grandmother. She was convincing enough, old or young: Una capitulated.

That evening in The Claremont bar where they were enjoying a pleasant, and purely social, evening, Maria nudged Una and said, 'Look over there – she's a split!'

Maria was speaking of a pretty blonde girl in a tight black dress, long-legged and giggly, leaning up against the bar, looking no different from many another of her kind, talking to the barman.
'What do you mean? How can you tell?' demanded Una.
'I can tell by her aura. There's two or three in there.'
'Like you and your grandmother?'
'Quite different,' said Maria, patiently. 'My grandmother just visits me when I need advice. Forget her. This girl has at least two female, one male, permanently resident. She could take my place on the team.'
'I know who that is,' said Una, thoughtfully. 'She's also Brian Moss's ex-secretary.'

Later she asked the barman if he knew the girl. He replied, 'She's resident here. Name of Lady Rice. You'd

301

never think it, would you, someone like her? But divorce affects some people like that. She'll wake up murdered one morning if she's not careful.' He looked Una up and down. He'd seen a few like her in his time, his expression said, at work in the bar. But he warmed to her, as most people did.

'Get her out of my hair,' he said. 'Save her from herself. She'd be better off going professional. She drinks too much.'

3

Restoration

'There's a difference between professional and amateur,'
said Una to Angel in the Whitehall offices, 'especially if
you're working for me. You must put the client first, not
yourself.'
'I always do,' said Angel.
'It's the "I" you need to forget,' said Una. 'My clients
pay you to be what *they* want, so they can discover who
they are. What you are is neither here nor there, and the
point is you must never try to know. The minute you
have categorised yourself, you're in trouble.'
'It suits me,' said Angel, and it seemed to her to do so,
though she couldn't be sure why.
> 'Angel,' begged Angelica. 'Don't do it. This is not
> for us.'

Angel didn't seem to hear: Angelica, angry, managed to
walk her into a door when she was leaving the room. It
was a sharp and sudden blow to the temporal lobes.
Angel felt quite dizzy. She put her hand to her head and
discovered a bump and a graze; but fortunately no blood.

'Do you have trouble with your physical co-ordination?'
asked Una, puzzled, when Angel had recovered.

'Not that I know of,' said Angel. 'I just didn't notice that the door wasn't open.'

'It's one of her other selves,' said Maria, who was sitting in on the interview. 'She's angry. That's not so good. She might be destructive.'

'Maria,' said Una, 'you are a better judge of the dead than the living. Anyone could walk into a door. Find a plaster for the poor girl, do.'

Maria fetched a plaster.

'Oh, hooray!' said Una. 'Here he is; our favourite architect!'

Susan's one-time husband had walked into the room: his beard, once black, was grey. He wore a baseball cap. He seemed furtive; a melancholy but friendly man in disguise, expecting a bailiff under every table, a Revenue man every time a telephone bleeped.

'I told you!' said Angelica. 'You need me! Now shut up and let me do the talking.'

'Humphrey,' said Una, 'I've done this completely mad thing: I've taken over the house where I was born. It's totally derelict. Maria tells me it's haunted, but she would, wouldn't she? I want you to do it over for me. Or are you up to your eyes in work?'

'I haven't exactly been up to my eyes in work,' said Humphrey, eyes fixed on the blonde girl leaning against the wall while Maria fixed a plaster to her temple, 'since my ex-wife put the evil eye on me, and I had to have electric shock treatment. What sort of conversion? Domestic or working? House of shame and sin or pleasant family home? I don't make moral judgements. What you

see is what you get; I am a defeated man. Who's this?
Haven't I seen her before?'
Una said she was new on the team so she doubted it.
But then, you never knew; it was a small world.
'What's your name?' asked Humphrey.
'Angela,' said Angel. 'Angela Maize.'
And it was true.

Una raised her eyebrows but entered this into her computer. 'Angela Maize, approx 120 lbs; approx 5'6";
approx blonde; good appearance, regular features, good-
natured, poor co-ordination, no distinguishing marks,
possible split personality.'

'Have I met you before?' asked Humphrey.
'No,' said Angel.
'My misfortune,' said Humphrey, putting her on hold,
as it were.
'But I can't take on any work,' said Humphrey to Una.
'It's impossible. Because I'm bankrupt; I have no offices
and no secretarial staff. You know that. You're playing
with me, the way powerful women play with helpless
men. Cat and mouse.'
'Nonsense,' said Una briskly. 'Payment in cash. You can
use Angela for staff. I know she has secretarial skills,
because I once saw her in action. I'll deduct her wages
from your fee. You can work from Lodestar House. Then
you won't hang about; you'll have to make it habitable.'

It was an offer Humphrey couldn't refuse. His kindly,
morose face broke into what was almost a smile.
'Suits me,' he said. 'Since the real world despises my
talents, I must descend into the underworld. Like
Orpheus.'

Angela just nodded and smiled.

'Angel,' said Angelica urgently, 'who is this woman? What have you done?'

'I don't know,' said Angel, pathetically. 'She's nothing to do with me.'

'Nor me,' said Angelica. 'She doesn't hear a thing I say. She just does what other people expect. She's a straw in the wind. She's what others want. It's my fault. I made you hit your head. I'm sorry.'

'I've never heard you say sorry before,' said Angel. 'I'm confused. I want to go to sleep. It's all such a battle.'

'Yes, isn't it?' agreed Angelica. 'We deserve a rest. She can't do any harm. Let's leave it to her.'

And, concurring for once, they drifted away.

Ajax said, 'Is no one at all listening? You can't do this. You will lose your narrator, your history. We'll vanish altogether . . . Angel, I relied on you. You are my vigour, my permanence through the ages –'

But he was talking to thin air.

4

Unification

Angela and Humphrey stood at the side entrance of Lodestar House, beneath the dripping stone arch. The key turned in the lock, but rusted levers did not engage; the tumblers jammed. The two of them put their shoulders to the door and pushed; the wood around the hinges gave. The lower edge of the door, reluctantly moving, scraped away a layer of mould on the stone floor.

'My God,' said Humphrey.

There had been an exponential growth within, it seemed, of entropic chaos. Congo's and Wendy's living breath, however old and feeble, had served to keep the worst away: now that was stilled, the forces of dereliction had taken over. Cobwebs now fell from the ceilings in mats, not flimsy strands; sprung floorboards gaped; wall beams powdered; entire steps of the staircase had dry rotted away into dust and tendrils. There was background noise of scuttling and squealing, a sound of dragging as if tiny dormice had grown overnight into major league rats and were already lining nests for yet more dreadful, upscaled progeny.

'This is nothing . . .' said Angela, thinking of Rice Court, but even as she said it, she forgot.

That evening, by which time Angela lay companionably side by side with Humphrey on Wendy's mattress – now on the floor, for the dealers, unasked, had cleared the remaining antiques, including the old lady's bedstead – Humphrey asked Angela for an account of herself.

Angela could give none. She had walked into a door, she thought, and now suffered from amnesia. But here she was, and it would do. She was as she appeared on Una's computer. An approximate person, with no peculiarities, saving a not unpleasant loss of memory. She had been kept in good order, apparently. Her legs were shaved, her hair recently washed. She had no complaints; why should he? He should just see her as a living doll.

Humphrey, a man who quickly brought all conversations round to himself, said kindly that he only wished he could develop amnesia, and start again. He tried to help her remember herself, but she had only her handbag with her, and within nothing more than cosmetics and an account from The Claremont. She had a memory of being brought to Una's Whitehall offices in a Volvo by a man who had driven off with her suitcases, and had upset her somehow. She had a feeling he'd said he washed his hands of her, he never wanted to set eyes on her again. But men did say that kind of thing, didn't they, when they meant the opposite? No other details. Presumably all clues to her identity had gone with the luggage. She didn't want Humphrey chasing anyone up, turning over stones; nor, when it came to it, was he eager so to do. A sleeping pill overdose, only just survived, not many months back, seemed to have dampened his own curiosity about the past.

'Some rich client, I suppose. The Claremont's famous for them,' said Humphrey. 'Una might know something, but why stir things up?'

They lay together for warmth and safety, the house breathing and cursing around them, some larger, chthonic, bad-tempered entity enclosing them in its womb. Both were fully clothed, for warmth. Humphrey claimed impotence. He could only properly respond, he said, to idiotic and helpless women, and Angela, he claimed, terrified him with her efficiency. It was true enough that, whatever her lack of personal memory, she had clearly not forgotten her skills. She was assertive and self-confident. During the afternoon, she had found and plugged in the telephone, located and mended burnt-out fuses so that now the electricity was back on. Warmth was beginning to creep back into the house. She had even unblocked a toilet. She had sent Humphrey out to the shops to buy pails, brooms, detergents and plastic sacks, light bulbs and six radios. While he was out she had left messages on answerphones all over London seeking builders' estimates.

'Surely that's my job?' he said, protesting.

'I can't wait around,' she said, 'for you to be sensitive and responsive. I've got to get things done.'

That was the kind of thing Susan had said to him. It wasn't surprising, Humphrey told Angela that night, that when her practised hand crept beneath his clothes it encountered only soft and helpless parts. What did she expect? This had been his wife's experience, too. Bullying wives get quiescent men.

Angela laughed and they both fell asleep.

Angela laughed a great deal: the ghosts retreated, the rats fell silent. Thereafter, she kept her hands away from Humphrey's parts; nor did he approach her. Neither of them mentioned this failure in lust to Una, who, once the house was halfway rid of its ghosts, would come over daily to discuss her ambitions for Lodestar.

Angela kept the six radios on, day and night, one on each of the landings in different parts of the house, playing music from different pop stations. The noise was dreadful, or so Humphrey complained. He wanted the radios tuned to one classical station, but she wouldn't allow it.

'The past is the problem,' Angela would say airily. 'The secret of happiness is to forget it altogether. Spring up anew every day. Treat your life like someone else's.'

'Pollyanna!' he accused her, loath to forgo his melancholy. He remembered vaguely once calling someone else Pollyanna, the trusting, annoying little girl who looks for good in everything; but he couldn't quite place whom. Humphrey's memories of his wife, his child who wasn't his child, his past life, were fading too; swallowed up in the black hole of Angela's softness. He thought he'd change his name, but he couldn't decide what to. He felt he was healing, though he couldn't be sure from what injury. Angela said she felt the same way. He moved slowly: he became lethargic. He needed to shave only twice a week. He felt that perhaps Angela was indeed sapping him of manhood, but only of the savage kind that sent black bristles starting out of his skin. He understood that he was happy. The house took shape around him, at Angela's bidding, with a little mild intervention from himself.

Angela had a computer set up in the back kitchen, which now served as the Lodestar office. She used Humphrey as the office boy, to post letters and contact tradesmen and craftsmen. He grumbled, but accepted his role. She took all responsibility, allocated no blame. She said he felt like her little brother; and that was okay with her. She was brisk but amiable. She billed Una for monies and Una responded without demur.

Maria came as Una's emissary, to deliver cash and collect receipts. Very little of Lodestar's finances went through official books. Many favours were undertaken in return for favours given. A plumber offered to do the work on an entire floor in return for a night with Angela. Angela would have obliged, but Humphrey objected. Let Una pay, he said. 'Why should you try and save Una money?'

So Angela said no to the plumber, but he was not easy about it. He drove nails through the pipes in his bitterness, so when eventually the water was turned on sprays of water spurted through one of the rooms. Luckily it was into the Golf Room – sand and grass merely squelched together into the mud that the golfers so love, and little damage was done.

'Why should the plumber think I would oblige?' Angela asked Una in surprise. She had almost forgotten the original terms of her employment. 'Nice girls are allowed to say no, surely? And, in any case, someone once told me – I forget who – that you couldn't tell a good girl from a bad girl just by looking.'
'It's obvious to the plumber the kind of house we are

creating here,' was all Una said, kindly, 'so he was just jumping the gun.' But she was aware that, as Angela's memory drifted away other than in relation to her work – where her judgement remained sharp, fine and effective – as her smile grew sweeter and vaguer, she looked increasingly available: like a ripe plum which would fall into the hand which closed round it, perfect and downy and not a wasp in sight.

Maria complained that Angela wasn't real: she was no more than a hologram. She was a person without conflict. She, Maria, couldn't think of anything to say to her because there was no one to say it to – she'd rather talk to a ghost any day. Maria hoped it was temporary. People got like that sometimes.

Otherwise, Angela basked in general appreciation. She lived without discursive or admonitory voices in the head; the incident of the plumber was soon forgotten. She and Humphrey clasped one another at night, though still merely for warmth, comfort and safety, as if they were each other's mother.

They kept the mattress on the floor even when there were beds available: long cloth draught-excluders kept plaster dust from creeping under the door. Angela thought of everything, now there was nothing much to think about, or worry about, or feel anxious about.

One day Una said, 'Another three weeks and we'll have our opening party.'
'Who will we ask?' asked Humphrey and Angela.
'Everyone we know,' said Una.

Angela sat and stared at the invitations, suddenly deprived of energy. Her mind was blank.

'Angel,' murmured Angelica, 'can you remember who we know?'

'Just about,' said Angel. 'Don't you bother your pretty head. I'll write the names and addresses for her.'

'I don't think I'll ask anyone,' said Angela.

'Then what are all these?' asked Humphrey, of the pile of stamped, addressed envelopes beside her.

'That's strange,' said Angela. 'I can't remember doing all that. Sometimes my left hand doesn't know what my right is doing.'

'It affects all of us,' said Humphrey, 'in one degree or another. Don't worry about it.'

She didn't.

5

A House Revealed

Now all the rooms of the house were open to inspection. Some shocked, some pleased: some seemed to stretch into infinity, some were small and closed. Some were inhabited by angels, some by demons, some by Una's Happy Boys and Girls, eager to oblige. Though many said it was only what Una had put in the champagne and fruit cup, some hallucinogen, that gave to so many this common illusion: that they had entered some other world where they could be themselves, where what you wanted to see, you saw, and no one would censure you or would band together to deny the evidence of your eyes, or curb your enthusiasms or object to your horrors. Some who came in together, separated; others who came separately joined up with others; some, a few, stayed hand in hand throughout the evening.

Angela opened the front door to guests: she was dressed in flimsy nothingness: a kind of pinkish Salome veil which draped over breasts and buttocks in an idle attempt to conceal parts she did not understand needed concealing any more than she would have done at the age of five. Nudity now seemed ordinary enough: the body a mere adjunct to the self: not interesting. Humphrey had said he liked the veil – it gave her an opalescent look which muted her air of childlike confidence and bounce – and she liked to please Humphrey.

'That kind of party! I see –' said one or two guests; but what other kind could there be, when you thought about it? Given by Una, in a house with many rooms.

Sir Edwin and Anthea arrived first, having mistaken the time by half an hour. They stood on the step in stubborn fleshiness: indeed, they lumbered in. Anthea had had her baby a month or so ago; a little boy. She had not recovered her figure. Edwin had put on weight, as if to keep her company. Angela took their coats.

'That girl will catch cold,' said Anthea.

'It's warm enough in here,' said Sir Edwin.

They accepted Una's champagne, and whatever was in that champagne, and Angela led them to the Wardrobe Room. Here Edwin changed into a ball-gown, the kind an opera singer wears to sing *Die Fledermaus*. Anthea chose a dinner suit, with crimson velvet cummerbund. They made an excellent pair. Angela took them upstairs to the Horse Room: the walls of the staircase agitated and moved as they passed by. Something or somebody was trying to emerge, flesh out of plaster and carved and gilded wood. Whatever it was didn't manage.

The walls of the Horse Room were stretched with blond hide, which could be made to vibrate and ripple when a switch was thrown. The major part of the room was occupied with a hologram of a fine black stallion covering a delicate white mare. Hay was piled upon the floor: a horse whip, a riding crop and a dildo were evident; a warm smell of horse shit and pungent urine, not altogether unpleasant, was wafted through the room by concealed fans. This room was Una's favourite, and to Angela and Humphrey the least interesting, although the creation of the hologram had challenged their ingenuity.

Here Angela left them rolling around, as if they were companionable children, beneath the horses' hooves, able at last to trust where in the real world only danger could be found. And a curious sight Angela found it: Edwin in his large-bosomed crimson opera gown, Anthea at home and elegant, but already only in cummerbund by the time Angela left.

'Angelica,' said Angel, 'are you there?'

'Only just,' said Angelica. 'I seem to have grown so old. Is something happening to time? Do leave me alone to sleep.'

'I don't mind,' said Angel, 'but I thought you might, so I woke you.'

'You told me you'd be sleeping, too. You're cheating,' said Angelica, suspicious even in drowsiness.

'I only woke for a minute,' said Angel. 'Honest. It was a shock. Your ex-husband's turned up, with his new wife.'

'None of that concerns me any more,' said Angelica. 'I'm sure I hope they can be happy. It seems profoundly unimportant.'

'If it's all right with you,' said Angel, 'it's all right with me,' and they both went to sleep again.

'Don't take too much of Una's champagne,' Humphrey warned Angela. 'I don't know what's in it, but I imagine some mixture of truth-drug, mind enhancer and aphrodisiac.'

Staff and guests mingled, behaving with various degrees of propriety. Some stood and stared, glassy-eyed: some found their pleasure in talk, in the excited exchange of ideas. Others slipped upstairs, singly, or coupled, with the Happy Boy, Girl or whatever of their choice. A few kept their own clothes; most made use of Wardrobe and Make-up; hardly anyone chose to remain in the gender in which they had first stood upon the doorstep of the refurbished Lodestar House.

Una was in a fine state of animation: she was riding Stephen White about the room, beating his patient shoulders with her fists. She wore a diamond tiara and a long white satin dress, hitched up to show scrawny but unashamed thighs.

'Angel,' murmured Angelica.

'An hallucination. Take no notice,' said Angel. 'Angela's doing fine.'

'She is not,' warned Ajax. 'She has schizoid tendencies. Whorehouses preponderate in schizophrenic literature. For God's sake, let me take some control of this body.'

But they'd drifted away, in their new unwary confidence; and Ajax was as helpless as Odysseus' craft ever was, drifting between Scylla and Charybdis, hoping against hope.

Lambert, on his way to be pinioned and beaten, dressed in pink silk top and navy miniskirt, was loudly objecting to Una's definition of gender as nature's error. It could hardly be the case, he argued: if you gave a man oestrogen, the female hormone, he'd grow breasts and his voice would rise, and if you gave a woman testosterone, she'd grow a beard and develop a temper, this proving the physical base of gender division. Una leapt off Stephen's ghostly back and called after him, 'And what is wrong with a person who has a penis and breasts? What is wrong with one who has a vagina and a beard? The mind might well feel at home in such a body.' She looked for Stephen, but he'd vanished.

Brian Moss and his wife were amongst the last to arrive. 'Little Elsie clung and clung,' said Oriole. 'She didn't want her parents going anywhere without her. You know how children are.'
Una raised her eyebrows. If she knew, she didn't want to be reminded. Oriole's hair was limp, her expression was strained and her eyes were small from lack of sleep. She wore a full-flowered skirt with an elasticated waist, a blouse, once, like herself, pretty, which also had been through many a badly sorted wash, and one reluctant string of chunky blue beads by way of party spirit.

Oriole looked around the Great Hall in some amazement: so different from the common scene of home: the measure of small achievement reckoned in fitted kitchens and CD sound. She preferred home. This place glittered in vulgar crimson and gold; over-the-top chandeliers hung from the ceilings; faded paintings – most of them bad – of men and women, sylphs and naiads, fauns and faeries, dryads and elves, in some form of intercourse or another, had clearly been brought from hidden basement stores, or attic cupboards and gathered here together. Fire and candlelight flickered on muted flesh-tones and intimate pastel moments. Erotica and strong colours, in art if not in life, did not go together: a general wanness pervaded all, yet added tone.

Oriole sighed. She had given up the study of art to marry and have children.

'What sort of party is this?' she asked. Her husband already drank from a full glass, but Oriole looked at the contents of hers suspiciously. 'I don't drink alcohol,' she said. Nor would she drink from the fruit cup when a glass of that was offered.

'That girl has no clothes on,' Oriole observed as Angela flitted by. But there was no one to say it to, for Brian had gone and she knew nobody else, nor wanted to, so she sat on a yellow velvet brothel sofa and waited for him to come back. Congo and Wendy sat on either side of her: no longer old, nor young, but in their prime. Oriole put out her hand to free her skirt from where Congo sat upon it – and her hand passed through his leg. She touched Wendy's piled brown hair and it had no substance. These happenings did not seem extraordinary.

'It's secondary smoking,' she told them. 'God knows what these dreadful people have in their cigarettes.'

'All things pass,' said Wendy.

'All too soon,' said Congo. ' But I'm glad they did the place up.'

'What about me?' asked Oriole, but they were not interested. She looked at her watch. It had stopped.

'Only holograms,' said Oriole. 'You're nothing but holograms. You don't frighten me.'

The six bedouins in white stood mid-hall and divested themselves of their clothes; folded them up on the rug: sashes, robes, undergarments. They stood gnarled and naked. Twelve little children applauded. The six masked women unveiled themselves, unclothed themselves, stood naked and beautiful, clustering, giggling, as if about to take a communal bath. The children applauded more. The men and women linked arms and performed a ring dance. Withered male scrotums bounced, nubile breasts likewise; children were enclosed. Then they disappeared as well.

'Someone has a strange sense of fun,' said Oriole to a man in fancy dress who now sat next to her. Congo and Wendy had gone. 'It must be some kind of art show.'
Her new neighbour was dressed as an executioner. He carried an axe with an ornate handle. She tried it with her hand, expecting another hologram, but the blade was real. She cut her arm on the edge of the blade; blood oozed out of the flesh, in tiny little bubbles, which joined up to make a trickling stream. Maria was at her side in a minute, with tissues.
'Have you seen my husband?' Oriole asked Maria. 'And I really need to call the babysitter to see if Elsie's settled.'
'Mothers!' said Maria. 'There's no curing them. You're a natural at the other world. You could earn yourself a good living as a medium.'
'Oh no,' said Oriole. 'It's Brian's job to provide. I don't believe in working mothers. Why have a baby if you don't mean to look after it?'

Maria went; abruptly and rather rudely, Oriole thought. She winced as the executioner unmasked a monstrously long phallus and Tinkerbell swung down and sat herself upon it, squealing happily. The pirate leaned up against the wall, watching and smiling. He had his boots off, which seemed to be exposure enough for him. Bare toes curled gratefully in the air.

'These people have no decency,' said Oriole. Milk spurted from her breasts. 'But I'm not breastfeeding,' she said. 'Where is Brian? He needs to be here.'

Ghostly figures moved up and down the stairs, carrying real-enough furniture. The faces of Tully and Sara appeared in ectoplasmic form, trapped in the ornate carvings on the staircase walls: how they stretched, writhing semi-stone arms to stop the profitable flight of possessions, but there was no stopping it. How Tully and Sara creaked and groaned.

'Look at that!' said Humphrey to Angela. She was eating the last of the strawberries from the fruit cup with her fingers; fingers so pale, you could hardly see them. Her mouth was splodged with strawberry juice more observable than her lips. 'You can stop anything but not the dealers' drive to make a fast buck.'
His hand was on her naked thigh. She kissed him; her all-but non-existent tongue in his half-existent mouth; she could feel but not see his now determined penis against her belly. And he was moving further from her as her belly was swelling too, pushing him away. She was doing it: she was the baby inside herself, growing. She did not like that but there was no stopping it. Even unborn, she could now remember, she had been insistent; so many of her in there determined to come to birth.

'Angel,' said Angelica, 'what's happening to us? This is dangerous.'
'She's all over the place,' said Angel. 'I'm frightened.'
'She needs us to hook her into the world,' said Angelica.
'She's lost her narrator,' said Ajax. 'Face it.

Angelica, hello. Angel knows me well enough. Let
me in. There's almost no time left.'
'Whoever you are,' said Angelica, 'if you can do
something, do it.'

Humphrey led Angela upstairs. Her foot hardly touched
the stair. Sara's stony arms passed through her waist:
Tully managed a cold rip with grey fingers into her more
substantial buttocks. Angela squealed, and with the
squealing solidified somewhat, as if in releasing sound
she released the anti-substance that afflicted her.
Humphrey, in anticipation, had returned properly to the
flesh. He was dressed as once Lady Rice had so often
known him dress – in a smooth grey suit which inhibited
any movement other than formal.

Humphrey opened room after room, searching for the
one which felt right. Angela looked cautiously over his
suited shoulder: little by little she was gaining substance;
if anyone were to photograph her now, there'd be no
doubt but that she was there.

In the Flower Room, Angela saw a naked Susan panting
and rolling on petals with a partly clothed Rosamund.
And in the Scout Room, Brian Moss engaged lovingly
with two young male cross-dressers. She saw Clive turn
towards her a face made brilliant and lovely with
make-up; he stretched out his arms to her but Humphrey
quickly closed the door. In the Computer Room old
Gerald Catterwall was tenderly embracing Una in her
prime. Angela longed for empty rooms and, in longing,
found them: or perhaps it was just that the drug was
wearing off. The next door Humphrey tried revealed,
once open, a cheap hotel room, serviceable and clean: a

narrow bed, white-sheeted, greyblanketed; dark, shiny veneered wardrobes; a tray with kettle, powdered coffee, wrapped biscuits, cups; trouser press: the opposite end from The Claremont. Horrible, but what other people had.

'This will do,' said Humphrey. 'If everyone else can, surely you and I will manage?'

Angela stood, undecided, in the doorway.

'Go in,' said Angel, Angelica and Ajax in unison. 'For God's sake!'

And Angelica's legs took them in, and to the bed, and Humphrey.

Oriole sat weeping on the yellow velvet sofa in the Great Hall.

'Brian had no business bringing me to a place like this,' she said. 'We so seldom go out. I was really looking forward to it, and now we're here he dumps me. I haven't even got money for a taxi home. I'm not well. I need to go home and take an aspirin. Everything seems so foggy in this revolting place.'

A couple were coming down the stairs: they looked real enough, and happy, and together. The man wore a grey suit; the girl, who was perhaps the sister of the one she'd seen earlier, flitting about with no clothes. But this one seemed reputable and pleasant enough, in jeans and T-shirt.

'You're Brian Moss's wife,' the young woman said to Oriole. 'Is there anything I can do? I used to work for him once. I guess I owe you a favour.'

'If you owe me a favour,' said Oriole Moss, 'then lend me the money for a taxi home.'

'Let's take her home,' said Humphrey. 'Let's get out of here.'

The three of them left unobserved: pushing past a middle-aged couple on the step, who stood there with a young girl, perhaps sixteen. She'd been crying, but spoke formally, firmly and politely.

'Mother will be inside,' the girl was saying. 'I'll be all right. Thank you for seeing me home, Miss Ruck.'

And then the three from the past were gone, except the girl's voice still lingered –

'If that's what a party is, it's loathsome!', but it might have been Oriole speaking; neither Humphrey nor Angela could be sure.

Humphrey and Angela booked in at The Claremont for the night. They had nowhere else to go.

'Welcome back, Lady Rice,' said the Commissionaire, but Angela didn't hear him. Humphrey did, but said nothing. In the elevator she said to Humphrey, 'Call me Angelica: Angela's much too singleminded a name. It never suited me.'

'You're Edwin's wife,' he said, as she lay in foam in the marble bath. 'Of course. That's who you are. His ex-wife, I should say. I heard he married again.'

'Forget all that,' she said. 'I'm no one's daughter, no one's wife. I am myself, started again.

'Edwin's ex-wife,' she said. 'Myself at last.'

That night, as new lovers will, they told each other their life histories. In the morning Angelica woke and listened for the voices in her head but there were none that she could define, let alone name: just an agreeable

324

kind of buzzy awareness, laid in layers, interleaved with the possibility of future, and she found herself reborn.

She looked out the window of The Claremont and saw Ram and the Volvo. He was looking up at her.

'Look!' she said to Humphrey, 'there's the man with all my luggage, back again.'

But Humphrey was asleep. She looked at him closely and saw he was much too old for her. She went to the window and waved. Ram waved back, and beckoned. She nodded and dressed and went down to him.

Fay Weldon

The Cloning of Joanna May

Joanna May thought herself unique, indivisible – until one day, to her hideous shock, she discovered herself to be five: though childless she was a mother; though an only child she was surrounded by sisters young enough to be her daughters – Jane, Julie, Gina and Alice, the clones of Joanna May.

How will they withstand the shock of first meeting? And what of the avenging Carl, Joanna's former husband and the clones' creator: will he take revenge for his wife's infidelity and destroy her sisters one by one?

In this astonishing novel, Fay Weldon weaves a web of paradox quite awesome in its cunning. Probing into the strange world of genetic engineering, *The Cloning of Joanna May* raises frightening questions about our identity as individuals – and provides some startling answers. Funny, serious, revolutionary, this is the work of a master storyteller at the height of her powers.

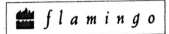

Fay Weldon

Growing Rich

Bernard Bellamy has done a deal. He's sold out to the Devil, in all his forms. In return, he is promised that all his wishes will be granted, all his desires fulfilled. One of them, young Carmen Wedmore, is proving to be quite a challenge.

Carmen lives in the new town of Fenedge, East Anglia, near her former schoolfriends Laura and Annie. The three girls dream of the day they'll escape their dullsville existence. While Annie flies off with a fluttering, blipping heart to the snowcapped peaks and frothy rapids of New Zealand to join the man of her dreams and Laura marries, capably moving the population graph a few notches higher, Carmen stays in Fenedge, under the powerful clasp of Sir Bernard and Driver, the Devil's agent. Disguised as a suave chauffeur, Driver cruises in his plush, shiny, sinister limo, stalking her every move.

But Carmen becomes ever more determined to ride out the temptations laid in her path and not to sell her soul. Will she eventually succumb? Or will the Devil, for once, not have everything his own way?

Fay Weldon's *Growing Rich* is a turbine-driven fantasy of love and revenge, values and morals: a witty and compelling elixir.

'Fast, funny . . . a glorious entertainment for the Nineties'
Woman's Journal

'Breathtaking . . . catches its reader up in a gale of good spirits and devilment that keeps on blowing from beginning to end'   *Observer*

'A typically Weldonesque tale of cleverness, with tongue-in-cheek asides'   *Good Housekeeping*

'Another Fay Weldon classic'   *New Woman*

'As exuberant as ever'   *Daily Telegraph*

'Absolutely hypnotic'   *Irish Press*

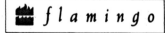

Fay Weldon

Life Force

Into the lives of Marion, Nora, Rosalie and Susan erupts Leslie Beck, an old flame not quite extinguished. Recently widowed, though somewhat weepy Leslie is still a man with the Life Force. To the four friends he is Leslie the Lucky, Leslie of the magnificent dong – his force forever pulls. Old secrets stir, old rivalries are resurrected and scores are settled as the friends are catapulted back into their murky past.

This copulative story of passion, jealousy, fidelity and faithlessness is Weldon at her most provocative.

'Weldon's funniest novel yet'   *Cosmopolitan*

'Weldon sends up all the novels of sex 'n' marriage 'n' kids in NW3 by triumphantly writing one of her own that is witty enough to finish off the breed'   *Mail on Sunday*

'Fay Weldon's *Life Force* is a scathing indictment of rampant seed-shedding and moral vanity. Through the voices of women Beck has seduced, Weldon joyously wields the scalpel, cutting deep into the sexual psyches of both men and women'   *Woman's Journal*

'A breezy book, often very funny and, as can be expected, full of energising satire'   *Times Educational Supplement*

'Weldon at her most wicked'   *Elle*

'Everywhere is the unmistakable zippiness of her narrative style'
                                                            Daily Telegraph

'Fay Weldon can tease, tantalise and scandalise better than any other writer today . . . Not recommended for the faint-hearted with something to hide'   *Financial Times*

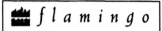

Fay Weldon's novels available in Flamingo

☐	THE HEARTS AND LIVES OF MEN	0 00 654508 4	£5.99
☐	THE CLONING OF JOANNA MAY	0 00 654593 9	£5.99
☐	DARCY'S UTOPIA	0 00 654592 0	£5.99
☐	MOON OVER MINNEAPOLIS	0 00 654510 6	£5.99
☐	GROWING RICH	0 00 654495 9	£5.99
☐	LIFE FORCE	0 00 654634 X	£5.99
☐	AFFLICTION	0 00 654683 8	£5.99

All these books are available from your local bookseller or can be ordered direct from the publishers.

To order direct just list the titles you want and fill in the form below:

Name: _____

Address: _____

Postcode: _____

Send to HarperCollins Paperbacks Mail Order, Dept 8, HarperCollins *Publishers*, Westerhill Road, Bishopbriggs, Glasgow G64 2QT.
Please enclose a cheque or postal order or your authority to debit your Visa/Access account –

Credit card no: _____

Expiry date: _____

Signature: _____

to the value of the cover price plus:
UK & BFPO: Add £1.00 for the first book and 25p for each additional book ordered.
Overseas orders including Eire: Please add £2.95 service charge. Books will be sent by surface mail but quotes for airmail despatches will be given on request.

24 HOUR TELEPHONE ORDERING SERVICE FOR ACCESS/VISA CARDHOLDERS –
TEL: GLASGOW 0141 772 2281 or LONDON 0181 307 4052

Printed in the United Kingdom
by Lightning Source UK Ltd.
132697UK00001B/20/P